# "a little work, a little play ..."

*Stories of American Men*

## Roslyn Willett

RWA Inc. Publishers 2015

# Contents

HOW THE DAY WENT    1

SKINS    25

THE FRANCHISE    37

A MAN WHO WORKS AS HARD AS I DO...    73

WE ALWAYS PLAYED WELL TOGETHER    95

THE CONNOISSEUR    117

NOT LEAST AMONG THEM    155

CLOCKS AND BONDS    165

OUTSIDE/IN    187

THE SYSTEM    211

OSCILLATIONS    237

TRUST    265

# ACKNOWLEDGMENTS

"a little work, a little play ..."

"Not Least Among Them" was published in the June 1994 issue of *Art and Understanding*.

"Skins" is in the spring, 1999 issue of *Papyrus* (Vol. 5)

"A Man Who Works as Hard as I Do..." was published in the October 1997 issue of *Words of Wisdom*.

"How the Day Went" appeared in the June 1998 issue of *Words of Wisdom*.

"We Always Played Well Together" was published in July 1998 in *Timber Creek Review*.

"The Franchise" was accepted for publication in an anthology, *America Laid Off*, edited by Linda Gibbs.

"Clocks and Bonds" appeared in Summer 1999 issue of *Timber Creek Review*.

"Outside/In" was published in *The Prairie Star* in June 2001.

"The System" is in the October 2000 issue of *Timber Creek Review*.

"Oscillations" appeared in *Phantasmagoria*, Volume 1, Number 2 in January 2002.

"Trust" has been accepted for publication in *Words of Wisdom*.

Cover image: Self portrait of Charles Keeling Lassiter (ca. 1975), acrylic on paper. Charles was a good friend and I own this self-portrait. - Roslyn Willett

# HOW THE DAY WENT

**7:30 am**     A few students were near the gated entrance to the Tyndall School in the east 70s, when Headmaster Woodrow Manning arrived, keys at the ready, to open the still-locked door.

"Hi, Dr. Manning," one said, "Can you let us in?"

He knew they wanted to get breakfast, not normally served till 7:45, and debated briefly before saying, in an access of friendliness, "Sure, why not." He was feeling good. There were frequent debates in board meetings and staff conferences about letting kids into the building when they could not be supervised.

But with a long day ahead of him, and a sweet evening behind him. Dr. Manning was in no mood to be harsh. He unlocked the door to his sumptuous office, one of a suite of large, square, high-ceilinged rooms on the second floor of the 1920s structure built especially for the Tyndall school by a wealthy board that wanted to ensure that its daughters had as good an education as the sons who went to the East's finest prep schools. No one on his staff had yet arrived, they were not due till 8:15, and he treasured this early time for the perspective it gave him on the often unsettling appointments and interruptions that made up a routine day.

He was smiling, as he sat in the high-backed leather swivel

1

chair. It was delicious to be in love, delicious to have that love returned and fulfilled. It was what made life worth living. Love enhanced the senses, perfumed every breath, brightened the eye, gave the body its reason for being. He and Genevieve had ordered dinner in from EAT, overpriced but satisfying, so that there was no possibility of their being seen together. Her two-year sublet was within walking distance of the school in a neighborhood that had been transformed after World War II from brownstones and small tenements into ugly but anonymous white brick high-rises. Perfect for a woman who was on an exchange program to teach French in a private school in New York while her counterpart taught English in France. Perfect for him; he knew his attention span. He was married, a father, had earned a Divinity degree before he went on to become an educator. And he was going to remain just what and where he was. Meantime, there was pert Genevieve, with her short skirts, finely muscled legs, narrow body and small high breasts, her sidelong glances and flirty smiles, her utterly French willingness to enjoy their pleasures without great expectations. Of course, an occasional gift, mostly small pieces of jewelry, made the evenings even more warm, as did a bottle of good wine with dinner. He knew how to do these things. He'd been doing them for years. To feel alive, he needed to be in love. He adored Genevieve. He would adore her until it was time for her to return home...

Now, to the matters at hand. He had appointments much of the day. His secretary had put his calendar on his desk just before leaving the previous evening. She knew he came in early. There was nothing unusual: a demanding parent, fund-raising, a troublesome kid, and preparation of a report on curriculum and cost-cutting for the evening's board meeting. His special, soothing, homiletic style, sweet reasonableness and accessibility were, he knew, what had kept him secure as headmaster for more than twenty years and would keep him there till he decided to retire. His was the longest tenure in the job after that of the founding person. (Even alone, he noted, he had become politically correct.) The founding person was, of course, the opinionated, terrifying headmistress about whom elderly alumnae reminisced.

He chuckled to himself. No one had ever caught him being opinionated or terrifying. He listened, he compromised, he did what was necessary. His days had enough variety to keep him engaged: it was not, after all, like tightening screws on an assembly line. The years had their base lines of summer planning for fall, welcoming new students, orienting new teachers, rethinking curriculum to match the latest in education fads and research, and integrating the trendy with the traditional. There were always budget problems, interviewing and hiring new staff, even an occasional necessary but deplorable firing. The year marched on with serious preparation for the SATs, guidance for creditable college acceptances, a ceremonial commencement and immediate gift solicitation from wealthy, grateful parents. Day to day, there were troubled kids, drug and other scandals, an occasional maverick on the board and unexpected breaches of the budget. All manageable.

When a job posed few major challenges, a man had to find another outlet for his energy. His predecessor had become bored with the school, his work, himself. His creative urge had culminated in his locking himself in this same sumptuous office for two years, writing erotic science fiction. Not he. His erotic behaviors were real, and not on school time. He gave the school full measure.

**8:05 am** His secretary, Miss Fabian, arrived, brisk and bustling, putting his usual Thermos of coffee already brewed and lightly laced with half and half, on its coaster-tray in the corner of his walnut desk. She poured a mug for him, and he smiled gratefully, "You're so kind to remember. Miss Fabian." She was old enough to be called "Miss."

"Do you want anything from the cafeteria before your first appointment? Scrambled eggs and a muffin?" He nodded. Miss Fabian was a jewel. For the first time, he remembered the kids he had let in before the cafeteria opened. Had they gone to the cafeteria?

"Take a look around the cafeteria and come back and tell me who's in there for breakfast. I let a few kids in early this morning. If they're eating and talking, fine. If they're on some staircase or landing, I made a big mistake." Staircases were the unsupervised venues for drug-dealing, a problem brought up at practically every board meeting. Board and parents identified it as the school's problem. But Tyndall was a day school; the kids lived at home. Blame shifted among the streets, the school, the family, the society, the failure of religion.

She was back ten minutes later, five kids in the cafeteria, no one remembered when they had arrived. He shrugged. "I'll be finished in five minutes, and you can get rid of the tray. Thanks. This is good." He was all business for his first appointment, an influential parent, a lady doctor who specialized in sexual disorders.

**8:30 am**       "Dr. Rasmussen, I know you have only fifteen minutes, so we'll skip the pleasantries. What can I do for you?" he asked.

"It's the science program. It needs revamping. My son is going to be a doctor like his father and me. Without good preparation in sciences here, he's not going to make it in a college pre-med program. Tyndall is excellent in many ways, but the school is not living up to its name. Tyndall, after all was an important scientist, a man who left his earnings from a U.S. lecture tour here to promote American science ..."

"Which sciences are you referring to, Dr. Rasmussen?" His tone was soothing. As soothing as if he were talking to a mourner. He had thought he was not really prepared to spend his life comforting, soothing and preaching after getting his DD, but it was how he spent much of his time, even here.

"Physics, biology, chemistry... what else?" she said impatiently. "I don't consider crap like botany or anthropology science. They have no predictive value. After you've learned their descriptive methods, it's all over." She paused. "Sorry about the language. It's early in the morning and I care deeply about my son's future."

"I'm so happy to have your input, Dr. Rasmussen. Would you like to work with us on science curriculum in the middle and upper schools? We're revamping it to include some of the latest..."

She interrupted. "You know I can't do that. Why don't you hire a consultant? At the rate you're going, I will have to hire a tutor. It's too bad, when the school's tuition is so high and its mission so clear."

"Some parents want us to stress the creative, as well, Dr. Rasmussen, and we've been trying to do that in teaching science, stress experimental work, the role of discovery in science, the relationship between insights in sciences and in the arts..."

"It won't work. That's not the way to teach science. Yes, laboratory work, so they will learn about keeping records and measuring results, but no to the other stuff. It takes too much time from what the kids need to know. And there's an awful lot of that."

He promised he'd look into it, maybe change textbooks, go into the newly-clarified structural relationships between physics and chemistry, chemistry and biology. She liked the last. Another satisfied customer.

But he knew better. The science curriculum committee's first task had been to meet with the lower school teachers to get their input. Predictably they had none. They liked buying the six-week segments on "science" sold by teaching material developers with teacher aids and workbooks for the kids.

The committee decided to concentrate on the middle and upper school where at least a few of the teachers had science backgrounds. In what? Physical anthropology, said the baseball coach who took kids to the Museum of Natural History where he was also a volunteer. He could teach anthropology, cultural, too, he said. But maybe that belongs in social studies?

Chemistry. We need a real curriculum in chemistry, the committee said. Not the old one that starts with the periodic table and the elements, but maybe chemistry in everyday life and a history of discovery in chemistry starting with the ancient Egyptians and the brewing of beer. Maybe a lab on fermentation processes. "A good mix of chemistry and biology," one wag said. Another lab on surface action and cleaning products; and another on corrosion processes. That ought to interest them. Predictably, the older people on the faculty called it pandering, and said you'd have to get back to the periodic table anyway. And besides, those were the things their maids dealt with. Biology was equally recalcitrant. Do you start with the cell and its contents and processes? Bacteria and protozoa — or the garden with plants, insects and vertebrates? Do you deal with the grand biological processes of growth and change, evolution and extinction; or the minutia of the cell, which was, of course, where the chemistry took place.

And in physics: mechanics or astronomy, the inclined plane and pulleys or the big bang and quantum mechanics? There was no end to it. Except God, and this was a secular school.

**9:00 am**     The Director of Development, Linda Chase, swept impressively into his office with a report on fundraising that he was to present to the board that night. Most of the school's expenses were covered by tuition that was as high as for many colleges. There was a modest endowment to take care of the unexpected. But this was arguably the most desirable school in the city, and money was always needed for new programs, and for scholarships for the sprinkling of underprivileged students brought from the slums to pepper the mainly salt student body. Parents, isolated themselves from the city's multi-racial population in streets, subways, and parks, demanded mixing. He thought about that for a moment. It was better than nothing, but not much. The gulf was too wide, but at least there was some real feeling when a little girl, who had suffered heroically with sickle cell anemia, finally died of it. He had presided over a solemn memorial service that elicited many tears, but how did tears weigh against the code words for minorities still used by some snotty kids?

An increase in the capital fund was needed to computerize the library and to fit the studios and theater with new technology. Plus, they had to add fast modems and Internet software to classroom computers, and get new analytic equipment and safety hoods for the labs. The lower school was clamoring for a larger facility for the nursery-kindergarten that had outgrown its limestone house a few blocks away.

"Linda." It was always nice to see her. She had been Director of Development for a smaller school across town till he hired her five years ago, and he had fond memories of her first couple of years on the job. Now they were good friends, who, understanding each other very well, had moved on. Her work across town had enabled that school to build an elaborate new plant that looked like the thing most appealing to kids: a tv set. That was the "built environment", a distinctive design, created for a passing moment in educational theory. It was an "open" school in spirit, but some of the "openings" were unplanned. The joke was that when you see a great new building, you can be sure the roof leaks. "How are we doing?"

"Good, good. The Merrin family foundation has awarded us a scholarship grant of $20,000 for ten years; and we have sent a mailing to alumni for contributions to the capital fund. We're getting average contributions of over one hundred dollars. Here's what we have so far."

A quick look at her impeccably organized tables sufficed. "Take it to be copied. We need eleven copies. For 6:15 tonight."

"What about the academic budget?" she asked. "It's not my job, but I hear you're cutting out some languages in favor of more computer time. Is that wise?"

He sighed. "Linda, I know. If they don't get the languages early when their ears and minds are ready for them, they won't ever. Computer stuff they'll pick up, of necessity. But, it's what the board wants."

She shrugged. "They're not educators. You have to explain..."

He pointed to the clock. It was an old argument in which neither of them invested much passion.

**9:15 am** He was awaiting the next one with trepidation. Here was the nursing office file. The kid came in frequently with headaches, vomiting and diarrhea, was depressed and unresponsive. What had he eaten? Where did he eat? Home, restaurants, school. No answer there. He was skinny, but lots of fifteen-year olds were. He was pale. His eyes looked all right. There were no tremors, postural or organic problems.

Academics: Very smart, but also cynical and caustic.

A handwritten memorandum, not official, from the headmaster of the upper school was what had pressed this case into his office. There were rumors this kid was a drug dealer, that he sat up late playing cards with other kids, that he took drugs himself, and was sometimes out of control. One parent had "heard" that Kevin was dealing cocaine in the stairwell. But cocaine didn't cause vomiting and diarrhea, did it? That seemed to be the work of Latin American hallucinogens, or was it? Coke was Latin American, too, wasn't it? He grimaced. Pharmacology was not something he wanted to know. And no one would be anything but opaque.

**9:30 am** The kid, a high school sophomore, arrived with his father, a city official of some sort. The boy was pale, freckled, wet-lipped. Not a healthy athletic type. He would be evasive and this was going to be very difficult. The father did not look like a Tyndall parent. Tyndall's selectivity had to do, in some measure, with the parents' desirability. This man looked tired and disheveled, his clothes off a discount rack and his shoes an outdated style. Dr. Manning observed that much but he could not just sit there.

"This is going to be difficult for all of us. Let's address it in the spirit of problem-solvers, without recriminations for the past, but with hope for the future." The kid's eyelids flickered, and he looked at the bookcase on the side of the office. The father nodded, a bit impatient.

"I thought we'd do this better with a father rather than a mother... Someone logical and cool... Mr. Sands."

"My wife's in Europe, in Prague, in fact, setting up a trading company, so you wouldn't have got her anyway," Mr. Sands said. "I should have left the housing department ten years ago, but I figured I might as well wait and get the pension and then go on.. It was a mistake." He was an assistant commissioner.

"You have a huge responsibility, Mr. Sands. It's hard for a man, alone. Do you have other children?" It was important to be empathic, gentle.

"One. But she's older, on her own. Kevin and I are buddies."

"Do you have enough time to spend with him?" This was too sticky. He had to get to the point.

"Be blunt, Dr. Manning. What are we here for?" Yes,

the man was an executive.

"I hate to have a meeting about rumors and possibilities, but there are too many of them for me to be comfortable about. The nurses' office and the faculty and one parent have an idea that Kevin deals drugs and takes them himself. Is that possible?" Kevin's eyes opened wide. His father was expressionless. "Kevin?"

"Everyone has taken drugs from time to time, Dr. Manning. I have. But I do not deal, and I am interested in them scientifically, and not on school premises."

Was this rehearsed? "Who is everyone?"

"Every kid here, I think, except maybe a few who get their kicks from high marks or higher math or breaking into protected computer systems. We get pass-along copies of the reports from MAPS and we read about the human bonding of ayahuasca and the ceremonial use of peyote..." He trailed off.

"MAPS?"

"Some kind of research organization into drugs. Very respectable," Kevin said. His father looked at the ceiling.

"Get back to 'taken' drugs from time to time. What drugs?"

"Whatever you can buy. There's a lot of stuff out there. The old stuff, marijuana, LSD, coke, crack, peyote, 'shrooms; and new stuff like Ecstasy..."

"I want to thank you, Kevin, for being open about this. I feel that I can trust you."

Kevin shook his head. "I don't really want to talk about it, Dr. Manning. I am interested in how drugs relate to human consciousness. My interest is scientific, but ..."

"But there's no way to learn more without trying. Is that what you're telling me? Is this some kind of spiritual crisis for you?"

"I would not put it that way."

"You say you do not take drugs in school or deal. Where do you buy them?"

"I can't discuss that."

Where does the money come from?" Dr. Manning looked at Mr. Sands.

"Not from me. Kevin gets an allowance that covers day-to-day expenses."

"Kevin?"

"I play poker, and I'm good at it. My father is, too."

"You use money you win from your friends to buy drugs?" Dr. Manning was a little shocked.

"Some of them get a lot of spending money, more than they can really spend," Kevin offered. "It's all right."

"If this is scientific, are you participating in any science fairs, writing papers, keeping a notebook, doing the science credibly?" Dr. Manning thought, this will either get him or it won't.

"Notebooks, yes. I keep a diary: dates, amounts, effects. There is no way to participate in a science fair with illegal stuff, even if you're only doing it with animals, not people, and how could the results be the same, anyway?"

"I have the picture. You want a 'quick trip' to enlighten-ment. None of this boring, longterm meditation and prac-tice that mystics have spent their lives on, assuming you're telling the truth, of course." Dr. Manning paused. "Is your notebook in school?"

"Of course not. Do you think I can carry it around?"

This was not productive. "Mr. Sands, can you see to it that Kevin refrains from the use of drugs till he finishes here? That's two and a half years, a lot of time, and I may be asking the impossible, but I cannot just let this go."

Mr. Sands said without a great deal of conviction, "I'll try."

"Kevin, is it drugs that cause your headaches and gas-trointestinal problems? Do they make you sick sometimes?"

Kevin shook his head. "Maybe, but it may be staying up late; it doesn't matter."

"Do you talk about your experiments in school? You know what you're doing is illegal; aren't you worried about the police?" He was beginning to sound like a fool, and he knew it.

Mr. Sands was not helping. He was not shocked, not angry, not volunteering disciplinary action. This parent withheld the proper social responses. The void was hard to fill.

"I don't want to ask you to withdraw from Tyndall, Kevin, especially in the middle of a semester. We do not want a scandal. I have to respect your truthfulness and not punish you for it. We have no real evidence; it would be unfair to force your withdrawal."

"My friends are here; I don't want to transfer."

"Well, then, don't push your luck, Kevin, you're faced with two and a half years of being above reproach. You're expelled with the next rumor. There will be no discussion of this meeting outside this room and with other students. There will be no more poker games. And there will be no drug purchases until they are legalized or you have a formal research grant from a respectable scientific institution. That's it." Dr. Manning was very firm. "You have an obligation to Tyndall from this day on. If anyone comes back to me with any new complaint, you are done for." He paused. They all stood up. The kid was very smart, and if he understood Dr. Manning's forbearance, would be the better for it. If not, well, he'd been warned. Dr. Manning was a strong believer in doing unto others...

"Wait. Let me ask a question. What about all the anti-drug programs, all the lectures and films we've been showing, the outside people we invited...?"

Kevin smiled, relieved. "Dr. Manning, they're so stupid, so anti- what we already know, so exaggerated that nobody pays attention. Lots of parents smoke pot, a few use coke;

nobody's brains are 'fried'. It's a human impulse to escape from the everyday; that's what booze, mysticism and drugs are about. 'Drug education' is a joke."

Mr. Sands nodded. He held out his hand, shook Dr. Manning's and finally said how nice it was to meet him.

**10:00 am**      He needed to think. Had he made a mistake? Should he have demanded that Kevin resign or be thrown out? He had let the kids in in the morning, he had not expelled Kevin. He wanted to give them the benefit of the doubt, not leap to judgment. It was risky business. But what about the historic Tyndall's own ideals of self-generated research into scientific problems as varied as the blueness of the sky, how sound goes through air, the motion of glaciers, and, he smiled to himself, the anatomy of screw surfaces. He was not supposed to think frivolously about the original Tyndall's interests in connection with his own. Ah Genevieve, how happy these days are.

There was the mail. Free computers if the school would just allow some computer time for commercial interests. No way. Tyndall could do without a letter from the psychology department at Rutgers that wanted to use Tyndall students for an experimental program in learning. They wanted to test left-handed students against right-handed. Why Tyndall students? There were private schools in New Jersey.

Next piece: The teachers and school administrators' pension fund's quarterly report. He filed it in his desk drawer. A few years more and he would be able to retire and perhaps pursue some scholarly writing. He had an idea about worldwide parallels in the history of religion, and ruefully rejected a parallel with George Eliot's pompous, ineffective Casaubon. In his school days, he'd been matter of fact about religion. Now, he was interested in myths and mysticism, and had been collecting notes in a file drawer for almost as long as he'd been at Tyndall. A book would make his reputation.

Arts-related notices: dance programs at the Danny Kaye playhouse, an opening at a nearby gallery, a calendar for the Metropolitan opera. Miss Fabian could put as much up on the bulletin board as there was room for and she would not have posted a fifth of what was received. He let her use her judgment because she liked to see and think about what might be most appealing to students and faculty. There was a special pile for her to sort.

A very large clipping from a parent about how computers were revolutionizing teaching, with ideas about artificial intelligence, different methods of teaching. He had no time for this kind of thing. He could attend a seminar once a year for high-level administrative people in secondary schools and get it all in one day. Meantime, he'd navigate through parental minefields with last year's barely remembered seminar material for a few months longer.

With relief, he noted it was lunchtime. He wanted another pleasurable flirty-serious interlude with Genevieve. But there was no way to eat with her without attracting attention. If there was anything everyone loved, it was gossip and just as the gossip about Kevin had put him in a riskier position than his activities seemed to have warranted (or was the kid an accomplished liar who knew just what he could get away with?) he, himself, could not afford a scandal. She might be having a sandwich in the office of the language department... But she could have gone home for lunch or shopping. He decided to eat quickly in the faculty dining room, and then spend half an hour wandering the faculty offices.

**12:15 pm**     He'd picked up a tray of chicken breast, noodles and frozen peas, typical cafeteria food, and a little carton of pudding and coffee, enough for midday, and left himself vulnerable to importunate faculty members who were eating in. Unlike the students, they could go out for lunch, but with time constraints. He was addressing his food with great seriousness, when the first approached: a physical ed teacher, female.

"Dr. Manning, despite all the Title 9 funding for girls' competitive sports, I don't think that's the way to go. We've been talking about it. A few girls like competitive basketball, field hockey, swimming and tennis. Some parents think we should provide horseback-riding, and competition. I don't think so. They can get that kind of thing after school or on weekends. After all, we don't offer ballet training. It's amazing that we have a modern dance program instead of gym..."

He looked up startled. "What is this about?"

"Physical ed. We're not doing the right thing for most of the girls."

"Girls? What should we be doing?"

"Just what we should be doing with most of the boys. Competitive sports are for a few natural athletes. But fitness for life, starting early. For coordination, pleasure, stress relief, strength. That's what people need."

"Uh, Ms. Cassidy. We have a curriculum committee – why don't you write a proposal and give it to your department chair to approve...?"

She would not let go. "Two sequences, with the boys and girls able to shift as they need to between them: Sports or fitness for life."

"Thanks. Get it to the committee." He had dismissed her. Another was heading toward him. At this rate, his office tour was aborted. A pang of deep disappointment made him bite his lip. He *did* want to see her today. Just to look and smile would make him happy. But no, an English teacher, a substantial old girl, probably left over from the era of the first headmistress, was plowing through the aisles of the cafeteria, clearly heading for him.

"Dr. Manning, you're pushing competition in physical ed, all that team and individual sport training. I want people to get the same thrill from English." (Could he put Ms. Cassidy and Dr B. together, he wondered, to subject their ideas to competition?) "Why don't we sponsor some medal or award for the best short story, essay and poem in each form? And then print them in a literary chapbook for each grade?" She was watching his face. "It doesn't have to be expensive."

"That's a lovely idea, Dr. B., putting emphasis on quality. But don't you think it amounts to a reward for what kids should be doing anyway, extending themselves? Time enough for them to get into the world and expect some kind of payment for everything they do."

She looked nonplused. Good. Silly old biddy. B for biddy. He smiled. "Some of the parents want us to place more emphasis on essentials like grammar and spelling. But I think you're the last of the English teachers who even know the fine points of grammar, much less how to teach it. Would you be able to organize a one-day training program for teaching grammar to the younger faculty so that they can pass it along? If it's a success, we might be able to hold programs for teachers in other schools. Then maybe our college application essays will avoid the dangling phrases and clauses, the mismatched tenses and subject/verb disagreement..."

"Dr. Manning, are you twitting me?" She was indignant.

"No, no. We do, yes, want to emphasize the creative in all our programs, even science, but there is a place for correctness..."

"I agree," she said, "but that's not what I want to discuss. These kids won't sit still for diagramming sentences, and I'm not sure that works anyway. They think the creative does not require discipline, only free expression. They all think that if they're creative, someone else, from another school perhaps, will edit them."

Impasse. This was an old story, and his lunchtime was over.

**1:00 pm**      The headmaster of the high school needed

a few minutes, Miss Fabian said. One of the city's week-lies wanted correspondents in the private schools, and they expected the high school's students to "dish the dirt", other-wise who needed correspondents. He did not much like the man, there was a whiff of danger in his presence. A bit of sado-masochism, no warmth.

"Mr. Williams, what can I do for you?" He was being too hearty.

"The kids think they'll get writing credits in the paper, and it'll be good for college admissions." That again. The whole business of teaching now was directed to college ad-missions instead of to learning. "I'm worried about their lack of inhibitions, of understanding some things should not be discussed... but I don't see how to censor their work a priori, especially when it's not on campus." Williams had dropped out of law school, and never let you forget it.

"What do you recommend?" That was the democratic way.

"We're just going to have to let these 'correspondents' have their say, I suppose, but maybe we should have a meet-ing with the other schools and see what they're doing. At least call their administrators. I'll do that." Williams had satisfied himself with a temporizing, temporary solution that was no solution, at all.

"What are you worried about, Mr. Williams?"

"It's not our academic program, athletics, or computer hackers that are going to embarrass us, Dr. Manning. You know what it is... the stuff about parties in country houses, orgiastic goings-on, drinking, drugs. These kids will do any-thing for the hell of it. They're rich, spoiled, bored..."

"Will we be more embarrassed than Dwight or Horace Mann, Columbia Grammar or Spence?"

"We're not as traditional as some, our students are not so controlled."

"Adolescents in this society are not controlled. They expect learning to be 'fun', their parents have their own lives. Let's just do the best we can."

"But when kids come in half asleep because they've been 'partying' on school nights, and drop off on their desks after lunch..."

"'Partying'?"

"It's the new word for hanging out in bars or at rock concerts, getting 'bombed' or 'wasted' and engaging in sexual activity if that seems the next thing. Cars, empty apartments, the country house — they all have country houses ... "

"I know that, Mr. Williams. Let's not let a whiff of envy seep into our evaluation of our educational role."

"Oh, all right. One upper school parent has a new rule for his kids. No kissing below the belt."

Dr. Manning frowned. That was not suitable for young adolescents. He gave it a moment's thought. The youngsters at Tyndall had nowhere near the incidence of teen pregnancy that the public junior highs and high schools had. Was that sex education or prompt and quiet abortions? Or, he smiled to himself, kissing below the belt? He maintained a solemn face to Mr. Williams. "If anyone in Tyndall wants to participate in this 'correspondent' role, they must first be 'A' students. They must also have a briefing with the headmaster about Tyndall, its goals, its methods, its student honor and tradition. Of course, we will emphasize their self-interest in being part of a school with a fine reputation. A school in which scandalous goings-on are reported to the public is not going to have a fine reputation, especially in college admissions offices. There is plenty of *good* news about Tyndall."

Mr. Williams nodded. "That makes sense." Dr. Manning detected a grudging approval. Mr. Williams was ambitious, and willing to learn from him how to handle sticky student business, biding his time till he had enough experience to become headmaster somewhere. It was a game of musical chairs for division heads, guidance counselors, the whole administrative hierarchy. Education was an expanding field for the ambitious who did not care to teach.

"There's been some talk about our bored kids' participation or admiration for slum kids' gangs. Have you heard anything about that?" Mr. Williams had been reading some weekly. Journalists in the city knew scandal sold newspapers. And magazines. No one read anything any more for information with which to live a better life; no, it was for juicy tidbits, titillating nonsense blown up out of all proportion to its importance.

"Mr. Williams, these kids start by stealing money out of their parents' purses and wallets, and then find more thrilling activity to engage in. They're too snobbish to spend much time with gang members. It's only a phase for a few. Let's not blow it up ..."

"Unless it blows us up..." Mr. Williams loved playing Cassandra.

"I want to thank you for sharing your concerns with me, Mr. Williams. We'll be all right. Meantime, I have to get ready for the Board meeting tonight..."

Mr. Williams smiled and left.

**3:00 pm**     The Board. He had to report on the budget, curriculum development, possible new hires for the next academic year, applications and transfers. There was plenty to prepare. This was his quiet time, five times a year, getting ready for them. An interesting bunch, chosen for their money and prestige, their business acumen and willingness to do good works. Also because they wanted to be on the board, as they wanted to be on the boards of the city's arts organizations, its museums, its civic councils. Thus, they could meet the best of all worlds at parties and fund-raisers, circulate from bay to shore in the Hamptons, ride with the stars in Millbrook.

Chairman: A wealthy international currency trader, with

two kids in the school, courtesy of nubile wife #2. He was a hard-driving but realistic man, who made serious contributions to education abroad. The others: the president of a small women's college, an ex-nun, one of two women on the board; a pudgy insurance company executive, the chairman of a stock brokerage, the president of a frozen foods distribution company who was a West Point graduate, the publisher of a chain of alternate newspapers, the founder of a real estate and construction company who was also a Tyndall parent, a well-regarded plastic surgeon; the president of an international retailing firm; and the last parent, a divorced mother of three who had inherited a fortune and the privilege of dispensing it via a foundation.

He liked most of them, knew they liked him, and knew that they respected his ability to deal with problems while maintaining a steady hand and a moderate pace of change in the school.

Miss Fabian on the intercom. The chairman was on the phone. "We're having dinner downtown instead of in the little room at the Carlyle. Please tell Miss Fabian to cancel our reservation for tonight and we'll meet you in the teachers' lounge at 8:30. You'll be able to have dinner at home, and I'm sure your family will be grateful. There's no need for you to ride all the way down to Broad Street."

He shrugged. They did that once in a while, generally when they were discussing changes in pay or the benefits package. Perhaps Mr. Andres was right. His family would be grateful. It was too late to set anything up with Genevieve, although, he thought, he could leave a message on her answering machine for when she returned home... They'd have a couple of hours... But no. He was pushing it. The day after tomorrow was all arranged, and she had a life of her own.

He called his wife: "Throw another potato in the microwave, Julia, I'll be home for dinner."

"Oh, how nice! We've missed you so much lately with all the school business you've been taking care of. Is the board meeting canceled?"

"No. They're meeting downtown for dinner, then coming up for an eight-thirty meeting so I will have to eat early, seven or so. Is that ok?"

"You know it is." He could hear the good-natured smile in her voice. "The kids are always hungry early, and want to get out, themselves. Even I do, tonight. There's an opening at the Museum of Modern Art I want to go to. It's one of the champagne openings, black tie and all, and I'm going with Jane and Oliver at nine."

Home for dinner, a homely dinner of steak and potatoes, salad and frozen yogurt dessert. Good for everyone, quick to prepare and no impediment to conversation. He loved the apartment the school had bought for its headmaster: one of the many perks he enjoyed. Four bedrooms, a real dining room, real kitchen, wood-paneled library-study and maid's room, four baths, high ceilings and a view of the park from some windows. It was a prewar, so there was no terrace, but who needed a terrace when all of Central Park was only a few blocks away, and the co-op had tiled the roof and landscaped it with potted trees and shrubs?

Julia was wearing her daytime uniform of faded jeans and a sweater, still neat and girlish at fifty. The kids, Woody, Alison and Jennifer pleasant and distant, preoccupied with a rock concert they were going to at Madison Square Garden, in their uniforms of faded jeans and sweaters, stylish, ugly shoes and later, leather jackets. Of course, they were still at Tyndall, another of the perks, but Woody was finishing this year, and the twins in three years. He and Julia had been saving for years, knowing that there are no bargain colleges, and that the tuition break at Tyndall would run out. They often discussed college costs — another educational issue, he thought to himself.

"How's it going?" Julia asked pleasantly.

"Oh, I don't know." He was suddenly tired, and wished he could just stay in tonight in the empty apartment, watch a sitcom on tv or read a book. "Too many issues to deal with; I sometimes wonder if anyone knows what kids should learn before they go out into the world, what we should be teaching and how. Do we want to train independent minds even if they go off the deep end for a while, or to stuff them with information so they pass tests? We're educating for an increasingly unknown future, using methods and styles of the past. But we can't adopt visionary ideas if the kids still have to take college entrance exams and their parents want them to get a 'good education' for the money they're paying. I sometimes wish I was back in the nineteenth century when we knew it all."

No one paid any attention. They were not going to contribute to his malaise or to an endless dialog on the natural man or whether philosophy, religion or anthropology made any contribution to moral development, or all the other subjects he thought were appropriate for the dinner table.

No, which Fifth Avenue bus went to Penn Station, next to Madison Square Garden? Should they risk a change in the weather without umbrellas? It was so uncool to carry them... They were bored with him, his wife as well as the kids. He was a little ponderous sometimes, even when he tried to be jolly, never sure what tone to take. No wonder Genevieve was what he needed. She set the tone, flirty, delightful, amused by Americans because they took life so seriously. She made him a different man, easy, sexy. He found a new self reflected in her, as he had found a different self, intellectual, moral or playful in each of the three or four women he'd been in love with before. Lifelong learning, he thought with a sigh of pleasure. He had an instinct for the right choice. His spiritual restlessness needed the refreshment of new passion. And none of them had made trouble. They were independent women happy with what there was, warmth and pleasure, and agreeable to a friendly denouement when it was over.

**8:30 pm**       He was going over his papers when the noise outside the door signaled the arrival of the board, one taxi load and right behind, another. Andres was first. "I'd like a word with you; let's go to your office for a few minutes."

He sat behind his desk, Andres on the sofa nearby. "You've done a very good, thoughtful, balanced job as headmaster here for over twenty years, Dr. Manning, but the board agrees we must have your resignation, effective immediately. I know this is a shock, but we can't allow you to continue. Unfortunately, it is your wife and children who will suffer. They will have to transfer as quickly as possible to other schools."

Dr. Manning was too shocked to say anything, but the involuntary, unmanning tears showed he understood. "What is it? What reason?"

Letting the kids in, allowing Kevin to stay in school, some financial peccadillo committed by someone under his supervision — what could not be explained, discussed?

"You don't know?" Andres looked at him pityingly. "You are setting an intolerable example for the students in this school. Intolerable. You are a role model, or should be, and we have irrefutable evidence that you have been engaged in an extra-marital affair with a member of the faculty here, subverting order, opening us to accusations of sexual harassment. It's bad enough that there have been complaints that no women have any power in this, which was, after all, an all-girls school not so long ago. Not even a woman on the roster for a speech at commencement! It's all sexist, and your having affairs with women in the school, is disgusting. They're under your purview, after all. What have you been thinking of?"

"No, no. That was never the point," he protested. "Never. I just fell in love in the most natural way."

"You're a married man. You're not supposed to fall in love."

"But half the people on the board ..."

"We're not moral examples. We're businesspeople or ... I'm not getting into that. How soon can you vacate your apartment, get your children out so they won't hear the gossip here, get out of your office? You have until the end of the month."

"I want to talk to the rest of the board about this before it is final." He had recovered a modicum of sanity. "Who? How?"

"I'm not going to discuss that either. Mr. Williams will be acting headmaster. Miss Duchamps will have to leave immediately, and we'll hire a substitute till the end of the semester."

In the teachers' lounge, one by one, the board stepped up to shake his hand and tell him how sorry they were that it had come to this. He had been a very good headmaster in every respect, but now he was teaching the children the wrong lesson and had to go.


End

# SKINS

**II.**     We talk a lot, he and I, across the years, across the Great Divide. We're so alike, living in the rhythms of the skins and the brass, dying in despair at what we have done and not done. He done dying, and I not yet.

I learned the skins from him, in a way, just wanting to, to be like him. Fascinated by the sound of my own knuckles on tables, trying the tinkle of spoons on half-filled glasses, banging the beat on a pot with a spatula before anyone would let me near his skins in the corner. Drove everyone crazy with the rumpus.

Learned about sticks and brushes, cymbals and footpedals, bongos and tomtoms by watching. There was nothing in the tympani section he could not play and he was as talented as the conservatory boys whose repertoire includes Oriental gongs, triangles and rattles as well as the dead thumps of the Japanese big drum.

Me, I do it. I call myself an instinctive drummer. I can't read. I play gigs with a nothing group, a few times a month, for what amounts to expenses and a little extra for good weed. But I love to play and on a weekend night, sitting on the top tier of a little bandstand, my wrists loose and easy, my head waggling lightly to the rhythm of the sticks, I mesmerize myself, even when I know those other guys have no distinction whatever as jazzmen. We play for weddings, anniversaries, parties – mostly for older people who know they're getting danceable jazz and know what to do on the floor to enjoy it.

Once in a while I join a pickup group in the village, playing for contributions in Washington Square. Or someone tells me that a restaurant, trying to flog a slow night, wants a jazz group to play for practically nothing. Tips maybe. Restaurateurs know how to take advantage.

I went to a classical concert at Juilliard not long ago with one of the many older women who think they'll get laid if they broaden my horizons, and there was Joey, a terrific jazz bass player pushing a bow across the strings in a Stravinsky piece. "Hey Joey," I ran up at intermission, "how come you're here?"

"I'm a junior," he said. "You're a terrific drummer; you could do classical, too."

I shook my head. "Not me. I can't read. I learned from my father."

"Could your father read?"

"My father could read flyshit," I said, proudly. "Not me."

"Why not? You could learn. Register for an evening course."

He did not understand.

**I.**      I could see it when he was small. He tried so hard to be me. But it was not going to work, no matter what. It is my fault, but it is too late for regrets. Growing up in the Bronx, near the Grand Concourse, between radical east with its Russian Jewish garment workers and bourgeois west with its cast of small businessmen and pampered women, I could be either or both. Yes, to City College and a music major; yes to radical statements in the cafeteria.

But it was jazz I loved. And jazz I played. No sense in finishing college when I could be playing, touring, flirting, gulping big hits of maryjane and enjoying the ride.

Not booze. Good Jewish boys did not drink. Not much, anyway, just to be sociable. But the needle, by and by, that was the best.

My family gave up. Especially when I found a cute, compact, vocalist/dancer with a dazzling smile, and skin like melted chocolate at a matinee gig in Harlem. Lura was her name. She went for me too, homely little me with my big Jewish nose, not much helped by the light mustache that I thought made me look hip. Maybe because I wasn't an ignorant stud, took her out to dinner. Maybe she was flattered that I was smart, white, a step up. When you're young, you think a warm response is love. I did. I brought her home, after trying to tell Pop and Ma who she was, how talented, pretty... That was it. They tried to forgive me later. We married at City Hall, with a couple of friends as witnesses. No one else.

II.     I hated living with my mother. She was never home, never came to school for Open School Week, or to walk me there or back, even when I was little.

"You're a big boy," she'd say. I was, too big. Too big, too fat, hungry all the time. We'd go to the supermarket and I couldn't wait to get home to grab the first box of weird cereal that came tumbling out of the bags to enjoy its crisp sweetness surrounded and finally drowned in milk. I loved cereal. And when you're hungry all the time because your mother forgets you, as long as you have some of that and milk, you can fill up. She didn't cook. We'd go out for pizza or hamburgers and fries or Chinese on Broadway. Sometimes, we'd order in if it was raining or very cold. Roxy (my sister changed her name from Rosie) hated the cold. She was born two years earlier than me. By the time I was born, they had split. He would visit when he wasn't on tour. But not much. We lived in a mixed neighborhood on the west side, and Roxy and I went to elementary there.

I loved the neighborhood, hated school. I was this big, fat

kid who never made out on tests. I could talk, all right, never shut up, my mother said. Roxy was smart in school, smaller, just as brown as me, overweight, too, but disciplined. I hated Roxy. She and my mother had some female thing between them that I never figured out how to be part of.

I knew I'd do better if I could live with my father. He'd visit, and I'd beg him. "Take me with you, dad. I don't care where. Take me with you." I'd grab his legs and hang on and scream when he was ready to leave.

My mother didn't want us and wouldn't let us go. He had to kidnap us, finally, and Roxy wasn't too thrilled. She was a better fit in that school than me.

**I.**          A white jazz drummer making a home for two half-black kids. I had to. My cute little melted chocolate sweetie was a lousy mother, a lousy wife. She forgot the kids, wanted to take off for the Far East or Europe or Latin America where she was an exotic. Liked hanging out late at night and could not get up in the morning. Impeccable about herself, but not about the house. Never cooked, never cleaned, never comforted them or me when we needed her. We were not meant for each other, I guess.

But where? Easy, but lousy. The Catskills. Get a job in a band in a big Jewish resort, live nearby and send them to a rural school. And where was my career? If I could not tour, how could I fulfill the promise of an early listing in a prominent jazz directory? I couldn't. Real jazz was down the tubes with my life.

I had two jobs, then, bring up the kids, earn enough to subsist on. Rent a house in the Catskills foothills, old wooden house, lousy plumbing, enough yard for growing vegetables and an apple tree and pear tree. A little chicken coop and a scratching run outside for the rooster and a couple of hens. Growing up in the Bronx, I knew enough to write to Cornell Ag to find out how.

I wasn't earning a lot – you play in a crummy band in the

Catskills, they think you're single and one of the benefits is getting laid. Part of my rent, I earned by helping the farmer we rented from. Chop wood, fix machines, clean the barn, ride the tractor. You could do that during the day, if you worked from eight o'clock on to one or two in the morning. Teach the kids to help.

Eli, junior. What kind of a name is that? We name after the dead, not the living. But if you have a shiksa wife, the kids aren't Jewish anyway. Not to my Orthodox family. Well, Eli, Jr., just Eli to me, wanted to help. He was a big kid who could dig, and chop, and carry and sweat. In winter, he could heat water to pour on the steps when they iced over, then break the ice. In summer, he could hoe weeds, replant lettuce and spinach and green beans. He was a good kid and followed orders. And watched me play the drums at home. Watched and watched, wagging his head, tapping his fingers and toes. His sister learned a little about moving from her mother. But not him. His body was clumsy. So he'd sit, smiling eagerly at me, forgetting to go to the bathroom till he peed in his pants.

He tried, but he was not really quick. Just earnest. Wanting so badly to be loved. He started early, collecting everything about me – pictures, programs, notices, stuff in the Catskill weeklies. I could do anything I wanted. He worshiped me. But no one else. I had fathered a big, rough kid that I had to worry about. I could not let him run wild; it would be too hard when he grew up. So his small, skinny, but still imposing, father beat the shit out of him for every transgression. And he cried and hollered and believed he deserved it.

Except when he didn't, when it was Roxy – like forgetting to flush the toilet. And when he'd convinced me it was not him, that ugly, triumphant shit-eating grin that Roxy had been caught.

I tried to teach him about manners, about classical music,

about dressing with subdued elegance, not coding himself with the fads the few others who'd settled in the area – cooks, musicians, civil servants – adopted from the city. That took. He was exceptionally neat. So many years of doing our laundry at the town Laundromat had fostered a culture of brightly bleached and blued whites, fabric softeners and all the rest of middle-class America's careful self-presentation.

II.          We lived like that for twelve years, moving from the Catskills to the Shawangunks, always near some big kosher hotel that catered to older people but had singles weekends and low rent conventions. Roxy still excelling in school and me just getting by. Daddy would ask me why. Wasn't I paying attention? I was. I just didn't get it. Didn't get math like fractions and percentages, didn't get much in history and geography, and didn't get biology or any other science. I could read, and I loved reading so Daddy focused on that. Learn lots of words, look them up when you don't know them. Mark them in your books to be sure. Make lists of new words. I did, I did. I looked them up, too. But I forgot them. He tried with the math, going over and over how to convert fractions to percentages. I'd have it. But it would slip away, always before the tests, not after.

"You don't test well," he'd say. "You're very acute and observant, but you don't test well." Right.

The hotels had services. Friday night and Saturday and on all the holidays, seders on Passover, feasts on Rosh Ha-shanah, and the night before and evening of Yom Kippur. Harvest festivals in a sukkah, every few weeks a new cere-monial occasion. Daddy took us to those. The guests would ask, incredulously, "Those are your children, Eli?" But he'd read the Hebrew with the other men, his body moving in unison with theirs, chanting the rhythms as if they had all gone to the same school.

The rabbis were always nice to us. The cantors, too. Cantors were big in the Catskills. A soaring tenor made a holiday. It was the one thing Roxy and I agreed on. We loved it all.

**I.** What do you do to kill the pain? Weed is ok to slow time for the accelerated bangs and pops a generation brought up on Gene Krupa expects from a drum solo. Weed is not a pain-killer. A needle. That's what the doctor gives you, that's what you give yourself. Morphine, heroin, the one legal for pain, the other not but available. A cooperative doctor – my back, my sciatica, whatever. Or a dealer. More expensive, less quality control.

The pain? The pain of living. Isn't that what it comes down to? I'd see some good-looking woman by herself on the streets of Saugerties or Woodstock or New Paltz. I'd smile, try to chat her up. And there would be young Eli, dragging me away to shop, "C'mon Daddy. I want my cereal." You can't make friends that way. Later, he'd rebuke me for flirting. When, then?

The pain of boredom with the music, boredom with the guests, boredom with the owners. Lura's maybe once a year picking up the kids to take to her lovely, tall, old aunt's place in Queens for a change of scene for two weeks. Two weeks a year for me?

The pain of never enough money, making do, living the humdrum life of the financially deprived. Cheap clothes, casserole meals, second-hand cars, working my two jobs, and an occasional third, working the kids' work. Light-headed and stupefied with the pain-killer, constipated and slow-witted and afraid to be irresponsible at work or at home.

And an occasional "cure". "I'm off it," I'd say, and mean it. Go through the runny nose, runny bottom, acute pain, try substitute drugs to hold on with. And then it would get to me again. I had no life, only pain, only responsibility.

And Lura, still cute, still talented, making out in Stockholm or Copenhagen, Tokyo or Manila. Could even put on little shows in the loft she'd taken downtown. She had nothing to worry about. Roxy was not going to go that way, and neither was Eli. Roxy was a scholar. Eli? I did not know.

And then, after the cure, the relapse. Just this once, I'd tell myself. I *need* it. I can't bear my life. The docs were kind. They'd write a prescription.

**II.**          In high school I was much bigger than Daddy. Bigger all around. I had disappeared one day when I was supposed to be working with him on the farm. I wanted to go to the movies. They had an old James Cagney playing and I loved that tough little guy. I came back and there was Daddy, taking the belt off his pants, ready to give it to me.

"No more, Daddy," I said, bawling. "You can't do that any more. I'm bigger than you. I'm a grown man." He shook his head from side to side, slowly. I could see the tears behind his glasses.

"You are. What am I going to do with you now? You're almost ready to go out into the world, and you don't understand, aren't ready."

"I am, I am," I bawled. "You have no faith in me. I work hard, I do what you taught me. I have only one year left to finish high school. Then I'll go to college, like you."

"College? Where?" It gave him something to do. Roxy already had a scholarship for girls of African descent to go to Bryn Mawr and study biology. She would go far, she said, with a doctorate that would take her to the Harvard faculty, and be world-famous for her research.

"Where? Anywhere," I said. "I'll go."

The counselor at school didn't think so. "I know you work hard. You're an overachiever," he said, confident that the word meant I did better than I was entitled to.

Daddy got a job in the Poconos to be closer to Roxy.

Playing again at a big resort, this one mainly for honeymooners. It had fancy, heart-shaped beds, mirrors on the ceiling, lots of foolishness, but the same heavy food as the Catskills. This one was more for Poles and three-day Polish weddings. Daddy even had to drum for polkas. What a comedown. But he picked up a few recording gigs with his old jazz friends on his day off. Jazz was coming back, and we were not so dependent now on his presence. I could cook for myself.

We had to find our services on Saturday morning in a nearby town. Daddy had taught me to read Hebrew and make a passable effort at translating, so even if I was not a Bar Mitzvah – he had not thought of that in time, and besides I was with my mother when I should have started – I could pass.

I could pass in lots of ways. On the telephone. You'd never guess then.

What was I good at? Drumming for jazz and dance. Talking. The college and career counselor said I'd never finish college, even if I could get into one. I knew I would, no matter what. By the end of the year, we'd chosen what was right for me. A little college in Pennsylvania that had a major in oral communication. Talk, preparing for talk, interviewing, radio and television, reading aloud, announcing for radio and television, doing commercials, developing the formats for music shows, MCing for special events. Just right in addition to English, a little of this and that, plenty of music.

I told Daddy we'd found it and I'd make it.

**I.** He's a good kid. Always was. Knew about helping out. Knew the value of experience. As soon as he had a career path in mind, he volunteered at a local radio station, learning about the equipment, watching the control room, seeing how they labeled everything so no novice could screw it up. He liked that. Always liked methodically fixing labels on connectors.

It was a dinky station, but they gave him an opportunity to announce, to pick up the AP wire releases and recite them for news on the hour. Especially late. And he was always willing to play the drums at a wedding or party in the area or when another drummer fell ill. Or me.

I was beginning to feel my age. Was this funny-looking, sad-looking guy in the mirror me? Thinning, graying hair, a little pot from sitting too much in crappy chairs when I played the drums, or maybe just from lounging in the recliner after taking my pain-killer.

He worries about me. I see it. I tell him I'm clean.

They're all just prescription drugs I need for arthritis, kidneys, sciatica, whatever. You open my medicine chest and it's a regular pharmacy. Not what other people have, eye drops and aspirin, Pepto-Bismol and antihistamines. I have the real stuff. Plenty. All my money goes to drugs. It's a good thing Eli works during the summer, helps out, bags groceries in the market.

I don't know if I can go on. I must go on. (Yeah, I've read Beckett. I read a lot, like Eli, Jr.)

**II.**      I knew it would happen. I was 18, just about to start college, when I got a call. I got to our rental house. There was our Ford in the driveway, and there was Daddy sprawled in the back seat, flushed and sweaty and dead.

I screamed and cried. Someone else had to call the police, an ambulance. Too late. They took him to the morgue in Stroudsberg. Cause of death? An overdose. Accidental or deliberate? Did he want to die? He did not say and left no notes.

High and dry, that's how he left me. No money, no insurance, no provision for a funeral. Social Security paid a death benefit (a couple of hundred dollars.) Roxy came for the funeral and we decided then and there to convert because it was all he had left us. Judaism and the caring community of an orthodox congregation that wanted us. We already knew a lot. It did not take long, and it was the best thing we did. That Congregation was so touched, they raised the money for my first year in college. I worked, begged, played drums, hit my mother for money a couple of times, even her nice old aunt in Queens, and the Jewish grandparents who just had to. I got through.

And no matter what I did, where I was, I asked myself. Did he give up? Was it deliberate? Did he just leave me like that, at eighteen, to make it by myself? Would he have been so cruel? Would he?

We're the same age, now, he and I. I hate my life, too. I want to be a father, to a white kid. I was married once. I'm not sure why. Yeah, I know why. She was an immigrant from Finland; to stay, she had to marry a citizen. I think I loved her, but we were like ships that pass in the night. She did not like my apartment, got tired of me quickly and left. After a while, we were divorced. No issue. I'd marry again in a minute: to any Jewish woman who would have a baby with me. Or any fertile white woman. These older women – they look all right, smooth skin, okay figures, but it's estrogens from the drugstore. They won't have children, and I spill my seed.

My father was a father, and I want to be a father. I have always wanted to be just like him.

I play drums, real drums, real skins, real whisks but only occasional gigs. I inherited my Dad's drum set; I have no room for it. Roxy keeps it for me, I think.

I have had plenty of jobs, booking guests for talk radio, running the technical side for famous guys who broadcast out of their upper west side apartments. But it all breaks up after a while. I am ambitious and independent and they have a hard time dealing with me. They want someone else.

These days, I talk on the radio, but only on weekends in a lousy station upstate. I even do my own jazz show on Sunday morning there in Poughkeepsie. They know my name, Eli Schwartz, Jr. And some people, having called me to MC at local events, even know what I look like, and recognize me in the city. Eli Schwartz, the *schwartze*.

I meet nice girls: I am a respected member of a small orthodox synagogue. I even advertise my jazzy difference in the singles column of a Jewish weekly. But the girls I meet won't take me home to meet their families. They say I'm cute; we have a great time on dates; they're crazy about me in bed. But even when I'm crazy about them, if they won't take me home, won't marry me, I get angry and break it up.

You guessed it. I'm an angry man. The system has given me nothing. I work like a dog, but I do not advance. In job after job, they make me a clerk, a gofer. I thought I'd be able to sell novelties, after all I'm a good talker. But not shrewd. I don't spot the gimmicks, the hooks that tie me up when someone offers me another lousy job. So, yes, I work during the day in an office. I am not unskilled. I know how to use some computer software, how to speak on the phone. I report to work on time. I clean my one-room apartment, I do my laundry at the Laundromat just as Daddy taught me to. Plenty of bleach and softener. No grungy sheets or underwear.

We're the same age, Daddy and I. I smoke an occasional joint. I think all drummers do. It's harmless. No needles, no sniffing. I hang out in a pizza bar and make friends. My mother and I, we hardly ever see each other. She is now Lu-Ra, still an entertainer, and pretty good. But we have nothing to say to each other and that's all right with me. I don't need her.

What do I need? A life. Or what?


End

# THE FRANCHISE

By the early eighties Richard Strayton was a success. A man who knew the value of appearances, he wore beautiful suits to the office and in the field. He favored pinstripes, custom shirts and severely rich jewelry. Thanks to his careful attention to eating right and getting plenty of exercise, his clothes fit him elegantly. His trimness was a metaphor for power when he dealt with customers and in social situations. He could see the momentary bellyward glances of the guys he'd gone to school with now when they met. "How do you stay in shape?," they'd ask. He'd grin ambiguously. He didn't have to answer.

Success had other markers, too: a new Jaguar for him; a little Aston Martin for his wife. The Jaguar said he'd made it. Only someone who took the trouble to understand such a car could afford to keep it. He did not need to drive it much, which was just as well, since it was often in the repair shop. He had a company-provided marshmallow — an Oldsmobile — for weekday use.

It was not just clothes and cars. A new home was required, too. People asked where you lived. You were judged by how you looked and what you owned. Lifestyle, it was called. So, a new residence should not be really new, just in the right place and better. In fact, a fine older home would

reinforce the image he and Gloria wanted. They knew some
of their moves were risky, but they were ready. Their old
crowd did not have much to offer anyway. Mostly school
friends, they had not advanced beyond where they started
— in family businesses and shops. So, he and Gloria moved
from Montclair to Princeton to make new friends. Montclair was a nice suburban town with pleasant middle-class
people, but now that he was making real money, Princeton was the place. The houses were larger and their grounds
had mature plantings. Princeton had a world-famous university with important academic people. It also had theatrical
and art activities, libraries and the Institute for Advanced
Study. To Gloria who had graduated from Douglass College
at Rutgers, thinking she might teach home economics; and to
Richard who had a BBA from Fairleigh Dickinson, Princeton
represented serious intellectual and social opportunity.

School. Richard's family had expected him to go to college. They knew it was not so much academic talent an employer would look for, but the simple steadiness that getting
a degree proved. He had not been an ambitious student.
His required science had been the one-year overview of all
science that the college offered business and liberal arts majors. His math, very much the same: an overview of math
for people who would forget it as soon as they passed the
course's final exam. Required English, required social studies, no foreign language. Yes, economics, business writing,
accounting, marketing and sales. A bit of corporate strategy and personnel management — and there you had it, a
bachelor's degree. No sweat.

His company had known what it wanted. It had chosen
its annual crop of sales trainees for years from the same pool
of local colleges, and their BBA graduates. He did not know
until much later that it specified to faculty advisers in the
business administration department just what kind of guy
— it was all guys then — it recruited. The company wanted

pleasant-looking fellows with grade point averages around 2.5 for sales jobs. It trained well, paid well, had a reputation for stability after the first arduous year, and had plenty of room for upward mobility. What could be better for guys who wanted to make money, were willing to learn and to work hard, and whose talents were still buried?

The company needed an annual crop because the hard thing about sales was that even in a good company, it took motivation to get up in the morning, call on people, learn how to turn their objections around into useful arguments for buying. The training was arduous, the pep talks incessant, "We have a major franchise in this company. We are THE institutional supplier of coffee and related products to the restaurants, hospitals, schools, factories and offices, colleges, even a few fast food franchise organizations in this part of the country. Remember that: a major franchise," the sales vice-president said.

Richard was not quite sure what he meant. Franchise. His company was not the same as McDonald's. So what was its franchise? It did not really matter, he decided early. It was a word sales people used to mean that customers knew who they were and what their company represented in quality and operating style. Good enough. The training at that time did not take place in classrooms. No. Richard was sent out with a "producer" — a man who understood the business and who would get a small percentage of his commissions for working with him. And who knew that the company protected its salesmen's territories so he need not worry that his trainee would supplant him or get a share of his customers.

He loved it. He loved the variety of their visits and the lore of food service and of coffee. He loved the names of the countries of origin for coffee, the names of the beans. He recited their characteristics and what kinds of food service they were good for with a joy in the detail that Mies had said was God.

During his early training period he lived at home with his family and entertained his father and mother and kid sister at dinner with imitations of foreign-born chefs' accents, and accounts of how he flirted with school lunch personnel. But that was all right. He was a serious man, who made sure he learned what he needed to.

By the end of the first six months, three of the trainees who had been hired with him had left or been fired. One had taken to filing exciting sales reports of visits to prospective accounts, accounts, he said, that were now giving unmistakeable signs of switching to his company, persuaded by the eloquence of the energetic salesman filing them. But the excitement remained just that; the orders had failed to materialize, and when the man was questioned, he said there had been personnel changes or that minor remodeling was taking place. It was not clear whether it was his or the company's discouragement that persuaded him to leave. Another had somehow totaled a company car in his assiduous cultivation, late at night, of a major Italian restaurant. Management did not think he should work such long hours, so they shortened his hours by axing him. The third had departed the northeast for an even more promising job selling real estate in California, a choice encouraged by his new girlfriend who had career hopes of her own that might better be realized in southern California.

The company gave Richard a little six-month bonus to let him know he was important to them. At the end of two years, he was labeled a "producer", qualified to train new hires. At the end of five years, he had a territory to supervise and spent more of his time in the office, preparing pricing schedules, maneuvering against competition, even conducting sales meetings for his territory and reiterating the magic words "our franchise."

And now, he'd been with the company eight years and

was a vice-president. He conducted the training programs, advised salesmen about when to visit each kind of facility to get the most attention from the owner or manager, discussed knowledgeably the various methods of grinding and roasting coffee for each facility's customers and their coffee drinking habits, worked with the ad agency on coffee promotions — tabletop and menu inserts as well as festivals. He even provided funds and mats for cooperative advertising where it was appropriate. Coffee was a complex business that people on the outside could scarcely grasp. Especially since the firm was diversifying into specialty teas and coffees and into dessert bases and pudding powders. They were part of their "franchise", selling easy-to-store dry products that marketing could differentiate from those of the competition, Standard Brands and General Foods, and lately Procter and Gamble.

What his company had was specialization, service and expertise. S-S-EX, Richard would hiss — these create our franchise, he told new hires. There was nothing the matter with a bit of friendly laughter during a hard-driving training session. Then he'd go on. No other organization provided as much at competitive prices. He'd conduct his sales meetings with such joy in the company's accomplishments and its future that the owners found it infectious. Indeed, it was not just they. The dropout rate for new hires dwindled, and the company, which quantified everything including the costs of hiring and training, was well aware of Richard's importance to them. It was better to spend less time recruiting new people and more on creating experts. During these years, however, Richard noted something disquieting. Despite the fact that their sales were up, coffee use was perceptibly diminishing. He knew he had to analyze the causes and think of solutions, but felt he needed to do some research.

He shifted his routines. Went back into the field at least a day a week to learn what was going on, following his own precepts for visits. Early in the day: school lunch ladies. He was no longer flirting with them, even in jest. The managers were usually sharp old girls who looked for bargains for the teachers' lounge and lunchrooms. Teachers drank a lot of coffee, and did not care much about quality. They drank it to keep their heads together, to socialize, to stimulate them a little way out of boredom. The teachers' lunchrooms and lounges used bottle brewers, only a few cups brewed at a time, so it did not lose its flavor on the warmer. Standard blends, even cheap blends using lots of Brazilian coffee were fine. Coffee was not served to students, of course, not even in high schools and not even in the south where it was commonly drunk at home by children. That was because U.S. Department of Agriculture reimbursements provided only for milk to students. Anything else was not subsidized and considered "bad" for kids, on a par with consumption of soda or candy. Richard liked visiting schools and looking at the grandmotherly ladies working in their simple kitchens assembling sandwiches, or preparing macaroni and cheese in big stainless steel pans. He liked seeing the kids who came for breakfast clustering at the steam tables and grabbing for their little boxes of cereal and containers of milk. He and Gloria had no children.

After schools, he had to be careful about timing. Next, he'd visit a hospital in the interval between breakfast and lunch preparation. The system in hospitals was changing — many tried to get food prepared in advance of meal assembly rather than try to coordinate the whole thing from preparation and cooking to service just before tray assembly. Dietitians, still the managers, were real professionals. They not only ran the kitchens, they advised the patients and even the doctors about nutrition. So there was a hierarchy of dietitians from the chief, generally a starchy, smart older woman, to the newest young things fresh out of college, and called, in deference to the venue, "interns". No one, however, called them "interns" in the staff dining rooms. The real interns might not like it. Hospitals used coffee urns, large capacity stainless steel devices with huge baskets for coffee in the top, spray-over water fittings to wet the coffee uniformly for brewing, steam-jackets to keep the coffee warm (it wasn't really steam, as it turned out — merely hot water which was used for tea, and being at a temperature good for keeping coffee warm, made a lousy cup of tea.)

Well, it was fine equipment and brewed a lot at a time because a lot was needed at a time. The trouble was that some unscrupulous competitors would provide these hugely expensive pieces of equipment in exchange for a commitment to buy their coffee. Which, as Richard pointed out to indecisive chief dietitians, meant they had to charge more for their coffee to make up their "gifts." Richard's company did not offer equipment. But the chief dietitians had arguments, too. Getting a new urn into their capital budgets was often very difficult, whereas no one scrutinized the price they paid for coffee. He'd nod lugubriously. Hospitals used a lot of coffee and brewed it differently for patients than for staff. Weak for patients, strong for staff. Some of the staff worked thirty-six hours without a rest. He'd get them when their commitment to the other companies was over. Meantime, the hospitality shops with their bottle brewers were still his.

It would be close to lunchtime now, and a bad time to visit anyone. There were always personnel emergencies and tensions. Right after lunch to late afternoon was the best time. The best time for fine restaurants, many of which used pressure or filter devices with his dark-roasted espresso; or hotels whose major meals were breakfast and dinner and wanted the richest, most aromatic blends. He could visit a college whose lunchtime rush was over, or an in-plant food service where three-part urns could not keep up with the demand, or a prison where watery coffee was designed to keep the inmates somnolent rather than charged up. And the ubiquitous coffee shops in towns on main streets, in road-side diners, on highways wherever an intersection promised traffic.

His informal questions and perceptions as he visited these places, talked to the managers who ranged from third or fourth generation family members steeped in the restaurant business ... to the hotel chains' Cornell graduates ... from executive chefs trained in Germany or Switzerland... to con-tract caterers' managers at the colleges and factories... to coffee shop owners, began to come to conclusions. He had noted, himself, that supermarkets were selling instant coffee to many customers. A major roaster had tried to introduce instant coffee to the food service business by saying their cus-tomers would not know the difference. Well, no restaurant or coffee shop anywhere that he knew about had adopted instant. They were still serving the real thing.

Why then had home consumption of instant affected the institutions' coffee consumption? It dawned on him, then. Instant, made from cheap beans was highly profitable, that's why it was promoted by the big grocery companies. But, because it was made from cheap beans and so heavily pro-cessed, it had much less caffeine. At least a third, maybe even a half less. It did not smell or taste as good, either. The new generation began to lose its coffee habit — without the caffeine kick and sensuous pleasure of flavor and aroma, why should they drink coffee? Richard even wondered for a moment if the rise of cocaine among drug users reflected the loss of the legal kick of good coffee. But most bever-age consumers found solace in the cola beverages that once sported coke — the real thing — among their ingredients. Their fizzy sugary *boissons* had about the same amount of caffeine as instant coffee and young people began drinking Pepsi and Coke at home for breakfast and lunch. And what were they drinking when they ate out, now? At lunch any-way: Pepsi and Coke. He was deeply alarmed at the trend and resolved to take it up with management and to develop a plan to counter it.

He brought his plan to company owners at a two-hour meeting. It was the first time he had really used some of the skills he'd learned at Fairleigh Dickinson, he used overheads he'd made on his copier — the data from the Coffee Brewing Institute, the charts of consumption over the past ten years, the numbers of people he had interviewed, and his conclusions. He had found the problem, and he knew what to do. So when the owners told him, "Coffee consumption is going down only one percent a year. There's nothing to be done about it," he said there was plenty to do about it.

He offered to help set up a country-wide marketing plan in which independent coffee roasters and distributors everywhere could participate. It would promote the "legal high" of good coffee. It would recommend small, quick coffee makers for people at home who only wanted a cup or two at a time. It would promote fashion, with special big two-handled cups for breakfast with lots of milk. It would recommend lunchtime refreshers and iced espressos and push the coffee break to management as well as workers. Coffee had major benefits in increasing accomplishment and creativity during the working day. It improved athletic performance, it helped to relieve headaches. It was a terrific biological product. And for those who worried about calories, top off the meal with a good coffee — you'll feel great and keep your figure!

The principals in the firm listened to him incredulously. "What makes you think even half of the roasters in the country would go for it? And the others would be getting a free ride," said one.

Another said, "It's the times. People want drugs and trouble. It's a rebellious spirit in this country now."

A third pointed out, "Independent roasters don't sell much to the consumer market. We're institutional coffee distributors. We would not be doing ourselves any good at all, just spending a lot of money for nothing."

He protested. "It's a long-range market we're trying to build. We could even offer specialty beans in gourmet shops and delicatessens. And make money..." Not one of them supported him.

Richard wondered if it was because they were third-generation in the business. Wondered if the energy and creativity and, maybe, anxiety, that had started their successful company and kept it going had petered out in this comfortable time. Well, no matter. He had his job, the company had its franchise, sales were still expanding and if he and they kept on this way, he might be their first non-family president.

He talked about that with Gloria at home. They were often home together in the most interesting part of the day. After dinner — whether eaten at home or out — their life was theirs. They played games, indulged in elaborate charades, assumed new roles. Gloria — what a nice woman she was — researched their games and plays in the library, in the museums, in fashion, art, history, movies — whatever she fancied. And he, enjoying the theatrical as he had even when he began his sales career and played customer roles, improvised in response. They had a wonderful time together. And if this meant lots of exercise of many kinds — that was fine. It was the secret, he thought, of his exemplary trimness.

It came as a total surprise when it was announced at an all-company meeting late one Friday that the owning family had sold the company. Sold it to a cola company that had a coffee roasting subsidiary whose specialty was individual gauze-bound humps of coffee on a tape for vending machines. When the money went into their vending machine slots, hot water was forced through one of these humps (thus they could boast, "individually brewed") and dispensed, very quickly, into a paper cup, producing a flavorless, odorless, highly profitable beverage, sometimes "whitened" with a mixture of soy products and vegetable oils. Richard was shocked, as were his colleagues.

The owning family apologized to them all. "You must understand," said the president. "We're the third generation in this business and we have loved it and carried it on honorably. But our children are not businesspeople: they are artists and musicians and antiques collectors and professors. When we go, the company would be sold anyway, and perhaps not into so favorable a market. The cola company is maintaining our franchise — they will keep our contacts up with the food service facilities we service, selling their cola and other syrups to our existing customers, placing their vending machines in out-of-the-way locations in plants and office buildings." A few eyes rolled up to the ceiling.

"The people who work in our plant will still work there. We want their expertise at blending and roasting. But, the cola company's sales department will probably take over sales for our organization — after all, they call on the same customers, and there would be an economy for them in selling our blends, too — so we have hired a very high-quality outplacement organization to take care of the rest of you. That, unfortunately, includes many of the marketing, billing and other inside people. We know you have worked hard and loyally for us, and we will do our best to make our parting an opening of new opportunity for you."

They were to clear their desks and belongings; and their severance checks, quite generous, almost a year's pay in Richard's case, would be in the mail soon. The outplacement company was setting up headquarters in a nearby hotel whose public space would be fitted for meetings and with temporary partitions for interviews during the six weeks of outplacement activity the company was funding.

"Outplacement." It was a new word. Employment agencies placed you "in." This was an opposite function: placing you "out." The first outplacement meeting was the following Monday in the hotel meeting room. A team of two persons, one male and one female, recited their lines.

"Companies have begun to downsize" (ah, another new word) "because markets are changing. Our job is to help you muster your resources to get jobs even better than the one you're leaving." (Yes, leaving.) "We will start by interviewing each of you, then go on to have you prepare a resume first, and then a 'network' schema for yourselves. A network will include all the people you know at work and at church and from school and any other contacts who can help you. We'll explain how to classify and work your network. You will have the space and phones here for doing that. You see, this is all organized, and you will not fumble at all in looking for a new position. That's what outplacement is all about." It was the woman first, perhaps to evoke motherly care for the orphaned children before her. Her name was Samantha Smith, and the outplacement firm was the biggest in the country, an affiliate of a major publishing company, she told them, so you knew they would not let you down.

Then, her colleague came on, calling the small group of executives including Richard, into his meeting in another room, while Samantha took care of the record-keeping, billing, service and other personnel. The man's name was Benjamin Grilli, and they were to call him "Ben." They were to sit around a table while he chatted informally about the outplacement process, and gave them assignments. In case they had not thought to bring notebooks, there were looseleaf books for them, full of ruled paper and even some graph paper for charting their activity. Each of them had a label on the cover, thoughtfully provided by the outplacement firm, which already bore their full names.

Ben said "You're a special group, with special skills, experience and education, and need a different approach to your careers. We're here to provide it, to help you discover who you are, whom you know, and what you can do. It will be systematic and painless – almost a voyage of discovery into a new world." Nobody laughed.

He then gave them assignments to do. Get their address books and Rolodexes in order, sort their business cards — the ones they picked up at business shows, at church, at Rotary or Lions or business organization lunches and dumped into a desk drawer or bound together with a handy rubber band. "This is your network. Start making a list now of all the people you know on page one of the tabbed section called 'network' in your looseleaf. Not just business contacts, personal contacts, even family. We've finally found a use for your brother-in-law," he joked. Everybody set to work. They were good workers after all. That's why they'd been promoted and kept on by the company, and were now in this program.

"Next," he said, "let's get started on your resumes. They will be an essential part of the process. Our point of view is that the resume has to sell you as the answer to a prospective employer's problems. It should not be just a 'where I've been' resume but a sales document. You have, of course, been keeping your resumes up to date, haven't you?" He grinned. "I guess not from the looks on your faces. You'd been promoted, you'd been rewarded with perks, you were secure. It is time to face the new reality. No one is secure now. Not me, and certainly not you, ever again. Even the president of a company has to keep his resume up to date now — he never knows when a headhunter will call or a search for a board member will offer him an extra 20K a year for a few hours of his time — and along with that, some extra pension money for a few years of service. That's part of what gives business its charm. Resumes. Did anyone bring his?"

Well, yes, one or two. They followed the format Ben had described as "where I've been," which would not do. "We will turn your head around so that you look to the future, not the past," Ben said.

Richard remembered Janus, from high school — who seemed to be able to look two ways at once.

"Your resumes will tell how you solve problems, what accomplishments you've been promoted for, how your salary escalated from the time you were hired to now... by percentages so that even if you started modestly the numbers will be meaningful. It will disclose the potential that your new employer will tap. Start thinking about emphasizing your accomplishments, then tenure and title. When you redraft the resume, we'll have a resume workshop. We have typists and copiers nearby. They can take your drafts and turn them into beautiful documents that we'll read appreciatively." Another grin.

"Now we'll do the interviews one at a time, for the guys who brought even rudimentary resumes — I'll call you. The rest of you — see if you can do a one-page yellow scratchpad of your career, education, family, interests, so we can get the interviews started even before the resumes are drafted."

The afternoon went by quickly. They were working, in a way, keeping the hours they always kept so that their loss of jobs, status, income and future would be apparent to no one — for a while. It was not till the next day that Richard was interviewed.

Ben said, "A marketing hot shot, are you?" Richard demurred.

"Too bad it's all been with one company. People think then that all you know is one product, and how to manage it. But good marketers are always in demand. You look good, better than good." He appraised Richard frankly. "The institutional market is growing, and some of the distributors are consolidating — the grocery distributors, Flagstaff, Sysco. Besides the broad line grocery companies like Kraft are getting into institutional. Shouldn't have much trouble. And in the meantime, while you're looking, you can be a consultant for almost anyone. Print some cards and a leaflet and you're in business." Richard was dismissed. He still had to revise his resume.

The network came into play. He was afraid to use much of the A list first — what if he fumbled with the really serious possibilities? Ben agreed. Start with maybe one or two of the A list and use B and C entries also till you learned what was successful. Richard's A list was the competition, the grocery distributors, the major food manufacturers. He had business acquaintances at all these companies — people he met at trade shows; and there were business acquaintances in the media and advertising who might be the source of leads. The B list was the people who cared: family, close friends. And the C list was everyone else: church, people he went to school with, anyone he met who had some business or even non-profit organization experience. Ben said that's how you organize your network.

He sent out his first letter, marking his lists with codes for who had received what. This letter was a straightforward explanation of the facts: his company had been sold, a considerable number of marketing people had been made redundant despite their previous successes, and he was now "networking" for leads. So no one was to believe (a) he'd been fired; (b) that they personally were responsible for finding his new job; only (c) that he was trusting them to think about whom they knew who might find a resume of such exceptional accomplishment interesting. In other words (d) would they network a few of their best for him, forwarding his resume with a letter of their own.

It sounded like a good way to do it — a chain letter of a sort. But, despite the fact that people did work their own nets for him and sent very nice letters which they photocopied to him, he had achieved only a few interviews in four weeks — and those were preceded by reluctant interviewers with, "There's nothing here now, but we like to know whom to call in case something comes up." Friendly, good-natured, unproductive.

He tried some of the A list again, and some others with a note saying, "I'm available for temporary consulting assignments in your office: marketing, distribution organization, sales training, even high-level organizational sales." This received some response. They thought he might call on his old customers to "convert" them to their organization. Commissions only. "How much, for how long?" he asked. No answer, no contract. No soap.

He was still in the outplacement unit, after all. It would not be right to betray people who had treated him well. He talked it over with Gloria. She thought it was possible that the old company would call him back when they discovered that the cola salesmen who placed vending machines were not good at real coffee. "Don't leave a bad taste with them. You never know," she said wistfully. He was a little romantic that way, himself. And there was plenty of severance pay to put into mortgage payments and the cleaners; he was still reporting daily to the outplacement unit, which, Ben Grilli said, had furnished all the tools he and his fellow executives needed and must now go into "crisis mode."

"What? We'll manage. We're capable people. Why talk crisis?"

"Well," Grilli and Stephanie said, "our contract ends in a week or two and we are supposed to provide crisis counseling if it is needed. We want you all to make a confidential list of your major worries, the things that scare you and your families. We will go over them one on one and no one but us will know."

More little visits to the cubicles, but the habits of a lifetime could not so easily be compromised. No one said anything about health insurance, about school tuition, about age and fear problems, about dissension at home . "I'm all right, Jack" sensibilities prevailed. No real man would say anything else.

The six weeks were over. Richard set up shop in his basement: a desk, old Smith-Corona portable typewriter, extension telephone. He hired an answering service in case some-one called. And had new business cards printed, "Richard Strayton, marketing consultant." A friend put out a press release, "Strayton Opens Consulting Firm." He mailed it to local newspapers, national trade media and a laboriously compiled list from Thomas' Register. It was only postage after all.

The notice appeared with a smiling portrait of him in a few trade papers, and in a south Jersey weekly. Friends called to congratulate him. Inquiries? Yes. From publications that wanted him to buy space for an ad, even just a "business card" ad. One from a startup firm that was going into men's soaps and wanted him to take an "equity position." Or to give him "stock" in exchange for his work. He did not think he could afford to be a volunteer. At the end of two months, with only two or three minor assignments — half days that he was billing at a modest two hundred dollars per diem — he realized that this was not the avenue to success. The anxiety was beginning to get to him. Working at home, even in the basement, made home the place to get away from. Evenings, dependent as they had been on Gloria's researches and the fun of acting them out, needed relaxed self-confident participants. Gloria thought they'd be better able to relax if she found a job. That was how she put it.

She had a college degree; she knew the library intimately. That was where she would inquire. But not in Princeton. Research was one thing; a job, another. She went to New Brunswick and was hired almost immediately for five after-noons a week in the children's division where her skills at story-telling, knowledge of fairy tales and fantasy and imag-inative recreations of different times and places were highly valued. And, of course, she could combine her work with ongoing research. Richard congratulated himself on a very creative wife.

But his problem... They had conserved the bulk of his severance pay. He was still answering ads for marketing and distribution executives. He was still "networking." But depression was getting to him. He was beginning to wonder if he would ever get back on the success ladder...

The outplacement firm got in touch after six months for a follow-up report. It was Samantha Smith. "Not much yet," he reported, 'T've gone into business for myself, and I've had a few hits..."

"Have you thought about a franchise?" she asked. He winced. "You have a business degree, after all. You'll probably do brilliantly."

A franchise, yes. The word was so familiar and homey. There was a franchise show in the basement of the Hilton hotel in New York the following week, and Richard, thinking the timing was terrific, decided to scout them all at once. Once there, however, he felt again the pain in his situation. There were uniform little booths, each offering a "package" of promotion material in a logo-emblazoned folder. Perhaps it was the uniformity of the packages that depressed him:. A letter from the president about "our franchise." A series of quotes from existing franchisees about their financial happiness. A few diagrams or photos of an existing facility, and most important, a financial breakdown of what the franchisors wanted, as well as a "pro forma" statement of what could be expected from the investment.

There they were: sign makers who could produce signs and lettering in one day. The franchisor said this was an ideal corporate transition, a "business to business" route to success. Next a lawn care business. Richard wondered if there was enough in it for winter. Or if you used the tractor for snow-plowing. Auto care. That sounded useful. He had traded the Jaguar in for a serviceable new Chevy now that he no longer had the Olds for everyday. Gloria had sold her car and was taking the bus to New Brunswick. These were good capital conservation moves, but Richard knew that everyone in the suburbs had at least one car and needed reliable service. The problem was that these auto care franchises were so specialized: mufflers or car washes and if you had not grown up with them, not so easy to adapt to. They were offering "master" franchises. He liked the idea until he understood the term — it meant you buy a lot of them and resell some to sub-buyers whom you supervised. The economics boggled his mind.

Here was an intriguing one: video yearbooks. Sell the idea to a high school or college and spend the year videotaping the kids in their home-rooms, after-school clubs, performances, athletic activities. Then transform the results into an hour's show everyone would want. He considered that real fun. But the firm wanted an investment of $15-35,000 dollars up front, and he'd have to wait a year for the payoffs. What could he do in the interval? Even if he sold the idea to ten local schools (was that a stretch?) and spent all his time videotaping at these schools fitting his schedules into intricate bits of time, would it pay off? Ten schools, fifty dollars per finished videotape, fifty student takers per school made a grand total of twenty-five thousand dollars in gross revenue for a year's work and the purchase of the raw tape. He didn't think he could make it. Maybe with a staff of part-timers, maybe with a large territory, maybe with really big schools in prosperous neighborhoods...

Kiddie Care. He could go into that with Gloria as his staff to begin. But the investment wanted was one hundred thousand dollars or more. They'd have to borrow. He'd think about it.

Here was another, a party store, a biggie. Their minimum investment was over $250,000, and they said the average revenue was over $1,000,000. Where? he thought. What kind of community can pay that kind of money for paper plates and crepe paper? He could not take a party store seriously.

Natural cosmetics. He loved cosmetics – for the appropriate moments and uses. Did he care if they were "natural"? Not much, but nice smells and packages were far from unpleasant to deal with, and the people who'd buy such cosmetics were probably good-natured and attractive. He liked that until he looked at the minimum investment, $240,000.

He moved along. Some of these little enterprises were clearly last-ditch possibilities for the guys offering them. Their packages scraped together by desperate men attracted to the idea by the possibility of up-front money. Richard felt for them, but knew better than to make eye contact. If he did, they'd harangue him for a while, waste his time.

Here was another neat one, he thought. A consignment business. Rent a barn, tell people you were starting a flea market, that they could bring things for resale. Used merchandise, tools, antiques, art, clothes. The guy called it "pre-owned" quality merchandise. ( There was no limit to the coverup words people coined for desperate reality.) The franchisor was offering a "system" for managing secondhands that would return a good living.

And here was a revolutionary auto technology that had no competition. What? No idle questions please.

An independent dealership in color tile and carpet. That would work. He could not work up any enthusiasm.

A travel agency. Yes. He liked that. Free travel went with it, and he and Gloria could get lost in new cultures. He picked up the package for that one. It was a distinct possibility, especially with a modest fee of only $39.5 thousand dollars. Of course, they'd not done much traveling. How much did this depend on personal recommendation? Where would they get clients? The package said nothing about national referrals from the franchising organization. He'd be able to use his networking lists for contacts; but he and Gloria would have to be trained, would have to join a society of travel agents... How did people get into these unfamiliar businesses and make a go of them? That was the real thing. He'd seen some statistics: franchises failed more often than other entrepreneurial activities. The promises and statistics in the logo'd brochures were sometimes fraudulent. What did he really know that he could do and afford to do?

There it was. Coffee. Where was a coffee franchise? There wasn't one. Coffee had a dwindling market; he'd done the research himself. Was there a franchise that knew about coffee? He went back to the franchise journal. Here was a booth with a magazine only about franchises. He realized that most of what he'd seen here were startups. He wanted a franchise with a track record if he was going to invest. There it was: not a coffee franchise but a franchise known for good coffee. A big one. The big donut franchise that everyone knew had the best coffee in the business. He'd been put off before by the donuts, but not now. He had to make a living. He wrote to Massachusetts.

There was a lot to learn: How to make the mixes for the various donuts, how long to keep them, how to decorate them, how to turn the last of the yeast-raised donut mix into "cinnamon rolls" when the yeast was too tired to make a fluffy donut. How to reheat the cinnamon rolls in a microwave oven for breakfast. And how to store the mixes, how to display the donuts, and finally — but this he knew — how to brew and hold the lovely mixture of Colombian and Brazilian arabica bean coffee. "Throw it out after eighteen minutes," the instructions were. He approved, even when it cost him money. The coffee was fresh and delicious all the time. He had to buy it from their approved supplier, but that insured uniformity, and that was what franchises were about – predictable quality wherever you found them.

Life settled into a routine. He was able to hire minimum

wage helpers, students, drop-outs, old people. They came and went (turnover, they said, would be over one hundred percent a year, but that was all right. It meant hardly anyone qualified for raises and promotions.) Gloria kept her part-time job in the library and helped out in the shop in the morning, and he and his helpers took care of the rest of the day. Donuts did not have much to offer in the evenings in his suburban town. The big business was mornings, very early, and a steady stream during the working day. He could set his hours as he pleased, staying open late Friday and Saturday nights. He had his own little side-businesses that nobody minded. There was a delivery service to businesses and meetings, and a breakfast buffet for local motels. He had other ideas, too, but they were emphatically nixed by the area supervisor. As were his other suggestions for improvement in the franchise overall.

He offered an idea to increase business for lunch and dinner that would require no expertise and very little additional space or equipment in the franchises' tight little structures: sandwiches to be made by the customers, themselves, with portion-controlled ingredients on paper slapped appetizingly on a wooden cutting board. Since the sanitary paper was between portions, the cutting board did not need a destructive turn in a non-existent dishwasher.

In response to this good idea, the area supervisor said, "The worst franchisees are those with a business degree. It's a real handicap. We surveyed 139 franchisees to identify the factors for success. And would you believe... only 27 percent of our best franchisees had business degrees, and 41 percent of the worst did!"

"What the hell does that mean?" Richard asked. "Who decided best and worst?" He was annoyed enough to call franchise headquarters and talk to the franchise relations man.

"Don't take it so seriously," the man soothed. "It's one

of those management fads. And they didn't really set up any criteria for best. Maybe they just like the guys who don't complain or get out of line." Richard believed that. The worst crime in a mindless business was rocking the boat.

Life as a franchisee had other disadvantages. He had to wear a tacky uniform and ridiculous cap when he was in the shop. The franchisers had no real respect for their franchisees. They conducted "meetings" in which the only contributions permitted from the floor were questions. They foisted experimental programs to sell ice cream or overpriced slices of defrosted cakes on volunteer shopowners who were so eager to try something new that they were willing to work extra hours "for the good of the franchise." Richard had to laugh. Most of the experimental programs seemed to him to be a waste of time. Something that genuinely increased business had yet to come along. Partly because the owners thought the name of the franchise had to describe it exactly; otherwise they would lose their "franchise". If it wasn't round with a hole or coffee, it didn't match their "franchise." The word had its own elasticity.

He and Gloria were living in a pleasant condo in New Brunswick, having sold the house in Princeton at a profit and invested some of the money in the franchise along with what was left of his severance pay.

After five years, he decided he'd had enough. It was time to sell the franchise. Maybe the real problem with a franchise was that you were paying for a job. The other problem was boredom. But they now had plenty of money saved, invested, ready to go to work again, and substantial equity in the business.

He should have done this long ago: he went to a career counselor. They did a careful assessment. Three days of testing that scared the hell out of him when they told him that the testing preceded the counseling. But it was time for courage.

Yes. "Business," they said. "You're good at it. You have the head for it. Numbers, creativity, organization, training, all that."

"Well then, what's the matter with me?" he asked.

"Why do you think there's something the matter with you?" the counselor fenced. "You were successful at the coffee company, very successful. It's the economic climate, competition, a new world, in effect."

Richard gritted his teeth. "Nobody wanted to hire me after that, as a consultant or as an employee." He was stating the obvious, he thought.

"We advise our clients about their capacities. But there's one more factor. We tell them, 'Do what you love.' What do you love?"

Ah. Richard was taken aback. Nobody had ever mentioned that before. What did he love? He smiled. He knew what he loved. But was it a business? Could it be a business? Could he make money with it? Start a prototype, find the bugs, iron out the wrinkles, make it into a franchise. He was still smiling.

The counselor said, "I seem to have struck a chord. Do you want to tell me about it?"

"I have to think about it." He was certainly not going to give it away now to a waiting world. Not before it was a refined idea.

He and Gloria spent weeks together working it out. It was the kind of teamwork they had developed over the years. And as much fun as anything they'd ever done. They'd start with a newspaper to be sold on newsstands and later by subscription. It would offer feature articles, classified advertising, advice services and... and ... whatever else developed.

It was not hard to sell the donut franchise. They had built a very good business in a very good area, had added services like donuts and coffee at high school and college basketball and football games, children's parties of donuts with additional beverages like fresh apple cider. These were all designed to overcome the beginning of the public suspicion that deep fried dough was not good for you. But the truck drivers, industrial workers and commuters in a hurry who were the mainstay of the business still came. The place was fresh, the plants green. They sold it in September 1987 for top dollar.

Gloria was using a computer at the library. She understood what it could do. And he, who was frying donuts during the first few years of PC development, caught up quickly. They bought a good machine and put in a terrific word processing and typesetting program. There it was, their first issue:

## KINKS

(Anything but Straight)

"Do what you love"

Gloria developed an anonymous column, "The Decorating Demiurge" which was intended to be a front-page feature. Her first was about setting up a modest medieval torture chamber in your rec room. Ropes, pulleys, all demountable in case the kids used the rec room too, ankle and wrist restraints (carefully padded), a flea market kitchen table with its leaf removed but the space remaining for a bit of suspense between end-pieces (she had to laugh at the homely joke; she had not been a home ec major for nothing), and a set of lockable filing cabinets which could exclude prying maids and children while accommodating the artifacts already mentioned and an assortment of lotions, oils, priapic and other devices. She had the idea that the filing cabinets, offered in an assortment of finishes and heights could be manufactured by a knock-down furniture manufacturer in Sweden and custom-fitted for their special uses. This gave them a mail order item.

Richard had solicited large numbers of display and classified ads by answering such ads in other publications. That, after all, was how the FBI managed its sting operations, and he had read it in the Wall Street Journal.

ESCORTS!

"FANTASY EXCEEDS REALITY"

(Was this a meaningful statement, he wondered. Perhaps it should have read, "reality exceeds fantasy." But the advertiser had sent fully prepared art, and it was one less job to do. If he had learned anything in the donut franchise, even maybe the coffee business, it was "Don't waste your time trying to change people's minds.")

170+ Women! 24 hours, 7 days! Immediate service. Major credit cards.

Accurate descriptions. SATISFACTION GUARANTEED.

MODELS INTERVIEWED DAILY. (He loved it. Was it fast turnover or expanding business? Another euphemism. Models, indeed.)

## FIRST IMPRESSIONS
Beauty, Style, Grace

COLLEGE GIRLS! Don't you deserve the best?

Je Reviens. Debut models and companions. (Did this suggest virginal persons?)

And, plenty more:

Man-to-man body action. Sophisticated, good-looking, friendly. Pamper yourself in a penthouse. Discretion assured.

Therapeutic, full relaxing body rub by student/model with great touch.

Class act: 21- year-old hot Latin ...

Exclusive for mature executives, safe location, Oriental.

Femme couchee — sophisticated.

Fallen angels: a theater for erotic art.

submissive julia's tales ... (not even assertive enough for capital letters?)

Creative bondage play...

Sensitive bodywork — this one had prices. Pretty reasonable: $75 for 1-1/2 hours, $90 for 2 hours.

And, of course, there were telepersonals, with separate phone numbers for men and women, a Night Exchange with privacy assured.

Plus for those who had not found what they were looking for, demonstrations and workshops, cross-dresser parties in New Jersey, and cleaning personnel who cleaned in the buff— "without rags", he thought to himself, smiling.

---

They placed their first issue, priced at a dollar, with newsstands, bookstores and video shops and sold out. Richard began to perceive several lucrative businesses in this niche market. There was the mail order business: whole fields of products quite unavailable or embarrassing to ask for in retail stores. He and Gloria began a card file that burgeoned as the weeks went by and their little weekly sold out. The second issue had a new piece by the Decorating Demiurge, this one inspired by an old Eddie Cantor movie, Roman Scandals. And the third: The Royal Canadian Mounted Police, and the fourth, for specialized tastes, Winnie the Pooh. There was no end to the Demiurge's creativity.

His first idea for mail order was condoms. There was much more variety on the market now. They came in colors, "thin", "big", with "doodads on the side." They were flavored, with peach, strawberry and passion fruit. Offered snugger fit, ribs, dots. Had exotic countries of origin: Japan, Sweden, Germany, England. Japan had the thinnest. With the condoms went the lubricants with juicy names like Motion Lotion and Astroglide. He could put out a catalog for the interested, and test it by inserting an ad in Kinks. If it worked, some of the men's magazines would be next.

Then another idea: the clothes and toys some people fancied and were willing to pay for. The Demiurge told them how to modify objects they could buy at Woolworth's or already had at home. But rubber stuff, swimwear, thigh-high boots, capes, masks, key chains, chastity belts, collars, and fancy underwear: That was LOVIN' LUXURY. Another catalog.

They were receiving correspondence from faithful readers who asked for sexual advice, no holds barred. It was time to delegate. Richard and Gloria could not do it all. They needed an employee, a free-lance writer. How do you find such a one? Gloria was reminded of Anais Nin, who wrote erotica to order for someone in the early '40s after Henry Miller found that writing to order vitiated his main thrust. They found someone by advertising in The New York Times, and considered the comedy of his advertising that "I Got My Job Through the New York Times."

His first columns were fabulous, they thought, since his experience of multiple relationships and his good sense in finding an informal board of consultants for the toughest problems created an additional flow of correspondence and subscriptions. KINKS was developing a reputation for being fun to read, and that created additional circulation in the area.

Richard went to see a First Amendment lawyer about offering subscriptions. He explained his business, and that he was devoted to good taste and circumspection, as well as a light heart. The lawyer laughed.

"What you want to be sure of is that you have nothing in it that has to do with children, and that you show no objects or materials in use. And be careful about illustrations altogether. The post office has to protect free speech but people get nervous about images. Standards for the acceptable vary in different places. Local taste is important with respect to your being harassed by suits, rallies, and boycotts. You'd win on the constitutional issue, but waste a lot of revenue and time, so just be careful."

Richard thought that was good advice. He and Gloria could proceed with their development of KINKS and its offshoots. He had a cute design done for the name — all knotty and twisted — which the letters lent themselves to, not being ultra-sinuous like Bs and Cs and Ss, although there was indeed a rounded final "s". Word of mouth had spread the publication further among the faithful, who were now sending checks and even cash for subscriptions. He put the money in a money market fund, leaving himself liquid for new ideas.

"Gloria, did you ever hear of audio tapes?" he asked one evening when they were earnestly working on a practical rehearsal for the events of the Demiurge's next column, this one inspired by Frank Wedekind's Lulu. It would be a multi-installment piece, ending with her possible death at the hands of Jack the Ripper, who, himself, might have been the hushed up protagonist of a royal scandal. What fun. Period costumes, multiple men (even multiple Lulus if that was the participants' taste) and a climactic death.

"Out of character," Gloria said shortly. She did not believe in mixing business with pleasure

"Tomorrow at breakfast, then."

Richard had a theory that cholesterol was necessary for brain function. He began every day with an egg, runny, sunny side-up. "Audio," he said between sensuous mouthsful. "People are carrying those little tape players in the street. They wear them on the jogging machines at the health club, in busses and trains. If they rent adult videos to play on their VCRs, why not audio? Much more portable."

Gloria, an apostle of good taste, said, "But not just heavy breathing, moaning, all that fake stuff. I would hate that."

"No. Stories. Stories with a plot, complications, wisdom, characters. Where is your Anais Nin when we need her? Or even Henry Miller, or D.H. Lawrence? We need writers. We need story-tellers. Maybe actors or cultured people. Should we rent or sell the tapes, or both? Where? In music stores or through catalogs or ads or what? It's not poetry, but maybe it could be. Even be sold as radio programming for the after midnight crowd." There were so many decisions to make, so many avenues to pursue.

They worked together marvelously, he thought. Gloria suggested that they advertise for writers in the Poets and Writers Magazine, not the Times. The Times would attract commercial writers who would not be so interested in art. They wanted art and to develop their own writers. Gloria said that was what the romance publishers did, essentially. And readers? They would advertise for actors. Very few actors made a living in the theater.

"We're a typical small business," Gloria said at breakfast a few weeks later, quite unexpectedly. "I've been reading books about running small businesses, and the U.S. Commerce Department and Small Business Administration are running seminars for small business. They all say the same thing: We're too involved, doing too much, thinking too hard. We're losing our focus on ourselves, too. I'm not having any fun lately. I want a vacation, away from being creative for other people. In fact, I'm going away, by myself."

Richard was shocked. What would he do without Gloria? Had she shown any signs of discontent that he had missed? He'd consulted her all the way. She was his partner in everything, and now she wanted to go away...

"How long?" He was breathing hard, could not catch his breath. What was going on? How could he cope with this?

"I'm going to Italy," she declared. "I'm renting an apartment in Rome, and I'll see what I do from there. You can send me one-third of the business' net for the next couple of months — I trust you to do that — and then we'll see. There are all those terrific stories about Italian men. I've never been to Italy."

Richard was speechless. She had been planning this for a while. It was not just a breakfast whim, but a full-fledged plan. She was leaving him for adventure. He could not stop her. And if he could not get her back, how could he, the publisher of KINKS, be sure of doing "what he loved?" She was leaving him with a business he could not leave, the responsibility for running it, the whole thing.

"Totally irresponsible," he said, without thinking. "You're my partner. You can't just run off."

"Why not?" she retorted.

Indeed. If that was what she wanted to do, what could he do? She had not asked for half, only for a third. It was fair. "What about the Demiurge?"

"I'll write a few of those before I leave. Easy enough," she said. "I won't leave you in the lurch. If I feel like it, I may send a few more from Rome. We'll see." She sounded so independent, so self-assured. When had all this taken place?

The joy had gone out of it. Richard went to the office every day, the office they had established as Super Communications Ltd. His ad appeared in Poets and Writers asking for writers for inspirational audio tapes that incorporated fictional elements. Inspiration, after all, meant breath and that was what he wanted, but not really heavy breathing, and it should have something of the divine in it. There turned out to be plenty of novelists whose books were not selling well, short story writers who had found a paucity of paying outlets for their stories lately. Fiction was not as popular these days as fact, and magazines were publishing less of it. Gossip, posing as fact, was more amusing and often more salacious. There were plenty of writers who were willing to try to write for an audio tape market and to incorporate the insights and pleasures of sex manuals without giving away their sources. The most ingenious jumped into ancient Chinese novels like the Golden Lotus, into the Kama Sutra, into Arabian Nights stories that they embellished with modern frankness. The familiar, the classic, and the Brothers Grimm's original, unexpurgated stories captivated the growing audience that KINKS was developing . The tapes were a mad success. Ads started coming in from all over the country for special services, for phone sex. Richard could even, he thought, have created some dial-up services of his own, plus... plus... There was no end to it. It was growing too fast.

Gloria had left Italy. He was able only to get in touch with her via American Express which forwarded her mail and her checks to wherever she was. She wrote occasionally — sent in her Demiurge pieces on time with few clues as to where she was or what she was doing. They were postmarked Majorca, Sicily, Mexico City, Hong Kong, Bangkok, Kyoto, Katmandu... Did she miss him? How could he tell if she did not say and did not tell him what she was doing?

He had tried to find a girl friend, tried hard. There were divorcees, even single women. Some were very pretty, prettier than Gloria, he thought. But where was the spark he wanted, the joy and creativity? His belly, he noticed, was going stack, even with energetic workouts at the health club. It was not the same.

When would she return? He asked, but she did not answer. He was working well, but new ideas no longer made his heart leap with surprise and pleasure. He was just slogging away, putting in his time, putting away his money. It was almost as bad as the donut shop. Now he knew. The donut shop was a franchise. He was ready. The development work was done, it was a proven success.

Six months later he had it, "KINKS", the franchise, a division of Super Communications Ltd. The package included "KINKS — anything but straight. Do what you love," a national publication customizable for additional local advertising and local editorial content. He had examined the way chains of weekly papers, and even some national magazines handled local material and ads. With computer makeup it was easy. KINKS, the franchise also offered the catalogs of exotic clothes, condoms and audio tapes. These, too, could be customized with the local return address for franchisees who would fill the orders.

There was to be an annual meeting for franchisees, and plenty of avenues for them to develop new ideas that they could use individually with the nationally developed lists, or get royalties on themselves from other franchisees who adopted them. But nobody would have access to the complete lists and shop outlets that were to be kept at headquarters. Royalties to Super Communications Ltd. were enough to run a lean headquarters, fund development when necessary, and make Richard rich. Richard knew how important it was to respect the franchisee, even while he controlled the whole package.

The first national meeting was held in the respectable auditorium of Richard's insurance company. The president of the insurance company, who had bought himself a franchise for South Jersey, took the platform.

"We're here because we, as a society, are finally recognizing the naturalness and validity of one of nature's basic drives. Nature provides pleasure to insure that we continue to do what we've been doing for a million years. We enjoy eating chocolate even though it hasn't much to do with basic nutrition. And we and the rest of nature enjoy sex for its intrinsic value in bringing us closer, and relieving pain, hostility, and emptiness. It's not only about reproduction. Nature is prodigal with her gifts and in wasting them, too. Our franchise is devoted to facilitating the yearning and legitimate desires that palliate most of mankind's humdrum lives, give them something to look forward to, something to look back on, a lifetime, if they please, of harmless adventure and love. That's what our franchise offers. It's for everybody to enjoy. A universal franchise!"

"And now, I want to introduce the man who has made this all possible, Dick Strayton."

"Richard," Richard corrected. "I have never allowed myself to be called Dick." He heard a giggle in the audience. Was it...?

"We have a major franchise. It lies in the heart and spirit and body of most adults and is there for us to mobilize into expression. Our franchise offers good taste, service, wit and joy. It is a franchise that speaks to the deepest part of humanity. It will not go out of style, it's not unhealthy (properly practiced), not fattening." He smiled. "My dear partner and I experienced the bondage of longterm development before we offered it to you. Now you can add your creativity, personality and pleasure. We do not expect a climax of growth but rather a prolonged carrezza of fulfillment."

"We invite you all to annual meetings to make perfectly clear that this franchise is planned to help you develop along with the organization and to create a climate in which there is plenty of give and take to enrich us all. Royalties can flow in all directions, not just one. This is one of the few franchises with an established system for franchisee input. It gives you a successful, needed, wanted business and lets you vary the themes like a great composer. We want you to have it all. And all we want is our modest percent, seven percent off the top, of your total revenues. The rest is yours."

"There are different styles all over the country – you can customize your franchise. It is your franchise, our franchise. We know and you know, most business is local, most relations are local, most sex is local and most stimuli are localized. Stimulate your franchise and it will return pleasure and money. That's what KINKS is about: Doing what you love. Just remember not to sully our image as an organization whose good taste cannot be called into question. Headquarters will be responsive to your inquiries about feasibility and safety, we promise. Meantime, I who have loved what I've been doing, will now see if I can go on, without the pressures of business and time, to develop further the philosophy and partnership that have brought us this far. We'll be in touch."

He scanned the crowd, not able to see much past the middle of the room. Was she in it? Intuition said "yes." After all, the "master franchise" was hers.

End

# A MAN WHO WORKS AS
# HARD AS I DO...

Roy Priest, that's my name. No, I'm not one. I'm a hard-working lawyer. I have an independent practice on Long Island, a place that was once New York City's bedroom area, and in some ways still is, but also has become an industrial and office headquarters in its own right, with plenty of small businesses as satellites to the big ones. A nice mix, still suburban and still in process of development, with the farms and fishing now played out. But to give it new cachet, we have the rich Hamptons resorts and a few wineries.

I grew up in hardscrabble Hicksville, born just after World War II ended. I don't think of myself as a "baby boomer," a member of one of those population slices analyzed by demographers to help clueless vice-presidents design their marketing strategies. They describe us in insulting detail: We are the progeny of affluence, but our gigantic cohort will make our lives competitive to the end of our days. We are spoiled and opportunistic. We grew up in a world of relative, rather than absolute, values, because our parents and our teachers, themselves straitened by the Depression, came to think that progressive education and happiness were more important than tough moral fibre and being unyielding right.

Which is all neither here nor there. I'm too busy for

that kind of stuff. I do whatever legal work presents itself — everything from real estate closings to wills, divorces
when they walk in the door, occasional work before NASD
or New York Stock Exchange arbitrators on behalf of plain-
tiffs or even member firms. But mostly, I'm a litigator, a
guy who takes on cases that are going to trial or will have
tough negotiations beforehand — criminal or civil. It's like
hand-to-hand combat, but cerebral, too, and when it's over
you know who won. It doesn't exactly matter who was right
and where justice lies.

Lawyering is grounded in moral ambiguity. You have
to take your client's side because the law says he/she must
be represented, no matter what. I protect myself from real
criminals: I do not think I could justify a real rape or murder
or other bloody act. I'm not a religious man; I'm not even
a Catholic any more. When you're divorced, you become an
Episcopalian, and look for God's forgiveness. The Church
will forgive (with suitable penances) most other things, but
not your wanting out of a consummated marital relationship,
unless you have some kind of Papal annulment. Which takes
too long. I am not a patient man.

We were not married too young, Serena and I, twenty-five
years old for me, just out of St. John's Law School, and she
twenty-five, too, a very good legal secretary in the office of
one of the county's premier legal/political firms. You know
the kind of firm. Active in Long Island business associations,
and exerting "pull" or "push" – some kind of muscle — in
local affairs. That's how cases come to you, and everyone in
the firm was a rainmaker.

Of course, I loved her. She was a pretty girl with a good
figure, understood my business, could provide tips for getting around and getting clients. She was good-natured and
just crazy about me. I was hired by the firm as an associate
with a prospect of becoming a partner in a few years, and
I was grateful to have a "place," not having made law re-

view or having very good connections of my own. We rented an apartment in a house in Hempstead, kind of a low-rent commercial suburb, and began to live our lives, enjoying our nights out bowling with a league, going to the movies, going on an occasional "retreat" with the other young couples of our church.

We went to church on Sundays, sometimes inviting our families over for brunch afterward: scrambled eggs, sausages, English muffins and plenty of coffee, plus a pitcher of whiskey sours that made everyone fun to be with. Then came the first baby. Serena took only a couple of weeks off and went back to work. Her aunt, a widow who needed the money, was glad to take care of Roy, Jr. at home, and Serena was still the best damn' legal secretary around

Then, less than two years later, another one — our darling Louise. And Aunt Florence was still kind and what we needed. Then, oh dear, Serena said, the third, Peter, and all the children under six. Too much for Aunt Florence, and time for a house and for Serena to stay home and run it and the kids full-time.

And there was Serena, home at last, with three nice little Catholic kids. Since she was no longer in the firm, I left it, figuring I'd do equally well on my own, but trusting that when the old firm was overloaded they'd farm some work to me. They did. And I had already developed a bit of a reputation — hardworking, bulldog. Didn't drink, didn't gamble, didn't fool around, just put in the time and research needed to win my cases. I had no laurels to rest on. I stayed late in the office, brought home work to do, networked as much as I could.

There was just one little problem. Serena didn't want to get into bed with me. "No more children," she pleaded.

"I'll use a condom," I offered. She'd shake her head.

"You get a diaphragm," I said, "or a IUD."

'No." She was stubborn.

"For God's sake! Then how about the pill? It was invented by a Catholic doctor!" I thought that would do it.

"It's dangerous — not good for you."

"You want to get your tubes tied?" I asked. She looked shocked, staring at me as if I had proposed doing it myself. And, of course, I hadn't volunteered to have my "tubes" tied. I had heard there were unpleasant repercussions.

That kind of home situation makes a man cranky. I worked too hard to be able to live with it easily. There were, of course, other solutions — any guy knows what they are, but they're not what a married man wants. I didn't have time to run around, I didn't have money to finance a comforting mistress like a Frenchman, and our suburb didn't have any ravenous married women looking for a little extra on the side. None that I could detect, anyhow. Besides, those things need a certain amount of sustaining attention. Even a good-natured married woman wants you to spend a little time chatting her up before the other routine. I'm a busy man, too busy.

So, I took up running and lifting weights, and what a prep school acquaintance of mine called private practices, fuming and yelling at Serena later that I was a married man and that this was utterly unbecoming my status.

Well, how long could that last? You'd be surprised. Years. Then I had enough. God's law was, after all, man-made. Other Gods hadn't made the same laws and maybe ours weren't the result of divine revelation, just Paul's and maybe Augustine's ideas that had been codified by time and tradition and a desire for order.

Serena had been sitting home, driving her car to shop and pick the kids up, cooking and cleaning. She had transformed herself into a plump eunuch, big belly stretched by three pregnancies, big bosom to project over the belly, and big butt to balance the front. She was not the brisk smart legal secretary I had married, but a woman who had let herself go, confident that I had nowhere to go but the same way.

I asked for a divorce, offered her the house, alimony and an allowance for the kids. But not forever. Only till they were fully grown, with a dwindling sum as each reached maturity. That was enough. I would not be in hock for more than fifteen years, I figured. Maybe even less. It had to be done quickly before the law changed. I had been putting a little aside — not reported on my tax returns and not easily traced. I knew how to accumulate assets as the problem developed. I did not want a new law to compromise me further.

There were plenty of negotiations. Serena did not want to hire a lawyer, but I forced her to – I did not want a settlement reopened on the ground that she had not had adequate representation. She was not offended. Maybe relieved. Was it guilt? It occurred to me she did not like sex. Had she been simulating passion and fulfillment during our early years together? Who knows what a woman is thinking?

I was at liberty all right, but still without the time to play with randy housewives or go through the elaborate games that Parents Without Partners or other singles groups in Long Island offered. I'd go to a dance at a community center or a church or a school. Looking them over, thinking did anyone interest me enough even to say, "Hello." No. Massive inertia overcame me when the moment arrived, and I'd waste my admission money standing at a cash bar, looking at all the expensive hairdos, vivacity, and painful high heels on display. Twice was enough. I tried a cruise. That was easier; the artificial closeness and all-day contact made the preliminaries move faster. But these women were desperate for something that was not me. An ideal: a lover, a money machine, the fulfillment of a romantic notion of their selves. I was too busy, and I knew it; this would only lead to harsh words in the long run.

So where does a busy guy find a dear girl to marry who

doesn't expect so much? Close by. A new legal secretary: a girl just out of school who has learned what to do, is fresh and gentle, and pretty. I was forty-five when I found her. She was not yet twenty, fully prepared to allow herself to be influenced by the virile, fatherly figure I cut in the office. We talked about her ambitions. She thought she'd like to learn to be a paralegal so she could provide substantive services. She loved work. She was happy to learn from me, so of course, I took to teaching her about the law, explaining why I did things the way I did and where she would find model forms and papers to help with drafting routine actions and motions.

We had dinner together to discuss cases: I needed a woman's input, I said, to draft my approach to a jury or a woman judge. Sharon was a good listener, not as interested in talking as an older woman might have been. She would sit at dinner, eating quietly, nodding, smiling and showing her small even teeth and a little excess of gum; her eyes glistening with pleasure at being consulted, a pretty, slender, dark-haired girl, undeveloped in the way girls are.

When I took her home, at first I kissed her on the cheek. After a few weeks, I tried parking the car on the way home, and turning, as spontaneously as if I had not plotted my move, for a warmer kiss, and another, and an exploratory hand, muttering with passion, "I think I'm falling in love with you." And she, so flattered and bemused that this older man, who knew where to eat, and could tell the difference between one red wine and another was in love with her, could hardly not reciprocate.

Even her family, a nice Protestant family, thought I was a catch, vastly better for her than the shaggy kids her age who were heavily into pot and not ready to earn a living. We were married, and now I had it waiting for me at home when I wanted it. It was wonderful. I could teach and show, and develop an innocent's passion into one that followed without primness or squeamishness wherever love led us. And Sharon could go to school during the day, part-time, of course, so she could take care of her papers and her home responsibilities without interfering with my schedule. I could come home late when I needed to work; everything was ready for me. I could get into bed, eager to release the tensions of the day, and she was waiting and joyful. I was so happy that I won even more of my cases, enough to think about, finally, investing in a mini-estate on the north shore where I could keep a couple of horses and a boat.

We had four wonderful years together, weekdays in a house in Garden City, and in the last year, weekends in a gated community farther out near Port Jefferson. I had bought our place from the blueprints and built it on three acres of level land, a handsome, modern two-story house and, hundreds of yards away, the horse barn for two horses. They could graze during the good weather, and we could ride the dirt roads nearby, and participate in the horse events that preoccupied the local gentry. Indeed, it seemed we were becoming local gentry. We had more friends and acquaintances for weekend activity than for weekdays. The local Republican party asked if I'd run for Town Council, and I said sure. I knew how it would affect my practice and contacts, and also how not to spend too much time legislating. There were no barriers to picking up more business out there, environmental, institutional. It was lucrative and almost restful, to provide "counsel" instead of battling other lawyers head to head.

Sharon was even sweet enough to say she was not yet interested in having children. There was plenty of time, and our lovely evenings and mornings in bed should not yet be compromised by early rising, nighttime feedings, screams and diaper changes. We could sleep late on the weekends, waken languid and sexy... Ah. I had three children; I did not need more, not even with Sharon.

But something was happening to my darling girl. There would be a brief flutter of an eye, a leg or a hand would be weak and clumsy. Then she'd be all right. And again, a few weeks later, the weakness, the flutter, the clumsiness. "I'm just tired," she'd say. "I'm working so hard at school, spending time in the law library, and shopping and coming home to fix dinner and do my homework. You know how it is," she'd say cajolingly, "after all, you did it in law school."

Her family finally persuaded her to see a doctor. Then the best neurologists on Long Island. She was distracted and frightened, but I thought, she's so young, it can't be anything serious. Wrong. The workup was finished and the doctor wanted to see me, too. We sat there stupefied, both of us weeping. Multiple sclerosis. "It goes into remission," he said, "especially in very young people, sometimes for as long as twenty-five years. Just take care not to get too tired or too hot. Stay cheerful, get a personal trainer in to help maintain muscle tone, and if it progresses, we may find some medication that will help, steroids. .."

"What's the prognosis, Doc?" I asked.

He shook his head and shrugged. "Hard to say. We'll just keep an eye on Sharon, but she has many good years ahead of her, and if you take good care of her, she'll be fine."

But what do you do when a happy girl loses her appetite for food, for sex, for horses, for the country, for other people, for her studies, and for getting better? She listens when her doctor and physical therapist tell her what to do. She smiles and says, "I'll try," And then loses her focus on the effort.

She goes shopping and comes home with prepared chicken or cold ham and cole slaw and potato salad for dinner. And ice cream. She drives only to the nearest mall, and parks in the spaces designated for wheel chair license plates. She sits in the same place on the sofa all day and all night watching tv movies and comedy and commercials with the same slightly abstracted expression. A delightful, gentle girl, gone into mourning for herself, unable to muster her resources. We drive to the north shore for beautiful spring and summer weekends, and she looks ruefully at her horse.

"Sell her," she says. "I don't feel like riding any more. I think it might be dangerous for me." I cannot argue. I'm not sure myself. I keep the horses – for a remission, I say to myself. They don't cost very much now, lots of grass, hay and oats. What I'm really hoping for is a remission in my own inexorable march to being an old man — no sex, no action, no life. I'm only fifty.

In bed. That's the worst. Her hands and feet are cold, her body is limp. She is willing, but not eager. Just passively letting me touch and kiss and nuzzle and hug, waiting for it to be over. Even a rapist likes a bit of feedback: Fear, excitement, screams, fight, heavy breathing, twisting, a change of position. Something. Here is nothing. I can't do it any more. Can't get it up, can't go through the motions. I'm as passive and limp as she is. I can't stand it.

Then she doesn't want to leave the house any more. Doesn't want to drive to our north shore villa, not even for a reelection party which the chairman of the Republican party out there is holding for me and two other winners. But I persuade her, gently. "Come, Sharon. Everyone will be looking forward to seeing you. You're walking well, you have nothing really to complain of, it's just psychological now, isn't it?" I plead.

She smiles. "I guess so," and agrees to go. We'll make it after all, I think. The party is great, champagne in the afternoon, huge crabmeat appetizers and hot scallops in white wine, a buffet. Of course, husbands get plates together for their wives — except the few husbands whose wives get plates together for them. "I'll get yours," I offer.

"No," she stands up, determined. "I'll do it myself." And she does, a little slowly, but ok. She chats with the other women, picking at her plate, gets up to go to the bathroom, does what any normal woman does at a party. But I'm watching all the time, and so are a few of the others, the ones who know. We're all cheerful and encouraging.

Things begin to get a little hectic, a little boisterous, and Sharon has had it. "Roy," she is pleading now, "Can we go home. I'm tired." She has made a heroic effort, and I am overcome with love and can hardly wait to get her home to make love.

But her hands and feet are still cold, still limp, and even though now she is trying to seem eager, she does not fool me. I remember the real thing. Is this how it's going to be the rest of my life? Did I leave the church, divorce Serena — who may be menopausal now and not worried any more about babies, I think ruefully — distance myself from my own dear children who have not really forgiven me – for the revival of youthful screwing so important to me, only to be now the nurse, daddy and confidant of a limp rag doll? Is it some kind of divine retribution for being a normal male? I can't answer these questions, but they torment me. They torment me while I do what I can for Sharon, while I serve on the town council, while I stay in touch with my three almost grown-up kids, and work hard to earn a living. Without that, it all falls apart. In truth, I am saved by work.

Some of it is out in Suffolk county, the last stop before England, I joke, even if it is really more the last stop before Spain if we go straight across the Atlantic. Some government agency has decided our gated community with its expensive land and fancy houses is a "wetland" and puts us on the map. The wetlands map, meaning our land is now supervised by the government. We can't build, can't fill, can't be our own masters. The gated community promptly forms a landowners association and I'm elected president. I understand their thinking. If I'm the president, and also an elected member of the town council, I give my lawyering services free. After the election, I make my little joke, "You have to understand:

If I'm still charging for it, I can't give it away!"

They get it. I'm retained at a fancy five-figure flat fee to do the necessary. It has to be done fast. Those bureaucrats know about citizen inertia. They've given us altogether only a few weeks to file a notice of appeal, then there'll be stiff time requirements all the way ahead for research, brief writing, answering their brief. The wetlands agency has its own legal department whose mission is to defend to the death its right to take us over.

But I'm in the middle of other big cases, litigation to break the final will of some infatuated old fool who left his fortune to the doxy who was his third wife, while more deserving family members wound up with keepsakes; a NASDAQ arbitration proceeding against the very largest firm on the New York Stock Exchange for inappropriate investment counseling. The firm thought it would be duck soup. Their internal counsel would take care of it himself against a pro se litigant. The pro se came up with a set of tables about his account activity and constant losses during the discovery period. He even proved that the "tax shelters" he was sold were idiotic in the light of his tax position. Then he asked for the firm's records about his brokers, about their previous peccadilloes, about the "incentives" for selling the firm's limited partnerships and closed end funds. Stonewall time for the firm, and my opportunity, if I did well, to get a lot of their business. And the usual torts (medical malpractice, falls in awkward places), real estate, wills, divorces... Too much for a single practitioner, and too much riding on my harsh bulldoggery to lay some of it off on other lawyers.

Who is going to do the research? The legal secretary I hired after Sharon and I married has been with me five years, and that's more than the usual tenure now in job-rich Long Island. She might be able to do it, but she runs the office, takes care of the word processing, the filing, the phone calls, even drafts a few routine papers for real estate closings and mortgages, under supervision, of course. Mary is a divorcee, no children, early thirties, with a pleasant smile and a good telephone manner. But I can't have her out of the office during the day, even if I hire a temp as I do when she is on vacation or sick, and she has never offered to work late for any reason. I respect that.

I think, I'll ask Sharon. She's almost a paralegal. It will take her mind off her troubles. Maybe give her some real-world motive to come back to life. She shakes her head. "I know I'm a real disappointment to you, but I can't concentrate — I can't focus on what I'm doing. I keep thinking that a fine man like you who works so hard and needs his energies restored at home should have a better wife than me. I know it looks as if I'm just sitting all the time, doing nothing. But I'm thinking, thinking about what to do. Give me the time to sort it out, and I'm sure it will come out fine for both of us." She smiles winningly. I hate that. She is trying to make me an accomplice by playing falsely on my fondness for her. There's nothing really the matter with her; she's just coddling herself.

Then who? I can file the notice of intent to appeal to the wetlands agency. But I have to give reasons, and I don't know a damn' thing about wetlands. I can postpone the NASDAQ proceeding for a while. The will — I have to negotiate right away before a judge decides. I have to threaten to prove that the old man wasn't in his right mind, that he was unduly influenced, that his other decisions show he was failing, that he'd made bad investment decisions, that he'd decided to build a new house when he was dying. I'm going to have to deal with the doxy's lawyer and show him who is boss. The adrenalin rises. That's what I love: the rush of hormones.

I work late, accomplish everything I need to, come home to my limp doll, order Chinese dinner in, and, some time during the evening, find myself in the bathroom, wasting another wad of Kleenex. But I haven't solved the research problem. What the hell. I've been giving money for years to Serena who has been sitting home, getting fatter and lazier and not facing the day when the money runs out. Why can't she put in a little time in a law library for me in return? Especially if I offer to pay for the time.

So I call the very same evening. "Serena, can you do me a favor? I need some legal research done in the library and I don't know whom else to ask. I'll pay for your time." It's important to me to seem reasonable, especially after all the hollering I did during the closing days of our marriage. She was one hell of a legal secretary. If I give her enough direction, she'll manage all right to do the research. And the librarians will help if she's puzzled. They'll be nice to a mature woman putting in a few hours for her ex-husband.

"I'm busy," she says.

"What do you mean, you're busy?" I shout. "I've been busy working my ass off to support you and the kids forever, and now, when I ask you a favor, you're BUSY."

It occurs to me that I am not a very likeable man. I can see that in the faces of opposing lawyers, clients, judges, even judges' law clerks. "You're not going to let him ,et away with that, are you?" one of them asked her judge recently. But he had to. I had the law on my side.

I realize I haven't seen Serena in a few years. I do not look for her when I stop by on Friday evenings to take the kids out for dinner. I try not to ask them about Serena, except maybe, "How's your mother?" They answer ok, and we drop the subject.

Maybe she is busy, I realize. But she does not amplify. I think it will not be long before her alimony and child support disappear completely. Does she have a lover? A prospect of marriage with someone else? Is she working in a store or a law office? It does not matter. She doesn't really interest me — only what she can do for me does. "Are you too busy to listen to what I need?"

"No, I'll listen. What is it?"

I explain the time constraints on the wetlands appeal and what I need to know, and she says ok, she'll be back to me in a few days. "As soon as you can, ok?" I say. I work all evening after that and all the next day on the will and get my strategy together, trusting Serena at least to figure out a few supportable challenges after checking the law, and the wetlands appeals manual.

Sharon is still sitting on the sofa, making her situation even worse by her depression and inactivity. But what do I know about how that feels? I know I can't afford to get sick, so I take care of myself; I eat right, work out in the basement on a treadmill, use weights and do pushups and crunches. I can go on for another thirty years like this, I think proudly, but I need a woman to play with, a nice healthy lady who is not interested in permanence, just a comfortable affair. I can't tell Sharon it's time to go. I'm a brute sometimes, like all litigators, but I can't do that. She is sometimes unsteady on her feet, is having vision problems, she says. I ask if she'd like to have someone to help her during the day, some pleasant woman to clean, prepare food, and give her an arm to get around. She nods. "Oh, yes. Then you can go away weekends without worrying about me." That's an opening, and I know what to do about it.

Next day, I give it a shot. "Mary, would you be available to come away and work with me this weekend on something I have to finish Monday? Sharon is staying home and I'm having an agency send someone in to help her." I smile. "We'll be alone most of the weekend. Will that bother you?" Very graceful, I say to myself. "You'll have a comfortable room and I'll get you home Sunday night."

Mary looks surprised, eyes me speculatively as if to read my motives. I'm as bland as butter. "Overtime pay?"

I am shocked. "Yes, of course," I say, challenged to do

the legal thing.

I pick her up Saturday morning, having already rented a neat portable computer for our collaboration. We have to shop for food — breakfast and lunch, anyway, I think. If all goes well, maybe we'll have a good meal out Saturday night; a little wine never hurts the kind of enterprise I have in mind. We're shopping for groceries in a supermarket a few miles away from my north shore village.

"Roy! What are you doing here?" I have never met anyone shopping. Never. And certainly not in this stupid little town. It's a woman, a skeptical one, from my gated community. She is my vice-president, having accepted the task because "we need a full-time resident."

"Shopping," I say, observing the obvious. "And what are you doing here?" I ask nastily as if I know a little something about her, too. It does not work.

"And who is this?" she asks. "Is Sharon ok?"

"She's home, not feeling too well. This is Mary Rossi, my legal secretary. We're working together this weekend on something I have to finish Monday."

She smiles. She knows about Sharon's disability. And I hate her brisk nod as she waves and pushes her cart down the next aisle.

Okay, I've been caught without having done a thing. Mary bites her lip, but I don't see what she has to worry about.

The day goes well. I'm going through depositions, thinking about new questions, getting trial books organized so that everything is at my fingertips. Mary takes it down as I talk. I need to see what I've said, so the first notes are printed on a little laser printer I've brought along. Then we can get to the beginning of a brief in a pending suit. We break for lunch, eating on the deck overlooking the spring-fed pond the developers have created in a modest swale on the property. Is that the wetland, I wonder? They created it and now it's out of their hands, a natural wetland? I'm not sure. Anyway, we have salad with cold shrimp for lunch, lots of good French bread, a melon and even a half carafe of local white wine. I don't think it's very good, but Mary volunteers that she likes it. And espresso after the wine so we're not too stupefied to continue. The sun feels good outside, the air is fresh, the horses are grazing a few yards away, and if I were not trying to make a good impression, I'd suggest that we hop into bed for a while, and then go for a swim.

But, I'm a serious hard-working man, and we have an awful lot left to do. Mary is as serious as I am. During the afternoon, I am only occasionally conscious of anything other than the matter at hand — catching up on paperwork. That's focus. It deserves a pun, doesn't it? Dinnertime comes and I offer a nice dinner at a charming, romantic hilltop inn, not much in the way of cuisine, but the prime rib is always good, and they serve Long Island merlot which is not as good as Chilean but not bad.

Mary says, "If we're eating out, I should change." She takes her time, and comes down very much the better for it: radiant makeup and a longish form-fitting printed dress with a short jacket. I observe she planned to have a change, knew somewhere in her heart that this was not an all-work-and-no-play weekend. I am encouraged and flattered. We still have work to do tomorrow, but not so much as to be overwhelming. There's time enough. And the weekend is justifying itself. But, I muse, between thoughts of where to go from here, it would have justified itself even if it didn't. I'm a winner, no matter what, and if "what" really takes place, I'm doubly a winner and for weeks to come, because we can do it again. I am not going to worry about my vice-president.

We have the inn's best — oysters, prime rib, asparagus and crème brûlée. And a full bottle of merlot. And a heart to heart conversation. How is it being alone, I ask, after a marriage ends. (As if I didn't know.) What caused the break? (Was it you or him, I wonder, but do not ask.) I do not know anything about how she lives, someplace in Roslyn. (By herself? A roommate, a family? A boyfriend?) She answers these questions without telling much. It's a two-family house, with one floor rented as an apartment. There was no financial settlement when they divorced. What do you do evenings? Volunteer work, to my surprise. She's a reading volunteer for children and adults in Freeport and nearby communities. I'm impressed. A good person with serious matters on her mind.

"And you? It must be hard on you — Sharon's illness when you've been so happy together."

I admit it. "But it's harder on her, so young and vital, to be brought to a halt this way." She reaches out and puts her hand on mine. We are talking warmly and comfortably together, a little flushed with the wine and the day's rapport when the check comes, and I know it's going to be all right.

There's still that awkward business of getting to it. In the car, driving back, I am pleased to be able to drive with one hand and hold hers with the other. She does not pull it away. We smile at each other quietly. When we get out of the car, hugging and kissing are the most natural things in the world, and it's easy to feel her body inside the thin dress. Very nice. I'm comfortable enough to joke, "Your room or mine?"

"Whichever you prefer," she says. I've put her in the spare room with a double bed, and a hallway bathroom. But no one else is in the house, and maybe we're being excessively delicate about the absent Sharon, but the guest room it is.

Mary Rossi is warm and generous in bed, giving, yes, but knowing where her own pleasure lies and comfortable with it. I'm grateful and happy enough for a leisurely encore, and smile at myself, "Not bad for a guy my age." I even think that after a few hours' sleep, I'll be ready for more in the morning. Well, yes.

And then back to work and we proceed with our legal work till a late lunch, after which we pack up to return to Nassau County. "That was great, Mary, great of you to come for the weekend and work so hard, and also, to make me so happy. I hope it was as good for you." I'm a little embarrassed by the cliche. "I'll see you tomorrow."

There's a spring in my step when I come home, and Sharon asks how my weekend went.

"Terrific," I say, "Mary and I got a lot of work done, and I'm so relieved to be ahead rather than behind. How was your weekend?" I'm paying the aide who has her own car, so I do not have to take her home.

"I think I've got it," Sharon says. "You know I'm really not going to get better. MS is not curable now. There isn't even any useful medication. All you can do is hope for remissions, and I can't subject you to that, Roy. You've been very kind and generous, but I know my illness is making this less of a marriage than you need. I think the right thing to do is get a divorce and let you find some healthy woman who will be there when you need her."

I shake my head, "No, no, Sharon. Don't do this to yourself or me," and realize I sound like a bad movie.

Sharon is not so critical. "It's fine, Roy. I've decided I need to be on my own, not some helpless invalid or dependent twit. This decision will be the making of me. I love the law, and being a paralegal is nothing compared with practice of the law, itself. I've been looking for the right law school, and I've found it, North Carolina Central University. It's exactly the right place for me."

"Where?" I am shocked.

"Durham," she answers, as if I meant geographically. "It's mainly for black people, but they will understand and be nice to me. They admit people who haven't finished college, they care about issues that some corporate law schools

don't. I can finish college while I'm getting a law degree.
They make it easy for people like me. And then, I will be
prepared to practice law for minorities and the disabled, and
the poor, all the people who don't rate much in most courts.
You'll see. Even if I'm in a wheelchair — but I won't be —
I can practice. Tuition is low. And it'll only be for three or
four years. After that I'm on my own. Can you manage that,
Roy?" She is a darling. She still has to apply to the school
and pass the LSAT, but that's not going to stop her. I am
full of admiration for her resolve, and relief at her solution.

Back to court early Monday on some business litigation
that I do not want to come to trial. But it looks as if it will
not be settled easily either. We wait and then we fence and
the morning is over. A stop for lunch and I get back to Mary,
who has the mail arranged on my desk. In it is a small bundle
on wetlands from Serena. She has done a Westlaw search of
the Article 78 decisions in New York State, and extracted a
few. She has read local challenges to wetlands designation
and extracted possibilities. She has mainly challenged the
competence of the technicians who designated our little swale
a wetland, and said that will do for filing a notice of appeal. I
get it out that very day, overnight delivery to Albany. Then
I call to thank her, and ask if she can carry this further,
getting from Albany the wetlands manuals for designation
of a territory a wetland, and then finding whatever else she
can. We have a couple of months to file a brief. I hear her
annoyance that I'm asking her to carry the load, but I tell
her I'm sending her a nice little extra check for her trouble:
Two hundred dollars. She can spend a day at one of those
middle-aged lady spas with it.

I'm too happy about Mary to give Serena much thought.
Mary is still spending her evenings with the reading-deprived,
and I'm preparing Sharon for the the LSAT. During the
week, Mary and I do not compromise our business relationship. We don't need to. But we can look forward together to

a weekend of reading and shopping, conversation, pleasant meals, a little work and an easy, lovely time in bed. Now that Sharon and I are planning a divorce, I am no longer being "unfaithful", I point out to Mary, so we can head for the big bed in my room when we arrive on Saturday afternoon, and enjoy as much felicity as we want on Saturday night and Sunday morning. With all the weekday libido saved up I can be a hero on the weekend.

Sharon comes through well on the LSAT, and why not, with me coaching her and her own time as a legal secretary and beginning paralegal? Now that we're divorcing although we're still in the same house until Sharon leaves for good, we are as loving as the best brother and sister neither of us ever had. She shows immense courage and resolve and I am almost unbearably proud of her. And Mary, she's terrific. Self-sufficient, good-natured, her own woman and mine, too. If this is how the sunset years play out, I can't complain.

The weeks pass, as they always do, and I'm ready to file the brief for the wetlands appeal, when this giant bundle comes with a brief already written and for backup, the federal and state wetlands manuals, the Soil and Water Conservation Service maps, a challenge to the competence of the wetlands delineator... the works. There was practically nothing left to do except put the outer pages on the brief and have it duplicated as many times as the appeals book says is necessary. Serena has done an amazing job. For a law secretary. For the first time, I wonder if she is working in a law office, back to being a legal secretary. Is that how she got the Westlaw abstracts? I owe her a lunch, I decide, a good one. I hate taking time out of my working day for lunch; a man as busy as I am... But I cannot invite her out for dinner. She may get the wrong idea.

Okay, lunch. We'll drive to the south shore, one of those great seafood places not too far out on the island, have a nice, big, slow, low-calorie seafood lunch (and I'll make the

time up over the weekend). It's the least I can do, busy or
not. I'll pay her, too, but she deserves a little extra, I decide.
Where do I pick her up? I phone her at home that evening
to invite her to lunch, and she sounds as if she's smiling.
"Pick me up at two on Friday" she says, at an address on
Old Country Road, not far from the court houses. I conclude
that she's working in a law firm. Indeed, she is, I discover,
when I get there. There's a short list of associates on the
door and at the top of it is Serena Priest. She's a lawyer? I
am stunned. But why not? She had plenty of time to go to
school, on me.

I tell the receptionist when I go in. "Mr. Priest, to pick up
Ms. Priest" articulating very carefully the new style honorific
for women of indeterminate marital status. I do not want
anyone to misunderstand. And there's Serena, trim as in her
twenties, well-dressed in a pin-striped suit with a short skirt
to show off very good legs, her hair tinted and coiffed, and
only a bit of jowl in her maturity. Pearls at her ears, pearls
at her throat, the good lady-lawyer uniform. "Serena, you
look great," I beam. "And you did a great job for me. No
wonder. Are you an environmental expert?"

She's enjoying how flummoxed I am. And I'm enjoying
her enjoyment. We're a pair of grinning fools, recognizing
each other after a long absence. Lunch goes swimmingly,
and it's too late to go back to the office, hers or mine. I
decide to take her home, without asking what about her car
still in the parking space on Old Country Road.

"Roy, I'd better get my car," she says. "If you want to
follow me home, come along. We'll have a drink there, and
call it a day, so you can get home to your new wife." I explain
about Sharon. I'll just call to tell her I may be a little late,
not to worry. I have other ideas.

Serena, with the help of a law degree and what – Weight
Watchers, a gym? — is just too nice to miss. And we know
each other so well. It's Friday evening, and I've been saving

up all week. There'll be enough for the weekend, and she can't be worried now about more babies. We have our drink and head exactly where I intended. This is great, I think, but how am I going to manage it all? Serena's an estate planner, an inside job for Long Island's affluent; no wonder I've never met her in court. But she's a good "inside" lawyer, I think. How do I fit this all together without making a sticky mess with Mary. I think, "I love them both; I need a way to adjudicate competing claims on me — but I'd rather an amicable settlement." I feel like a middle-aged jerk.

I am a middle-aged jerk. But my ladies will have none of it. Serena likes living alone, and being independent. Mary has no ambition to remarry. The two understand me and each other, and do not mind, in fact, prefer, sharing. And I'm still strong and healthy and will stay that way forever, I think. (I'm joking, but if anything goes wrong, I have two to look after me.) I also realize that, yes, I'm a disagreeable man, but I must also be some kind of role model, with two lady lawyers spawned directly by my example.

I was in court the other day, and there was that law clerk, (the one who said to her judge, "You're not going to let him get away with that") talking to another lawyer where she thought I could not hear her. "Watch out for him, Roy Priest, a really nasty trial lawyer. They're all testosterone-intoxicated, but he's the worst." I grin. "Right-on, lady."

End

# WE ALWAYS PLAYED
# WELL TOGETHER

"They always play so well together." We had long weekend visits back and forth during childhood, my mother and her sister getting together for the lady talk they so enjoyed, our younger siblings, two each, fighting and screaming, crying about "sharing" toys that were unshareable, bloodying and muddying each other. But not Tim and Michael. Not us. Mom and Julia would see the two of us with a board game like Chinese checkers or Monopoly sitting on the porch when it rained or at the backyard table when it was warm, and tell each other so.

. "Do you two want some cold milk? With cookies?" Aunt Julia was always tentative. It was a feminine thing to be then. Mom, too, was not very definite, especially with the boys. If we nodded, one of them would bring out a tray. If not, we'd be asked again in a little while. Boys needed their calcium for strong bones and good teeth. The girls didn't need to be reminded. Neither did the younger boys, roughnecks in a way, who had no problem heading to a refrigerator and nabbing a Coke, even drinking it out of the bottle. Milk, too, they guzzled out of the container. When you're playing hard and sweating, you get thirsty. That was summer, the best time.

Michael and I had been born just a few months apart, but Michael was always taller, thinner and quicker, with eyes deepset in a face that was all sharp planes and bones. I, a little shorter, squarer, and slower but with plenty of endurance. That showed up when we played tennis: he'd just stop after a few sets. "That's enough." I'd have gone on much longer.

We visited back and forth all year: Long weekends during holidays and intersessions, overnights at other times. It was a long ride, that's why we stayed weekends, we coming in the big Chrysler from Stamford, and heading down to Silver Spring where Michael and Julia lived. Or they, driving north with the other kids in a Ford wagon to our Connecticut city. Either way, Michael and I were inseparable.

Back and forth, but not so often as we grew up. Michael and I asked if we could go to the same prep school. In Connecticut, we thought. Choate. Forget it, we were told. Too expensive. There were good high schools in Silver Spring and in Stamford. "What's with you two?" Dad asked. He was a management consultant, often away on assignments in Texas and California. We were just comfortable with each other. We talked about books and authors and exchanged magazines (Michael loved Esquire and I was addicted to Analog Science Fiction). Michael found Hermann Hesse and gave me a paperback of Steppenwolf. He found Kafka too, and I had bad dreams after reading Kafka's "In the Penal Colony." One weekend, I picked up a book of Paul Bowles' stories, and together we experienced the same frisson of fear and attraction reading "The Delicate Prey." We watched old horror movies on tv, "Dracula" and "The Mummy" and laughed ourselves silly, but were fascinated, anyway. By this time, I was on my school's swimming team and Michael was a runner leaping hurdles for his school's track team. There we were: Nice, clean-cut American boys going to parties, fooling around with our dates, going to camp as junior counselors and thinking about our futures.

We could have gone to college together, but by that time our interests had diverged. Michael went to Yale and majored in art history. His father, Uncle Len, was an economist at the Agriculture Department. I think he forecast crops and crop prices. He thought Michael had chosen a good, steady field, no big ups and downs, opportunities for consulting and for writing books.

Me, I picked Cornell's agriculture school. It was a top university, and I loved the idea of food and crops and proper use of land. Maybe I was influenced by Uncle Len. My dad thought it was ok, too. Not as strenuous and iffy as his field. You didn't have to worry so much about pleasing so many people. After so many stressful years of smiling warmly at the principals of his firm, adopting the latest in management fads so he could offer them knowledgeably and making the most of his "contacts," he could see the merit in dealing with something basic like the land.

It did not dawn on us even in college. Michael managed to lose it first. He even talked about getting married when he finished school. His girlfriend was a good-looking "townie" in New Haven, herself a student at the Culinary Institute. Gina was earthy and created dishes for Michael, he said, that were designed to develop and enhance the libido. I could not believe they taught things like that at a cooking school. He laughed, said it was her Sicilian grandma who was an herbalist and witch. She taught Gina to cook like that only for her husband so that there would be many children.

I was envious when he wrote about it. My libido had not yet found a suitable object and I did not like jokes about developing calluses on my fingertips. Ag had very few women. I tried bars: Michael said you could pick up girls, but I was overcome with shyness, and had a feeling that women who hung out in bars knew too much and would sneer at me. Home ec majors? They were nearby but hopelessly unattractive, I thought. I found a girl at last during a practice swim.

Would you believe, an engineering major, lean and blond with the deep chest swimmers develop. After a few weeks of post-swim heart-to-heart conversation, usually in bars, we decided that it was time for both of us. She invited me to her room in a shared apartment, provided — she was very stern — that I brought along plenty of Trojans, along with a bottle of Scotch. We spent a good part of the weekend in bed. It was a good-natured game of sex, cooperative and friendly, but we were both played out afterward, and felt rotten. Too much whisky and swollen faces, which earned us some derisive looks on Monday. Well, now I knew, and it was a great relief. Ellen and I dated sporadically after that, fighting about politics, and reconciling with bouts of booze and sex. We were good friends.

Late in the winter of our senior year, Michael phoned, "Let's go to New York for Easter week. I've reserved a room at the Yale Club, and we can put it all on credit cards."

What a week it was. We took a bus down to Greenwich Village on the second day, having reserved Day One for the Metropolitan Museum. Michael had it all planned. First the crafts shops, he said. They turned out to be leather shops with gross brass trims. "You want a suit?" he asked. I shook my head. Who would wear stuff like that? Then we went into a noisy bar for delicious hamburgers. I was distracted by a ceiling festooned with what looked like dangling dirt. It was part of the decor, and apparently never fell on the grill. Next, a bookshop. Instead of the silly magazines I was accustomed to seeing under other guys' beds, this was all men, with photos of penises and testicles that were nothing like what you saw in a locker room. And the customers: guys in couples kissing each other full on the lips, singles eyeing each other's hardware and the kerchiefs dangling from the pockets of their tight jeans.

We might have known all along. We went back to the Yale Club and our spare twin-bed room. Michael brushed his teeth, took his clothes off, and slipped under the covers of his bed "OK, come on. We don't have to be shy with each other." We kissed, and it felt right, easy. We explored with our hands each other's torsos and hips. I was trembling when Michael ran his hand along the inside of my thigh. This really was it, I thought. I knew I loved Michael, I had always loved Michael, but this was lust, Michael was my alltime object of desire.

Cousins. We could stay together for the rest of our lives; we loved each other. What about Gina and Ellen? They were nice, but it was not the same.

We were bolder as the week progressed: found a waterfront bar and showplace that featured mind-boggling acts: fistfucking and even a cowboy boot shoved into someone's behind. Not for us. Not any of that. We preferred the oral route, and we were not into the rough stuff.

"What could we do together? Something that we could work at and live by?" Michael asked. Our career possibilities were so different, there seemed no way to blend them, but Michael had the idea, and once he did, we were on track to make it happen.

I went to work for the Soil and Water Conservation Service in a Hudson Valley county, teaching farmers how to get the most from their land, how to handle their swampy patches, how to dig a pond for their livestock, and recommending truck farm varieties of vegetables to sell at roadside stands in summer. It was good work. Michael interned at the Met Museum, then found a job in an antiques shop on Fifty-Seventh Street in New York. We spent weekends together in his apartment or mine, going to all the parties we were invited to, flirting and dancing with new girls. We both loved to dance. We spent holidays with our families, looking like, dressing like, and actually being the conventional young men we were.

But we were making plans. Saving money and getting

ready. I actually found it. I had been asked to measure the oxygen content and clarity of a little stream that was channeled through a small paper plant in the eastern part of my county. The water flowed in clear and out white and turbid, not a good sign. Lots of sulfur and other chemicals made the water unhealthy for the cattle and farms downstream. I talked to the plant manager. "You'll have to correct that."

He shook his head. "We know. It's too expensive. We'll probably close the plant, instead." They were not wrong, but the town would suffer–no jobs, few prospects. The trains had stopped running there a few years earlier, wounding it, and this would be the final blow.

I walked to the town's central square. Directly ahead of me was a beautiful two-story square brick building. Empty. To the right, a workingman's bar with a neon sign "Genesee", to the left, an Agway hardware and seed shop, and, still on the square, a liquor store and an automatic laundry. That was it. The side streets had a few fine buildings: old houses and a Grange hall, no longer used. Not far away, there was an auction hall, with a sign offering a farm breakup — cattle and machinery. A tired little town. I wanted to revive it.

Michael was full of ideas. We drank champagne a few weeks later, toasting each other and what we were going to do, giggling blissfully at how we would mesh our lives and the town's, our skills and the town's needs. We had been prowling around the Village again, and found in some decorative accessories shop, a pair of waving beige ostrich feathers. When we returned, we unwrapped them and stuck them in the backs of our tabbed, button-down shirts, so that they waved above us. Our logo — the ostrich feathers. We laughed till we were breathless, drunk on champagne and our own madly witty postures with the feathers. What fun this was going to be. Hard work, yes, but if you love what you're doing, it's more like play.

It was time, since we were borrowing some start-up money

from our families, to break the news, as gently as possible, together.

Michael to my mother: "You've always said how well we played together. We do. There's always been this bond between us; we're not just cousins, there's more. We're like Tchaikowsky, Noel Coward, Michelangelo, Proust..." He stopped, waiting for my mother to show she understood. She did, finally.

"Ah," she screamed, "did we do this to you, my dear sister and I? What did we do wrong?" She rocked back and forth in her chair. My father nodded. He knew who was to blame, but it was too late. "Let's just get on with it," he muttered.

"We love each other, we'll stay together the rest of our lives, like any couple," I said. "We'll work together and live together. It's all right. It's all right," I pleaded. "And when we visit on holidays and family occasions, it will be just the same. No different. I promise."

"But, we'll know, and then everyone else will know." That was my mother.

"Not if we don't say anything, don't discuss it. We'll be living in the country, far away. No one will pay any attention, except maybe to the wonderful things we'll be doing."

"All right, all right." My father again. "Do you have a business plan? Do you even know what a business plan is? You'll need one later because what we're going to lend you won't make it. You'll need the banks."

We were over the hump. Next, to Michael's family in Silver Spring, a replay. Screams and tears from Aunt Julia, and "Both of you? How could that have happened? Everyone else in the family is normal. Everyone, grandma and grandpa, all your brothers and sisters, all our brothers and sisters, your fathers. Do you want to see a doctor, or a psychiatrist? Maybe we should put the money in that, maybe if you stop seeing each other so much, you'll find nice girls and marry. Don't you want to have children?" She wept.

We would use the two ostrich feathers as our logo — one on each side of the name of the store: "The Major General Store" that we hung over the entrance on the square. We had to laugh at the name — but who could forget it? In both front windows, we announced that our shop would be open early in November, stocked with marvelous food, beautiful music, antiques, jewelry and handmade things at every price level. We placed our announcement in the local papers and invited everyone for punch and cheese and crackers on our opening weekend.

That was the easy part. Then we had to do things we had never done before. I knew a little about farm buildings, construction and tools. Ag majors were supposed to. We bought lumber from a local saw mill, paint at Agway, old-fashioned wood-burning stoves to heat the place, and built our own ductwork to vent to the rear of the building. Our large brick building was actually a relic of a 19th century general store. In it, we had found the most beautiful mahogany display cases and counters, as well as floor-to-ceiling shelving. I scraped the floors with a rented machine, uncovering wide maple boards, and finished them with polyurethane. Michael washed and oiled the display cases, bought antique lighting fixtures to replace the fluorescents "some tasteless fool" he said, had installed.

We talked as we worked. "You know more about biology — what do you think?" Michael asked. "It's not hereditary, is it?"

I shook my head. "Nobody knows. The latest idea is that there's a hormonal imbalance in the womb. But ducks and cows, all animals..."

"When I was in Portugal looking at the Braganza porcelains," Michael said, "I went to the zoo one Sunday in Lisbon. I never saw such a variety of activity — big ones with little ones, males with males, females with females, in one big ape cage. Maybe we're all capable of anything."

"I guess how we're defined depends on the culture." I said. "I've been looking for clues in Mary Renault's novels. From ancient Crete to Alexander the Great, she insists on the same thing: We're mostly bi, like your bored Lisbon apes, except Plato; he only swung one way."

"Maynard Keynes was exclusively gay for years, then he met that Russian ballerina..."

"I like that. We could try open marriages and share our kids..." .

Michael muttered. "Not likely. Not me, anyway. I'm Plato."

Finally, our furniture was moved in upstairs, creating a modest apartment. That was a real commitment, to each other and the shop. Surplus furniture went into the shop's stock. We'd have to have heat upstairs eventually, but for now, we bought an electric blanket at a yard sale, and found a usable electric heater at the town dump. And we fixed up a bathroom where there had been none, hiring a local plumber to install the pipes and valves, and digging a waste line out to a septic field behind the building. We did not have a door on the toilet for months, having to shake our heads sadly when customers asked. We arranged with the bar owner to send customers to his facility.

We brought in all our albums, lp and 78, and a record player in a back room and played operettas, our favorites, to keep us company, while we worked and thought. Of course, we sang, too, how could we resist? If someone came in while we were working and said, "Oh, that's pretty," we made a note to order an album. What else would we sell? Local products: Shapira's teas and coffees, New York State hard cheddars, and homemade preserves, especially of local wild fruit. We had no refrigeration and could not sell anything that might spoil. But, yes, we could put canned goods on the shelves, nice things like artichoke hearts, olives, gourmet oils and vinegars, imported brands of pasta. We had daily deliveries of homemade bread, pies and cookies. Michael shopped the house sales and went to local auctions to buy small furniture, and old glassware, silver and jewelry. With his decorative-arts-trained eye, and a sharpness inculcated by his father, he developed smart auction strategies and a haggling patience I found embarrassing.

Opening weekend was a mad success. Our pressed glass punch bowls and cups were spoken for before the end of the day, a lot of silver jewelry, good local pottery and Shaker imitations, knit throws, and every other thing, including many of our collector albums were bought while we chatted up the customers.

The townspeople came in droves, drank up the punch (asked for the recipe) and munched a lot of cheese and crackers. They were happy to have us; we livened up the place, bringing business and tourists to their town. Farm people, mostly, they understood we were what we were, but they could see we were nice and discreet. That was all they wanted. And we had already hired a plumber, bought lumber and paint, contributed our modest bits to the local economy. The big spenders came from the suburbs near Albany, from western Connecticut and Massachusetts, from the fancy environs of horse and dog country, and they thought we and the shop were great fun.

But it was not just the shop that was on our minds. It was the whole town. We could rebuild it. After a year, we wanted a big loan. We were making money. Our records showed that. We wanted to buy the Grange building and turn it into a movie theater and a place for live performances as well. We wanted to buy a big old house and turn it into a guest house, a place for bed and breakfast. We might set up a smoke house for local birds, beasts and cheeses, maybe even farm-raised trout. And auctions. We had some ideas about them, too.

"Whoa," said the bank's commercial loan officer. "Don't get intoxicated by your little business. You have to prove you know how to run a bunch of disparate businesses. We're not going to stick our necks out. Just a little at a time. When you manage that, you get more."

We shrugged. Ok. We were together, we were making money and having fun — yes, we played well together, worked well together. We hardly ever left our little town except to find antiques and other stuff to sell. We had an ideal relationship, neither of us looking for anything or anyone else. It was interesting that in shopping for fabrics and antiques, we came across other two-young-men businesses in our rural area. One couple rebuilt old clocks, refinishing and repairing them. Another couple restored old houses, buying wrecks and putting them on the market for a profit when their tasteful work was done. Still another had a graphic design business for fashion advertising. And, of course, there were antiques dealers. We were all pioneers in a way, and recognized it. But we had no reason to get together. Each couple had its own life, busy, loving, creative and isolated, and too reticent for discussion of our shared mystery.

The bank lent us enough to buy the Grange building, an old meeting hall for local farmers. It had good bones, but needed a new roof, new floors, new walls. We wanted it to be mainly a theater. We built a fake proscenium (cut and painted wallboard, decorated with trompe l'oeil swags of red velvet, tied back with painted gold cord — one of Michael's triumphs). Our bleacher seating came from an ad in a local "pennysaver." On each side of our "proscenium" we put the real things — large vases of ostrich feathers, our two originals supplemented with bouquets of softly waving new ones — in black as well as beige.

There was no real audience for live performances yet, but movies, yes. We had our own take on what to show. We bought a movie screen and a projector, set up our bleacher seats, and ta-da, we could show musical oldies, Jeannette MacDonald and Nelson Eddy, Fred Astaire and Ginger Rogers, Dick Powell and Ruby Keeler, Shirley Temple and Bill Robinson tappin' together, Show Boat and Green Pastures, and Busby Berkeley's bloated extravaganzas. Sometimes a print broke, or there were projector problems, but we had a patient, friendly audience.

There were rumblings after a couple of years. A far-away war, student protests, violence on campuses. They did not touch us. No one would draft us. Inspired, perhaps, by the kids, and even the women's movement, gay men rebelled against official harassment in Greenwich Village. That was important, but not to us. We hardly ever visited there now. There were more important things on our minds. Michael wanted to get on with restoring the town. He had his eye first on a three-story American Gothic mansion left by the paper mill family. He could make it into a museum-piece guest house, assembling furnishings and details with an art historian's eye, and transforming himself into a caring host. It would be a great business, he said. Antiquers traveling up and down Routes 22 and 7 would want to sleep in our dream house. In fact, he said, "Let's call it The Dream House." They would linger in the area, and spend more money.

Back to the bank. "Interest rates are going up. We can't offer you six percent any more, and besides you're carrying a big load for a small business. Property values are up, too. The town and county will tax you on higher valuations," the bank manager said. "You guys have a pretty good record, but we've had some defaults lately. How about adjustable rates on a refinanced package?" He explained adjustable rates. We did not exactly understand, but went along. The Dream House became a reality. And even more tourists came to shop.

Then came the oil embargo. That affected us. Cars were stranded gasless on the road. Gas stations had long lines when they were open. But many of them were closed. Who would go out for a drive to visit our town if they could not be sure of getting back? It all happened so suddenly, like a cosmic hand sweeping our game pieces off the table, like a war or a plague or a falling asteroid. Revenues fell by sixty or seventy percent, and we were in deep trouble.

I tried to cut back on our expenses, reduced staff, cut purchases, but the big thing was the mortgage, and just as our revenues went down, our variable rate went up. We had to do something to raise money. As usual, Michael had an idea. "A foundation. That's what we need."

"We have foundations, we need to refurbish the super-structures," I said. I wanted to be funny, but as usual I was a bit lame. Michael poked me. Affectionately, I thought.

"A charitable foundation. Something tax-advantaged. But can a foundation support a business? No, of course not. The business has to go into a foundation whose purpose is to restore the town. We pay ourselves salaries as administrators, and everything else is the same. Or is it? Did anyone ever do this before?"

"We need a lawyer," I said. "We've been a Mom and Pop business, not even a partnership. Maybe we should not..."

"It's all right," Michael said. "There's a fellow in the antiques business near Spencertown who used to be a lawyer. He'll set up a foundation for us." He did, and suddenly we were a tax-free non-profit. Michael gloated. "We'll have the most fashionable parties in upstate New York, inviting people for dinner and dancing and musical performances, but only people who understand invitations that read "Black tie and long dresses." He giggled. "We'll have one of the wineries donate its best wine for program credit: Cascade Mountain or someone like that. We'll get Quattro's pheasants, local smoked trout from the Culinary Institute... In fact that's a terrific idea. We'll have the Culinary cater the dinner and carry it all in and heat it with Sterno. But the service will be elegant."

We were amazed. Our rented tables covered with rented tablecloths were full, each seat went for one hundred dollars, and our black-tied, gowned customers listened to our local opera singers, yes, we had two current and former stars of the City Opera living in the neighborhood who volunteered (when they were pressed into service) to help save our little town. Elaine, greatly admired by Ned Rorem, sang excerpts from Carmen. Mirella from Butterfly. We had a small orchestra of volunteers from the Hudson Valley Phil. We did not want to push our luck too far. But we had a disco guy playing oldies on his own sound system for dancing, and the ladies and gentlemen really did have a ball.

We had decorated the Opera House to a fare-thee-well, taking out the bleachers but leaving the proscenium for our singers. Even we admitted it was campy, but that was part of the fun. It was our BALL. We were the black-tied hosts, one greeting the arrivals, and the other announcing in 18th century court style who was arriving so that some start was made in helping the crowd to circulate and get to know each other. "Oh, are you so and so from Williamstown? Didn't we read that you had donated your prints to the college museum?" Or, "Is that your lovely daughter? Does she go to Bard? I thought I'd seen her in a theater piece there..."

We netted a few thousand dollars for the foundation which was a help with the bank. Not enough. So much work for so little. When we were cleaning up next day, I said to Michael, "How are we going to come up with the next payment? We can't have a fund-raiser every week."

"We can get grants now," Michael said cheerfully. "I'll write grants applications for The Major General Foundation's support, and we may be able to get federal and state money for our restoration." A genius, I said to myself, smiling fondly at him. He had such good ideas.

Well, yes. Michael went to a library in Albany and found

a book of Foundations that give grants; he got in touch with our Congressman whose staff forwarded copies of federal restoration financing legislation. And with local and state officials to see where we could feed at their troughs. There was plenty, we thought, but it could not happen quickly. Meantime, I drafted a fund-raising letter to our customers explaining our new membership program and benefits. That brought in a few hundred a week. Not enough.

We were still showing the wonderful movie musicals of the thirties, forties and fifties but the audience was dwindling. Even our rural area was getting television. Sometimes we ran a sparkling Astaire/Rogers film for an audience of three. Taste was changing, I realized. We loved Mayfair and our audience preferred mayhem. I thought that was a good line, and said so to Michael. He grimaced.

Then he said we needed publicity. "No. Money." I corrected. "Money." Michael applied for an award for "Business in the Arts", a program carried out by, of all things, Esquire Magazine. We won in the teeniest business class and made Esquire. So what. The news and photos were counterproductive. They made us look prosperous, like philanthropists ourselves!

Michael was away a lot, researching our grants applications, talking to people. It would take time, he said. The grants business was at least as competitive as any other business. We were not getting any. They wanted us to look better financially. If we looked better financially, would we need their grants?

We were still running The Major General Store, the Opera House and now our Dream House resplendent in olive paint and white lace. The gas shortage was easing, and we thought with lower inflation and time, we'd be over the hump. The problem was we weren't making enough money, and we could not show that to our customers. We had to be there for them: smart, cheerful and obliging.

They came because they liked us and what we sold. They wanted to support what we were doing. They knew it was important to the town and to its people, to the area and to all fading, hopeless places. And it was important to them, too. It gave them a glamorous local destination that offered something special at the end, something they could talk about.

But we, the authors of this pleasure, we had an odd place in it – a little exotic, a little clownish, to be referred to, tactfully, as "those two young guys" — as much a part of the interesting display as the ostrich feathered Opera House, the impeccable guest house, and, of course, the mahogany cases of The Major General Store. We were there and theirs to be shown off. We knew it in a way and played up a little, only a little, to their expectations. That's what it meant for us to be storekeepers, fundraisers. We had to be their pet gays. "Pet" as in "precocious", "entertaining" and "titillating." We knew it, and refused to know it at the same time. That was part of our game.

And we kept it going despite the fact that we were losing it. Bills were coming due and we could not pay them. The monthly payments were slipping behind, and the bank was warning us that this could not go on. They were warning us by mail, at first. Then they started telephoning. I could not stand it. I woke up one morning and before breakfast, I started screaming at Michael. "How did we get into this? It was you. You didn't know when enough was enough. I saw this little town that needed a new business, and then you ran away with it. More, more. Guest house, opera house. Maybe another guest house, the auction house. The application for a business in the arts award. We couldn't afford the whole damn' town — there isn't enough here."

"Oh shut up," Michael said, still a little frowsy from sleep, and heading to the toilet. "You sound like an old fishwife. Everything we've done you agreed to. Now, you're blaming me. Typical infantile behavior instead of taking responsibility for your own part in it."

"I'm talking about the variable interest rate mortgage," I said, "the piling up of more and more debt. You're the guy who arranged it with the bank, arranged the consolidation into this awful wreckage. You're the leader. I'm the follower." I jumped out of bed to follow him.

"Well, then, if you're such a good follower, shut up and get out of the way." Michael said, quite brutally. He did not speak to me the rest of the day. And left at five o'clock and stayed out till noon the next day.

How could I ask where he'd been? Had he gone to New York to arrange financing? To see something to buy? "Are you all right?" I asked when he returned. Solicitude never hurts even when you feel hostile; it becomes a counter in a game of give and take.

"Of course I'm all right, I had to see someone in New York," Michael said.

"A doctor?" I asked, almost hopefully.

"You're just like your mother, faking concern when you're really angry!"

"Don't bring my mother into it. Where the hell did you go?" It was out.

"I guess I have to say it's none of your business," he said slowly. Then it was clear that the time of doting, of unquestioning ease between us was ended. It was not play any more. If we wanted to stay together, working on our projects, keeping shop, making love, it was going to take real work. The game part was over.

"Okay, then let me say a few things now about what is my business. We used to be able to go to house sales and pick up wonderful stuff — paintings, sculpture, jewelry, furniture, books. Not lately. We're paying too much for what we buy. I've been relying on your sense of what's good. Now I want to know: Why did you buy that table?" I gestured at a

Sheraton console. "It will take too much time to refinish it. We won't get enough for it to make it pay. Why are you making all these decisions that put us deeper in the hole?"

"I've always made the decisions," Michael said coldly. I was shocked. I thought we had made them together, a partnership, a loving partnership.

I tried to ignore the break. Talking about the day, the movie, the merchandise. I cooked dinner, young filet mignon from the no-hormones beef in Pine Plains, local vegetables, everything we enjoyed. But it was no good, not even with a Bordeaux we had been saving for a special occasion. Michael had a sour, closed look and took it to bed turning his back on me. I put a hand on his shoulder once. But he did not turn.

A phone call from Albany. It was our banker, our "banking relationship."

"I'm under orders to visit you and find out what your plans are. We cannot keep carrying you. Will day after tomorrow be all right?"

So soon. We knew then we were on the edge of the end. A lump of dread formed in my midriff. "What are we going to do?"

"Do? Do?" said Michael. "What do you think? We'll see what he has to say, play for time, think of something, do what we have to do."

Well, of course, that was bravado. There was nothing to do. The bank was getting a court order, the county sheriff was going to post a "Seized" sign on all our property – that was not our property after all — and it was all going to go at auction unless some savior came to buy the mortgage beforehand. The bank was shopping our property to vulture real estate people now and we had a few weeks before we were ordered off the premises.

It was the worst thing. I could not have envisioned anything more awful. I kept looking at Michael for confirmation that we were experiencing the end of the world. He looked cheerful. How could it be? "What will we do?" I asked.

"We?" he said. "I'll go to New York first. But, then to London. I've been considering us, and I've realized, I'm tired of this, bored with you, ready for something new. And I think I've found it. A year or two ago, a young Italian whose father sent him here to Yale during the wave of kneecapping in Italy wrote to ask me about Chinese and Japanese porcelains. Well, we met one day in New York, and it turned out that he had a contract with Rizzoli for a picture book about porcelains in American collections and he wanted me to help with the text. We've been seeing each other, and I think I'm in love with him."

I felt as if I was dying. But no, I only wanted to die, and even that was unbecoming and melodramatic. He was throwing me over for a younger man, one with European glamour and a rich father. I turned away. I did not want him to see the tears in my eyes. There would be plenty of time for weeping, wondering how it could have happened, replaying our lives together over and over to see where I had made a mistake. Brooding about how to live now.

The next few weeks were a nightmare. We had to pack our personal things and ship them — where? But what was personal? What was his? What was mine? Michael was generous.

"I don't need any of this stuff," he said. "It costs too much to ship it, and I'll be able to buy good things in London and elsewhere. You can have all the furniture and household goods." I broke down and wept. "It's all right," he said. "I still love you; you're my cousin. Just not the same way."

Oh my God. His cousin.

"Put the stuff in storage till you decide. It isn't such a lot." Michael again.

I went home for a week, back to my family in Stamford. Mother was kind. She brought me meals in my old room, and did not try to make conversation.

The rotten bank conducted its rotten auction. They wanted to get their money out of our debacle. Those bastards did not know they had broken us up, and in doing so created their own catastrophe. They never got their money out. Our merchandise went for practically nothing and there were no bids on anything else. I was glad, spitefully glad.

And then? The county put the property up for taxes a year later, and some speculator got it for practically nothing. His game is waiting. I waited a long time before I could go back to take a look. Saddest place in the world. Everything closed and dusty – our Opera House and the Major General Store, and our Dream House. The town was deader than I had ever seen it. Dead, dead, dead. I was sad and pleased at the same time. As I would be, for example, if Michael were to be dumped by the still young, rich Filippo, for a younger man.

We can meditate here about games and life, about playing life as the ultimate game: Our text, The Bead Game by Hermann Hesse. Or focus on the bank's losing gamble that it could attract a better "player" for its bad deal. Or on what happens to a life game when one player, like Michael, picks up his pieces. (Relate this to the sound of one hand clapping.)

We can open up a whole new game: the mating game. Is it, as Helen Fisher has suggested, one we play for genetic variation by wanting to switch partners every few years? Because, if that is truly built into our genes, gays are playing with a marked deck.

I live in Vermont now, keeping a new general store, "Tim's". Vermont cheddar, maple products, church lady cookbooks, hand knits from everywhere, and country furniture. By myself. I take no risks. Not with finance, not with lovers, not with seeing Michael because it is too painful. He tries to visit on his infrequent returns to the U.S. His and Filippo's book was published. They're considered experts; they live together; play together in London's fun places. I guess our little town and I were just foreplay for Michael's bigger game: The one where he plays Magister Ludi with his next, or maybe last disciple.

End

# THE CONNOISSEUR

Henry Shields was born in Oregon, a victim once removed, as he put it later, of the British Law of Primogeniture. His father, whom he loved and respected, was a younger son of a titled English family, and had, therefore, not inherited the family's great house or its lands in Surrey. They had all gone to the eldest son and later to his heirs. Henry's father had gone to a good public school and then to Cambridge, where he chose, finally, to study medicine. Then, before the turn of the century, he had married a young woman of excellent family, and thought about where he might practice. He could have remained in England, but England was no longer the place for accumulation. Besides that, he wanted the variety of a family practice, rather than a well-paid but narrow Harley Street specialty. He had inherited a decent income, and might inherit more, so the question of where to go hinged on other factors. Not India or Ceylon, South Africa or Rhodesia. One could sense the possibility of future trouble in those places. Besides the climate...

No, if one were heading to a distant place, one wanted it not too foreign, where one could work without fear, a place with a wholesome climate, and with plenty of room to build an estate for one's descendants. The United States spoke English and had a legal system similar to the one he'd grown up with; the northern part of its west coast was as cool and damp as most of England, and land was there almost for the taking.

He wound up with ten miles of pristine Oregon coast, plenty of timber and other income-producing property, and three sons and a daughter. His children enjoyed a comfortable upbringing with many British friends, and a few of German extraction whose parents had seen the same opportunities. They adored the shore, the mountains, the forests and the rivers, and developed strong, healthy bodies, an interest in northwest Indian tribal culture, and an appreciation of the pleasure of smoking and eating your own salmon.

Henry had a fine education, first in a boys' school in Connecticut where he learned Latin and history, and more about British tradition and the family. Then he went home for a degree from the University of Oregon in Eugene. He studied nothing to prepare him for work. He did not need to work. His father had amassed a fortune simply by being in the right place at the right time and knowing the right people. Henry was, yes, a member of the landed gentry.

He did not want to follow his father into medicine. It had its disgusting aspects and required constant availability for patients, with office hours, house calls and hospital visits. Henry considered law, the only other gentlemanly profession, but no. He did not like the prospect of dealing with clients who might have performed questionable acts or of thinking ahead to protect them from other people whose practices were ignoble. He did not have a head for business either; his money was managed by the bank's trust department.

Since he was not going to work, it was time to leave Oregon, which, however beautiful and however much his family had put down deep roots in its moist soil, was not the right place for a cultivated man. There would be plenty of Shields to maintain the family presence. His brothers and sister had married, he even had a niece and a nephew and he knew there would be more. And, perhaps, in time, he too ...

First, a trip to England. He had been before on family visits to Surrey to see his father's family; to see his mother's in East Anglia. He had played cricket with his cousins in regulation white, had visited Bath, had toured the British Museum and the National Gallery. But these visits were not comfortable. He spoke with an American accent; his manners were not authentic, he did not quite understand local references and snobberies. This time, he stayed in London at the Hyde Park Hotel, breakfasted in the Buttery, was introduced to his club by one of his cousins, and there introduced to the man who changed his life: Col. Basil Russell.

The colonel had done what the younger sons of other good families in England did: he had gone into the Army, had put in his time in India, had fought with distinction in France in the World War, emerging only with a weakened left arm, and had, by the late twenties declared his Army career over, and that he had no interest in politics. He, too, had inherited enough to obviate the inconvenience of having to earn a living. He had set about cultivating his taste in the galleries of London, Paris and Geneva. Col. Russell was thirty years older than Henry. Like Henry, he was a high church man. They both liked God, the ceremonial aspect of services, and the social style of their obligations. They hit it off very well.

It was in London that they decided to move to New York. The colonel already lived there part-time. He had a delightful pied a terre in a residential hotel in the east '30s. Rents were low, the service was excellent, the neighborhood had pleasant restaurants. He asked if there was another apartment on an adjacent floor for Henry, and there was.

The colonel provided entree for Henry to the seasonal pursuits of New Yorkers. Despite the depression, there were debuts, winter balls, charity affairs, the Opera and the Philharmonic. The colonel was very much in demand, as a distinguished middle-aged, well-fixed, single man is likely to be in any society. He introduced Henry who became, as he put it, a man about town. When he was asked where he was from, since many of his tradition-conscious acquaintances could not place him, he said, very simply, "I'm Henry Shields of Oregon," as if it were a manorial estate. In a way it was. The timberlands, orchards, cattle spreads and fisheries of his father's genius paid him a princely income.

He and the colonel went everywhere together. They ate breakfast, lunch and dinner together. They dressed for dinner, and often changed afterward for late evening parties. On Monday nights they went to the Metropolitan Opera in formal dress, since they were members of the male-only Metropolitan Opera Club. Going to the opera then in the old Met at 39 Street near the headquarters of the New York Herald Tribune did not necessarily mean listening and applauding. They knew and recognized the members of various claques, but were not fanatical enthusiasts. Sometimes they would hear a whole opera, but it was not uncommon for them to spend part of an act sipping champagne with other young men in the Grand Promenade.

During the day, Henry and the colonel visited the auction houses and dealers in rare books, Oriental rugs, medieval and Renaissance art, and antiquities from the dawn of time in Egypt and the middle east. The colonel was teaching his protege while he continued his own learning and refined his own connoisseurship.

At that time, Henry Shields was a young man, somewhat above medium height, slim, with pale skin and light brown hair, dressed in the British style in the clothes he ordered from London, whose shops had his measurements for shoes and shirts. When his tailor sent a representative every fall, he chose his new fabrics, ordered a blazer along with two or three suits, although the older clothes in his wardrobe were not yet worn out. For late spring and early summer in New

York before he departed on his annual pilgrimage to visit his brothers and sister in Oregon, he made do with clothes from Brooks Brothers. The London tailor had no suitings for a New York summer.

He adopted during this time, from the colonel and from New York society, a manner quite different from the rough-and-ready style of Oregon. He held his head up, and turned slightly to one side or the other from the frontality of his torso so that when he conversed at a party, it was as if he had been held back in his advance toward some goal and was only permitting the conversation to slow him. His tilted head, the sidewise look "down his nose," as his critics described it, was a standard for the polite snobbery of his social position. He rather liked the image it gave him.

In the course of their years together, he and the colonel were instrumental in founding the first ever Oriental rug collectors society. They called themselves the Hajji Babas. They counted knots to the inch, distinguished among the many tribes of West Asia and their mountainous habitats, understood the looms on which which these masterpieces were knotted, identified the vegetable dyes the tribespeople employed, knew the meanings of the patterns, some of them going back to the time of Genghis Khan and even earlier. They recognized the heraldic patterns woven into great carpets for use in the grand homes of the west, and the indigenous patterns as well as the asymmetries of prayer rugs on which the faithful bent five times a day toward Mecca. None of this was easy to learn; the era of books about the crafts and arts of Asian peoples had scarcely begun. They did not, of course, collect the weavings of North Africa or Europe or of the machines of the west. Two good things about these beautiful, flexible objects was how easily they could be stored and used. Their respective apartments had rugs tossed across their sofas, covering their tables and pianos and beds, and hanging on the walls as well as the obvious –

covering their polished parquet floors. No matter what their origins, or where they were placed, the patterns and colors created a feel of lushness that he and the colonel found sensuous, exotic and satisfying. And when there were no more surfaces to cover... why then these exquisite weavings folded upon themselves into neat bundles, easily unfurled for the admiration of their friends, easily stored in mothproof chests.

But they collected more than carpets. Col. Russell was interested in antique glass, fine small shapes, some exquisitely iridescent, from ancient Egypt, Mycenae, Mesopotamia, and Rome. Henry had illuminated cases built into his rooms to hold his cache of glass, plates and bowls, medallions and pitchers, some whose surface brilliance had been softened and blurred with wear and cleaning, but many as bright as the day they were made, and still others whose mineral inclusions had aged into shifting rainbows of glorious color.

Then there were the Renaissance bronzes that could be picked up at auctions and estate sales: finely detailed equestrian heroes, saints conquering dragons and demons, bronzes of youths and dalliance. And there was so much interesting research to do on the sculptors, major and minor, that this too, occupied their days. The auctions also came up with other great prizes, early Renaissance paintings, pieces from Italy's myriad monasteries and churches, stolen or officially sold, no one cared greatly.

And, finally, books. Mostly monkish manuscripts, hand illuminated with the tendrils, birds, scenes of everyday life, and visions of their cloistered copyists. Henry was on the mailing list of every dealer of ancient books and manuscripts in New York, and was contacted by Mr. Foyle from London when he came across a fine manuscript that he did not want for himself.

It was a very satisfying life in many ways, but as the colonel aged, he preferred staying at home with his fireplace and his beautiful things. Henry found himself visiting the colonel, taking his meals with him, but not going out with him. He knew no one to take the colonel's place. He had to think about the unthinkable: being alone.

The colonel was not going to Newport for the summer, he said. He preferred to remain in New York and continue his reading and studying. Newport was becoming too strenuous. Henry offered to remain in New York with him; but the colonel said no: Henry had to visit his family in Oregon as he always did during the summer. See his nieces and nephews, his brothers and sister, his still-flourishing father and mother. The family ties had to be maintained. That was what life was about: the family.

Of course, the colonel died, quietly and tastefully as he did almost everything. He had a quick, neat heart attack, and succumbed in bed one morning. Henry had dropped in to pick him up for breakfast, and to his surprise, the colonel was not yet dressed.

"I'm not feeling well; a little nauseated, and I'm perspiring. Could you brew a cup of tea for me, Henry?"

"Toast with it?" Henry inquired.

"Just the tea, with a little milk," the colonel replied.

Henry went off to the kitchen. He returned ten minutes later and found the colonel dead. It was very hard on him.

A few weeks later, a member of the Hajji Babas came to see him about a worthwhile project. "I have a nephew who is interested in non-theatrical films – for schools, museums, ladies' clubs. About art and travel and current events. He has a camera, 16 mm, I believe he calls it, and thinks we should allow him to make a film about our middle eastern carpets. He says he will use some 'footage' from museums and the National Geographic Society and put it all together. He needs investors. We will syndicate the movie. Do you think you can become part of it? It is certainly worthwhile, don't you think?"

"Well, yes," Henry replied, beaming. "Who is preparing

the script? Someone will be talking, will they not?"

"I had not thought of that. How clever you are, Henry."
Henry smiled modestly.

As it turned out, each of the Hajji Babas contributed his
own insights into his carpets which were photographed in
turn, in each separate home, by the nephew. The nephew
assembled and cut their remarks, intercutting with shots of
how the tribes did their weaving, mostly women, and stored
and carried them on camels and horses, and displayed them
in their tents. A fetching combination of information and
lush visuals. The continuity was read by an actor.

Henry was charmed. He liked the idea of non-theatrical
films. They were made for themselves, for their audiences,
for education and pleasure, not for the hoi polloi and not
to make quantities of money. The people who made non-
theatrical films, Richard de Rochemont and others, were
gentlemen. He set about learning about equipment, the language of film-making, the disciplines of production and distribution. Then, he wrote the first book ever written about
film-making as a technical art. It was not a best-seller, but
it remained in print a long time, and in its minor way, made
him an authority.

But, despite his new interests and new friends, he was
lonely. His sister took him aside on his annual visit. "Henry,
you should have a wife. You are not as young as you were,
and you need a companion and children."

"I have not yet met the right girl," he demurred.

"You have not really looked," she said. "You spend your
time in New York with the flighty society girls or here... I
will inquire, if you permit me to."

He frowned. "I will find my own wife," and realized that
was a commitment of a sort.

He was introduced to Ruth Holm, a tall, handsome blonde
with the slender legs and ankles the British had tradition-
ally associated with good breeding, at a benefit. It was Fate,

she said. She had lived in New York for years, but never attended these things, preferring less formal company and entertainments. But she had a house guest who wanted to see New York, and there was this invitation...

Ruth had an exceptional complexion, very fair and quite poreless; blue eyes deep-set under a straight brow, a good nose, and full chin. He very much liked the way she looked with her pale hair, broad shoulders, good carriage and fine legs. He liked her voice, too. It was a mellow contralto, and when she spoke, it was often with an informal, self-deflating humor. Henry, who was really quite shy in a well-bred way, often talked that way, too, no matter that he looked sideways.

"You're not from New York, either, are you?" he asked.

"Of course not. I'm from the hinterland, Minnesota; Minneapolis, in fact. And you?"

He acknowledged that he had come from even further west. Henry had no trouble ascertaining that like many Minnesotans, Ruth was of Scandinavian extraction, Swedish back a few generations. That was a relief. The Scandinavians – mostly, he thought, the Norsemen – had invaded Britain and northern France many times. He might even have had some of their blood admixed with his own Angles and Saxons. What did Ruth do? She wrote children's books about dogs and horses, about Indian lore, about ice fishing from huts built in winter on frozen lakes, about canoes and sky-blue waters. They were illustrated by a friend of hers with pretty pastels, and offered as a package to her publisher. She wrote mysteries, as well, but not under her own name.

He could tell she liked him, too. They dined together and chatted, went to the movies and the theater, attended parties and visited galleries and museums. Their relationship was cordial and affectionate. They knew each other for months before he learned that she was an heiress. Her family had founded one of Minneapolis' great wheat milling companies. Other family members still managed it, and when she went home, she visited with the Peaveys and all the other milling families. Henry was also tastefully reticent about his own fortune. No vulgar discussion of where the money he lived on came from. There were only two small flaws in their growing warmth. Ruth was not an art lover, and she was a Lutheran.

He did not hold these against her. He would teach her about art, and introduce her to the Episcopal Church. First, the church. He took her to church with him on a Sunday in autumn when he had returned from the Coast. "Why is that man swinging that smoking pot?" she whispered. She knew she was being funny, but also serious in her own way. She liked a less gaudy service. In fact, she told him later, Scandinavian Lutherans were very plain, very spare, very austere. Church was not a success. Neither was hers for him. But since she only attended infrequently, it was less consequential. He attended his superlatively dramatic services alone.

Art. When she lived with beauty she would come to appreciate it. Music, too. He took her to the Opera, Otello. She said she preferred musical theater. Well, he thought ecumenically, it was, indeed a minor art form, and the singing and dancing were fun. He had made a mistake starting her with heavy Verdi, he thought, even though she knew the story, and did not need to follow the plot. He should have started with something amusing like The Marriage of Figaro, or more instantly accessible like Carmen.

He and Ruth agreed they got along well, were very fond of each other and that they would enjoy being married. He went home with her to Minneapolis where her sisters made a splendid wedding in the home of the eldest who was married to a surgeon at the Mayo Clinic. He could talk comfortably with this brother-in-law, comparing his father's practice with the Mayo's world-famous activities. Ruth wore a long white dress, a veil, all the accouterments prescribed for a virginal first marriage – it was, after all, her first – although she was certainly in her thirties- and he wore the obligatory white tie. His Oregon family showed up en masse, staying in downtown Minneapolis hotels. All the little girls were flower girls, the little boys pages. Ruth threw her bouquet at her maid of honor, a dear school friend who had also not married.

They did not need a honeymoon, they decided; not right then. They would go on a trip later in the year. When they returned to New York, Henry would help Ruth pack her things so that she could move into his beautiful apartment. But, he realized, that would not be so easy.- He had carpets, sculptures, cases of glassware, paintings, books, antique furniture, all sorts of stuff everywhere. The colonel had made Henry his heir. He would have to clear some out to make room for Ruth; to make her feel at home as if the space were hers as well as his. He was a very considerate man.

Henry called a representative of the Metropolitan Museum of Art. He had met him often at auctions and parties. "I want to give some of what I have here to the Metropolitan Museum. I want to discuss with you what your collections need that I have, and then to make my own decisions." He was very precise.

The man looked and made notes. He made recommendations after conferring with curators and museum administrators. A question arose as to whether Henry would donate money as well to help maintain his gifts. Henry said his capital was all invested for the long term in real property, and not available for a major donation. No one in his family depleted capital. They lived on income. The man was disappointed, but understood. Henry donated quantities of ancient glass, illuminated manuscripts and books, many old carpets, some fine furniture of the eighteenth century, a number of bronzes, and several Italian Renaissance paintings. The Met was quite overwhelmed. He was, they said, named a Fellow in Perpetuity of the Museum in consequence of his gifts to them, and they put it in writing and on a plaque. He was quite thrilled. "A fellow in perpetuity" – that was a long time.

It was clear, however, after a short time, that it was hard for Ruth to work at home since Henry was accustomed to being at home for some of the day, and although he worked on his films and his studies, he talked on the phone, wandered back and forth, stopped in the kitchen when he wanted a drink, found it hard to keep to himself when Ruth wanted to work. She explained herself very carefully: "Henry, I love you, but we can't both work at home in this place. I will rent a small studio and go there during the day to get my writing done. We will meet for cocktails, and enjoy our evenings and weekends together."

"Ruth, dear, I could office elsewhere. I do not mean to drive you out."

"No," she said firmly, "I want a little studio."

Although this was not the most carnal of marriages, Henry had his heart and mind set on perpetuity. And after three or four years, Ruth announced that she was certainly pregnant. Henry rejoiced. Ruth joked about impending changes in her figure, but to Henry, she would look like a Jan Van Eyck madonna, and he was deeply touched and reverent. Alas, in her third month, when the only perceptible changes were in the fullness of her breasts and a faint waterlogging of her tissues, she began to bleed. They rushed to a small private hospital nearby, but the baby could not be saved. Her doctor told Ruth she was really not built to carry children despite her strong physique and good health. Her pelvis, he said, was too narrow and would create difficulties. Henry experienced a spasm of pain when he heard this. It stayed with him, especially when he realized that Ruth did not mind nearly as much as he did. But he knew she was disappointed. To console her, he spent hugely on a set of diamonds: a necklace, earrings, a thick bracelet and diamond clips for a decollete dress. Whatever she wore, she would be radiant and beautiful.

They transferred their hopes to the midwest and far west, doting on their nephews and nieces on both sides, taking them out when they visited, buying gifts, making plans. Their brothers and sisters were sympathetic; after all it was sad.

Their delightful Park Avenue-in-the-'30s neighborhood was changing. Huge office buildings were going up on Madison and Lexington, even on Fifth. The streets were crowded now during the day with business traffic and clerks and secretaries. The comfortable residential hotels were being bought by chains and subtly altered to appeal to a transient crowd of businessmen. The grand old Murray Hill Hotel had closed; the airlines put in a bus terminal opposite Grand Central; Lord & Taylor offered inexpensive clothing on the second floor, and some of the other stores changed their merchandise too, including Ruth's favorite, Peck and Peck. She still liked trotting into Altman's for lunch in Charleston Gardens but it was beginning to be seedy, and Henry no longer enjoyed a look at the antique Chinese and Japanese porcelains on the main floor before they rode upstairs.

It was time to move uptown into a quiet, residential area. Henry made inquiries; he still belonged to a couple of men's clubs. Another member handed him a prospectus for a beautiful new building that would go up in the east sixties, occupying the long block from Third to Second with an undulating white tower and its own driveways and gardens. With such a structure, they could not be cut off from light and air no matter what other buildings went up nearby. The building was a co-op, a very WASP co-op, the other member said; Henry and Ruth would have no trouble getting in, of course. It was an offering by a major insurance company which would also manage it. The services would be splendid like the best kind of residential hotel; the lobby would reflect the comfort and security of the residents and provide a convenient place for rendez-vous. All services would be in the basement; mail would be delivered to individual apartments. And the Third and Second Avenue facades would have the finest restaurants and retail shops so that everything needed for the good life was nearby. Someone was even building Manhattan's most luxurious movie house virtually across Second Avenue. Henry rejoiced. He loved movies, and was delighted that this theater would have a lounge where patrons could sit sipping Colombian coffee and eating tiny pastries before and after a film.

They chose a spacious three-bedroom apartment, the two spares to be their in-home studies as well as guest rooms; two baths, a spacious kitchen with a dining area, and a real dining room. Henry was not willing to part with some of his old furniture, an eighteenth century fauteuil with original, but slightly ragged period tapestry covering, velvet sofas, and his beautiful carpets. He had new cases built into the living room for what was still a major Egyptian glass collection. He hung his Giotto triptych on a wall. But Ruth had something to say, too. She ordered a shoji screen from Japan for the livingroom, and furnished her own study in Italian modern style. They had borrowed the money to buy the co-op. It was not a problem; they had very large incomes, and paying their monthly mortgage and maintenance fees would not create a hardship.

At least, so they thought. But, the proliferation of nieces and nephews and a third generation meant that there was less for individuals. Henry's brothers all worked. Henry's sister had married well. Henry could no longer subsidize what began to seem a hobby – his non-theatrical films. And Ruth's books. Only a few children's books were highly successful. Royalties on Ruth's books amounted to only a couple of thousand dollars a year.

Their early-evening cocktail hour began to seem self-indulgent. They started buying Sherry-Lehmann's house brand of gin for Ruth's little pitcher of martinis and a house Scotch for Henry's straight up on the rocks. They ate in for breakfast and lunch, ordering their groceries from the high-priced and not too scrupulous Gristede's nearby, and checked its bills after they realized the manager sometimes left small, expensive items out of their delivery, or charged for two pounds of butter when they ordered one. But, even these economies were not sufficient. It was Ruth who said to Henry one day, "Henry, you must get a job."

"A job?" He had never worked. Who would hire him now, a middle-aged man, with a thickening waist, and a suddenly bothersome case of gout? His pale face now looked jowly and a little sweaty, obscuring his fine features. He was less careful about his clothes these days, since he went out much less frequently. He now ordered his shirts from Brooks Brothers since his figure had changed, but the button-down style of the collars no longer suited him. Ruth had not noticed. He had abandoned his heavy British shoes for comfortable Maine loafers...

A job. Ruth suggested scanning the "help wanted" columns of The New York Times when his calls to old friends turned up nothing suitable. She also said that first he must develop a resume. He did not know where she had learned so much. He visited a resume service which found wonderful things in his background: "independent non-theatrical film producer? author? exceptional background in the arts? founding member of...? Fellow in Perpetuity of..." Well, yes, he nodded. It was all true.

He was hired to head the film and slide film department of a new advertising agency that could see a future in producing its own ancillary marketing materials for clients. The agency was housed on the ninth floor of a fine old building

on Park Avenue near forty-seventh street. The building had
been a residential hotel but was now rented to fledgling businesses, consulting firms and non-profit organizations. The ad
agency had been organized only a couple of months earlier,
by a man who had had a financial disagreement with the
owners of a larger agency where he had worked, and had
negotiated his own exit with a partner and a two-year pay-
out on the clients he had taken with him: A gentlemanly
arrangement that had created no scandal. The man, Roderick Denham, was the "account executive", the outside person who talked to clients and kept them happy, sold them
new ideas and campaigns. His partner, the "inside person",
Julius Minton, was considered a good copy person, and better at handling employees and the flow of work in the agency.
Their skills were complementary, but the agency was named
only for Roderick Denham, who, after all, had brought his
accounts with him. Julius had no accounts. This was the
way ad agencies worked, Henry learned. The copy people
never saw the client; they were kept hidden because they
were sometimes odd, not socially acceptable.

Henry was considered a great prize by Roderick. He had
entree to the upper crust of New York, and with his fine
manners and background, would make a great account person himself when the agency expanded. Henry had thoughtfully invited Roderick and his wife to his home for dinner a
few weeks after he was hired. He had assumed that was the
proper thing to do. Ruth did her part. She ordered a wild
goose from one of the game purveyors on Second Avenue, and
stuffed it with a juniper-flavored bread stuffing. Her family
always sent wild rice, enough for the year. And she fixed a
salad and ordered pastries and her favorite breads from the
bakery on Third Avenue. They refilled and consumed the
pitcher of dry martinis several times before sitting down to
dinner. Roderick's wife was learning interior decoration to
keep herself busy, and she found Henry's antiques and Ruth's

Italian study very interesting. The meal was a considerable success. Roderick admired two Renaissance bronze sculptures, and Henry, wanting very much to do the right thing in this novel situation, offered to lend them to Roderick to display in his office.

The agency had a corner suite of executive offices that had a view of Park Avenue, a screened waiting room, and several smaller offices that looked out on a now paved-over interior court that had once been a garden. Henry had been given one of these smaller offices, furnished, just for now, he was assured by Julius Minton, with a second-hand desk, swivel chair and side chair and an empty bookcase. A similar desk and two chairs occupied the opposite corner of the small room. No one was assigned to it. There was nothing on the walls. It was a very plain, undistracting environment. The agency had no current plans for films or film strips, but Henry was assigned to study the accounts, and to think about what kinds of films could be sold to them, and to develop proposals. These would be embellished by the art department with illustrations.

There was a supermarket chain, a dogfood account, a clothing manufacturer, a floor-covering company, a plastic tableware molder, and a few smaller organizations. He read their files and made copious notes on a long yellow pad. But inspiration came slowly. Meantime, Roderick asked if he would mind writing some copy till the movie production work came in. He did not mind at all. Found it rather simple work, easier than trying to think up a movie for these organizations.

He had a routine now: get up and get to work on time, walking, in fact, a little over a mile to the office whenever his gout did not bother him. Sit at his desk, mulling his copy and his movie ideas, saying "good morning" cheerfully to whoever passed his open door. The agency had only ten employees.

He usually ate lunch alone, finding it a pleasant time to have a bottle of beer with a sandwich and catch up on the day's newspaper. There were a few small, dark, quiet bars in the neighborhood that served food. Additionally, about once a week he joined two other writers, a man and a woman who worked separately down the hall, for lunch at a place called the Divan. Thus they got to know each other a bit. Now, since he was a working man, he did what British working men do. He stopped at a neighborhood pub on Lexington Avenue for a beer and some sociability before going home. This gave Ruth time to finish her work and to prepare dinner if they were eating in.

Julius Minton walked into his office one day to say that he had hired a girl for a few days to write a background booklet for one of their clients. She was an experienced copywriter, he said, but he was not sure they would want to hire her permanently. Henry was puzzled. He had been hired by Roderick, and his job was permanent. He sorted it out, finally. There was a difference in social status that made Roderick hire him, whereas cagey Julius was only trying this female person out, and when her project finished, if they did not want her, there would be no hard feelings. Then Julius said, "She will share your office." He was taken aback. He had supposed he had a private office.

There she was on a Monday morning, a small, thin, dark girl who had worked for J. Walter Thompson for several years, and lost her job when the food company whose products she worked on had shifted its account to Leo Burnett in Chicago. He shook her hand when they were introduced, and she said, quite formally, "How do you do?"

"Very well, thank you," he said, making a polite joke about the dual meaning of the formality. She looked serious and did not respond. There was no further conversation. She sat down at her desk, opened the folder of background material she had been given, and began to read and make notes. Within an hour, she was typing. How long was her task supposed to take, Henry wondered. At twelve o'clock, she stood up, said, "I'm going to lunch, Mr. Shields," and left. Everyone else in the agency used first names, even the partners.

She had finished her writing and had clean copy ready for an anniversary booklet for the dogfood company on the second day. Plus, a folded paper format, and suggested illustrations. "Do you want to see this?" she asked.

"I?" Henry could not think why he should. She looked at him seriously, nodded and went in search of Julius.

When she returned, she had another assignment. They went on this way for two weeks. Once the slim young man who worked on the floor covering account and the somewhat older woman who did the supermarket company ads invited her out to lunch with them. They ate in a place known for spaghetti and meatballs, she said.

"We usually eat at the Divan," he said, "and have Chicken Divan. I prefer roast pork and mashed potatoes." Then he worried. Perhaps she did not eat pork.

Roderick came in to see her one day, "What's this? What's this?" He seemed agitated, waving her dogfood booklet and quite redfaced. "What does this mean?" He read out loud, "Twenty-five years ago a dog could eat like a pig; now even a pig can't eat like a pig: he's on a balanced diet, too."

She said, "It's just a little joke to open up Twenty-five Years of Canine Nutrition. It's true, and it's funny. Don't you like it?"

"Not a bit," Roderick said. "You'll have to change it." She nodded, and took the copy back. Henry thought it was funny, but he realized that he did not have to deal with the client; Roderick did.

The next time Henry ate with the two down the hall, he jocularly referred to "the little Phoenician" his officemate. He was too embarrassed to say the other word. The older woman understood; she was English, and wrote radio copy, having been with the BBC. The man, a native of Brooklyn, looked puzzled, "Phoenician?" Henry did not amplify, and the subject was dropped. No one wanted to be too friendly with her; why invest energy getting acquainted with someone whose tenure would probably be short?

It was different at the end of three weeks or so. Julius offered her a permanent job. She was quick, versatile, productive, and no trouble. Julius had liked the canine nutrition piece, but he knew better than to defend it when Roderick disapproved.

Now, she was a fixture in Henry's office, and he knew she went out to lunch at unfashionable twelve rather than fashionable one. That she had few lunch dates, made few personal phone calls, looked at the ceiling when she was thinking, went to the ladies' room infrequently, did not fuss about clothes, hair or makeup and left promptly at five to walk home to a small apartment on the lower west side in an area she called Chelsea. He did not know anyone who lived on the west side, and only ventured there himself for the opera or theater.

Her name was Celia Baron, her married name that is. He asked what her maiden name was. Shaw, she said. But no, it was not spelled that way. It was spelled Shore. "Where is your family from?" Henry asked politely. Everyone always asked where people were from.

"I was born in New York, here," she replied.

"But originally," he persisted.

"Austria-Hungary, when there was still such a place."

"Ah. My family came from England, and now we're from Oregon."

"I've never been there," she said.

"Where?"

"Either place." She went back to work.

It took months for them to become more friendly. Henry had not, to his knowledge, ever made conversation with a Semite before. But there was, after all, some precedent. Queen Victoria had had Disraeli, a Prime Minister whom she liked and respected. And had there not been a Lord Montague...?

He called her Celia, and recognizing the precedent of the agency's partners, she uncomfortably set about calling him and the others by their first names. He saw how carefully she made herself inconspicuous with dark dresses or suits, plain hats and leather gloves, and low-heeled shoes for comfort in her long walks home. But, he noted, she was very pretty with fine, regular features, clear olive skin, brown eyes and dark hair. He was reminded of Sir Walter Scott's Ivanhoe with his beautiful Hebrew girl, Rebecca, who of course, could not be the chosen one when there was a Saxon Rowena in the story. Thackeray, of course, had not been so inhibited, and wrote an alternate ending to Scott's romance, choosing Rebecca as the loved one. Henry thought about that: Ivanhoe could not choose Rebecca. His children then would lose the purity of their heritage, and would be confused about who they were, half-breeds, mutts. No. Ivanhoe had made the right decision.

One day, on impulse, he asked if she would join him for lunch in a little dark bar named John's. "How nice," she said. "I usually eat alone, and walk around trying to find a place that doesn't make me feel uncomfortable reading. I'll pay for my own, of course."

That was scrupulous, he thought, glad that she had voiced the least embarrassing rule for their meals.

At lunch, she was unexpectedly vivacious, asking what he recommended and ordering it too, but with coffee, not beer. "I love roast fresh ham, but I don't much like the gravy," she told the waiter. "Maybe a spoonful, that's all. And none on the potatoes." She finished her green beans. Henry usually left his.

They talked about the book he was carrying, Victorian England: Portrait of an Age by G. M. Young. Yes, he liked it. That was what he read, history. He had just finished a book about the Middle Ages by a Dutch historian, Huizinga. They talked about Northern Europe's medieval cuisine with its root vegetables and cabbages, herrings and hams, breads and soups. She told him about her grandmother's cooking, and he said that it was very like that of several centuries ago.

She had not read as much history as he, but he could see that she knew what he was talking about.

They talked about food because he was still concerned about her possible dietary restrictions. "No," she said. "I was brought up in a family that paid no attention to dietary laws. Those restrictions might have had some meaning two thousand years ago..."

What did she read? Serious fiction, anthropology, philosophy, economics. Yes, he thought, the folklore said "they" were intelligent.

He winced on the way back to the office. "What is it?" she asked.

"It's my gout – the purines assemble in crystals, you know." He was embarrassed.

"In your foot, near your big toe like all the caricatures of Merrie England?" He nodded. "I will look it up, and see what..."

"The doctors do that," he said. "Very competently. There is no cure. One must simply be careful about what one eats, take one's Benemid and drink dilute alcohol like beer instead of Scotch."

She came in the next day with something interesting: not about a cure, but that there was some correlation between gout and a high level of intelligence. He was pleased to have been identified by her as intelligent. "Do you ever ask yourself if you'd rather be dumb and not know or notice very

much; or be smart with all the pain brought by awareness?"
What an extraordinary question, he thought. He never asked
himself any such thing.

"What about you?" he countered. "Would you rather be
bright and sensitive or stupid and thoughtless?"

She smiled. "There is nothing that gives me more pleasure than the intricate workings of intelligence – wherever it
is." Of course.

The office was moving. Roderick and Julius called a
meeting to let everyone know. The beautiful old building
was to be torn down, and Union Carbide would build an
office tower in its place. No one, however, would be incon-
venienced. They would move into new quarters on Madison
Avenue only three or four blocks away, into an old office
building just south of Brooks Brothers, where there would
be room for expansion.

They had private offices now, Henry right next to Celia in
tiny spaces constructed with the movable walls that flexible
office planning required. They even had doors. The walls,
however, were of panels and glass that went up only seven
feet in a space eleven feet high. Henry said, "Illusion is all.
We have the illusion of privacy." But they did have something the offices on the opposite wall did not have: windows.
A single window each, that moved up and down, permitted luxurious control of their own environment. This was
meaningful because it had suddenly become the rage to design new structures without windows altogether as AT&T's
Long Lines had done, or with glass curtain walls that were
immovable like those in the new Lever House. Such new
buildings allowed their architects to shut out light and air in
favor of man-made and man-controlled environments. But,
Henry had read, working in the AT&T building was like
being confined underground in a mine; and he had himself
visited Lever House. The same air conditioning served the
toilets as the offices, and recycled the smells. No, this old

building was quite satisfactory, as many old things were, despite the fact that the windows offered no real view – just that of a dark, narrow courtyard.

They were becoming good friends, conferring about writing problems and photography, chatting about movies, and making only oblique comments to each other about Roderick's insatiable woman-chasing and about Julius' pretensions, copy delays and ultimate uselessness as an agency partner.

"Come for dinner. I've talked about you to Ruth and she wants to meet you. Bring Lawrence, and we'll have a pleasant evening together." He was surprised at himself, wanting to entertain them, but why not?

Celia brought a bottle of very good French Pouilly- fuisse to go with the Longchamps-cooked chicken dinner Ruth ordered in. What a pleasant couple they were, he thought, admiring his books and manuscripts, talking about having met Mr. Foyle in his beautiful refectory in Essex, and about having climbed to his tower so that he could show them his most valued manuscripts. Now why would Mr. Foyle have served them sherry and shown them his manuscripts? He did not know how to ask, but Celia gave him the answer. "We were really privileged. An English couple we spent some time with in Italy invited us to stay with them in Great Braxted, and then took us around and introduced us." English? He was astonished. Did the English couple not know? Apparently not.

They admired his collection of ancient glass, his fine old furniture, his paintings, bronzes and his carpets. They had exceptionally cultivated tastes, were the products of quality education. "Where did you learn all this?" he asked. School, the museums, reading... where did you learn anything, Celia said.

The evening was a success, the most entertaining he had had in months. He showed them his and Ruth's bedroom with its double bed and matched nightcaps on the pillows.

"Nightcaps?" Celia chortled. "I have only seen them in illustrations for nineteenth century novels."

"Why, of course," Henry said. "One's head gets chilly when one sleeps. We always wear them."

The conversation went from culture to amusing stories, to food, to movies. Celia said her mother loved mysteries and Ruth admitted writing them, and offered Celia a couple of paperbacks for her mother. Celia said she and her mother had foraged on Fourth Avenue below Fourteenth Street every Saturday when she was a child, buying second-hand books four for a quarter, and coming home with troves of E. Phillips Oppenheim thrillers, S.S. Van Dine mysteries, Somerset Maugham and Jack London, Sinclair Lewis and Pearl Buck.

In the office, new people were hired, and Roderick asked Celia to give up her windowed office to a new copy writer, a man who would be reporting to work the following week. She could have an office across the way without a window. Celia had stared at Roderick, not trusting herself to say anything. As soon as he left, she knocked on Henry's door. "What should I do?" she asked. "I have been here for two years. Roderick even told me he had told the new writer I was the one for him to 'beat.' I should go into his office and tell him how ridiculous it is for him to want me to hand over my office to some male person who has not yet produced anything. In fact, that is what I am going to do."

'Do you want my advice?"

'That is what I came in for," she said.

Henry smiled ruefully. "Don't."

"Don't what?"

"Roderick pays the rent, he pays your salary – the other office is the same size..."

"No. It is not right. I will simply tell him I do not want to move. I like my office. If he and Julius want to fire me..."

But they did not. The male writer was assigned the office across the way.

As in many agencies, perturbations were frequent. A new writer was fired when management perceived that he might be homosexual. Celia was indignant and took it upon herself to treat him to a lavish lunch as a farewell gesture.

All the writers had the opportunity to plan and develop presentations for new clients, but only Celia's brought in new business. Roderick did not promote her to account executive –he was convinced no client would accept a woman in that role. Celia said, "If you have confidence, they will. Why don't we try it and see." She said it to Julius first, and he said he would talk to Roderick. She did not expect much of Julius: he was not straightforward. She was quite right. Roderick would not hear of it.

She told Henry she would ask Roderick to have lunch with her so that they could get better acquainted, and then perhaps he would have a more favorable view of her. Henry shook his head; her effort would do no good. She said she had to do it, and did. Roderick refused flatly to lunch with her. "But you eat lunch with everyone, everyone. I will pay for lunch," she said. She told Henry about it afterward. "Then he looked really grim and closed the door, and flushed red-faced, said to me, 'You think I don't like you because you're Jewish; you think I don't like you because you're from New York; you think I don't like you because you're female. Well, yes. All three.'" She was close to tears.

"He's not a nice man," Henry said.

Another crisis arose out of the files. Celia kept her files in the file drawer in her desk. Roderick wanted them centralized. Celia said no; she needed them- she could not work without them. Roderick backed down again, but his mutters could be heard all over the agency.

"Why don't you fire her?" his latest secretary/paramour asked, and offered her logical solution to anyone who would listen. Roderick could not. She did too much work, and was endlessly creative.

On one of his lunchtime rambles, Henry stopped in at H.P. Kraus, a rare book dealer, and impulsively decided to buy a manuscript, a very attractive one, at a reasonable price of one thousand dollars. He asked Celia if she could lend him the money for three months; he would pay her one third each month. He did not want Ruth to know he had been so extravagant; they did not have the income they formerly had, and neither of them would touch capital. It was all right, Celia said, and wrote a check. In fact, it took him a little longer to repay, and to his embarrassment, Celia had to remind him of his debt. But he was encouraged enough to buy another... and another... always affordably-priced, and always with an advance from Celia who was good-natured about it, and knew he would pay her back even if she had to nag a bit, as she put it.

Easter was approaching, and Henry asked Celia if she would like to attend Episcopal services with him. She was his friend and he would enjoy introducing her to his splendid church.

"Henry, I could not. I am a Jew; I do not really like the history of Christianity, or indeed of many other religions. I am a Spinozan. I do not believe in a God separate from the processes of the universe, nor in a creator outside the universe, nor in a hierarchy. By most standards, I am an atheist." She was troubled and thoughtful and clearly did not want to hurt or disappoint him. But in this, as in her professional life, she could not do what did not seem right to her. "An atheist?" he said. "You are the most religious person I know!" He was surprised by his own statement, but now that he had said it, he knew he meant it.

The agency had finally managed to sell a movie to a client, and Henry proceeded to do the research and script himself, hired a cameraman and actors, and got it rolling.

The film was a deliriously episodic treatment of the same
family's mealtimes through the ages – a dining room-oriented
Antrobus family like Thornton Wilder's in The Skin of Our
Teeth – taking them from gnawing on bones in the cave to
communal clay pots and wooden platters to varied meals
on gold and silver and exquisite china to, Henry cackled,
the culmination of civilization – unbreakable melamine for
home and school lunch. Along the way, there were heroic
battles derived from King Arthur and Shakespeare, unpleasant goings-on among the Borgias, a Chinese revolution, and
a sumptuous meal in a tent like the one in which Rudolph
Valentino seduced Vilma Banky. The film was entered in the
American Film Festival, an orgy of non-theatrical films, and
Roderick bought a table at the Festival's annual banquet.
Henry told Celia about it afterward. "There was Roderick with Mrs. Roderick with whom he otherwise has little
congress. And Ruth and I; and Julius with his peroxided
lady... We were all in evening dress. Imagine." Celia nodded. "It was an awful evening. I said to Ruth in the taxi
home – 'Why didn't you wear your diamonds? It was the
perfect occasion.' You know Ruth. She said, 'Henry, they're
beautiful, and I love you for giving them to me when the
baby died. But Henry. Those people would have thought
they were zircons. And anyway, you know I like jewelry
that clanks.' Isn't she funny? And does she not understand
perfectly how those people are?"

Celia laughed. "I like jewelry that clanks, too. Big pieces.
Mostly silver, mostly from Mexico."

Modern Talking Pictures distributed Henry's film to clubs
and schools, and Roderick talked up new possibilities but
none materialized. Henry was reduced to supervising photo
shoots for other clients' print advertising.

He conferred with Celia about a photomontage for a
client, and they and the art director decided on a series of
shots with what the art director called, "The all-American

boy – tousle headed, freckled, gap-toothed..."

Henry relied on the photographer, an old hand at this, to pick the model. After all, he dealt with model agencies all the time. The photographer arrived with his stationwagon and equipment; they picked up the boy, and then drove to their location. Henry supervised the shoot with misgivings, and then brought the proofs to Celia. "Ooh," she said. "The kid looks a little adenoidal. Roderick will hate spending the money, but maybe ..."

"Well, who knew John would choose a boy who looked as if he was about to burst into glorious womanhood?" Henry was upset or he would not have joked that way. He did not like failure. And, indeed, Roderick made a fuss. He even said he did not think Henry was earning his salary and that he was hiring another new business person because Henry, with all his contacts, had brought in no new business.

Disheartened, Henry stopped in at his Lexington Avenue bar, "the swamp" he called it, for his daily chat with an old friend, Dr. Oliver St. John Gogarty. He had been meeting Dr. Gogarty at the swamp for more than a year when he first mentioned him to Celia, who knew as soon as he said his name that he was the model for Joyce's Buck Mulligan, the pudgy, Greek-quoting medical student who ascended to the top of the Martello tower in his dressing gown and shaving cream at the beginning of Ulysses. Dr. Gogarty was still practicing, he said, but pub life was as necessary as food and sleep to him. Henry was delighted that they could talk together most days. Today, he let Dr. Gogarty talk; he was depressed.

"Ruth, there is something wrong at the office." He told her about it. She listened seriously, sipping her martini, sitting on the sofa in front of the Japanese screen, her broad brow furrowed over the deep blue eyes. When he finished, she sat still for a bit more.

"Henry, Roderick is bored with you." He marveled at her

insight. "You must wait a bit so that you do not look hasty or upset, and then resign."

Meantime, Celia and Lawrence invited a few people from the office to a party in their funny floor-through near Tenth Avenue. Ruth brought her own homemade tuna fish salad in a one-quart plastic container that she had saved after they ate the ice cream. They had a splendid evening despite the fact that the new new business man was invited, too, as well as the other writer who was told Celia was the one to beat. It was a big party, very informal, ravioli and sauce, and green salad on the kitchen table for people to serve themselves, and a jolly little bar in the foyer.

Ruth found a friend there, a tall blonde woman named Eva, a Norwegian sculptor who was a friend of Celia. Celia had two excellent terra cotta pieces that Eva had built: a head of a black man, very naturalistic; and a torso of a naked woman, arched and twisting. Ruth invited Eva for drinks and they became close friends, visiting back and forth during the day. Eva had been a WAVE during the war, had been married twice, but was now single, and childless. She talked in a breathless voice, smiled beautifully, and looked enough like a heavy version of Ruth to be her sister. He was glad Ruth and she were so close.

The time had come for Henry to resign. It was obvious that his career was not advancing; he did not like working for other people, and he would not do so again. He typed a letter of resignation and gave it to Roderick, who nodded when he read it. It was a tactful letter that said he had enjoyed working in the agency, and had learned a great deal, but it was time for him to return to his own projects. His Renaissance bronzes were a bit of an embarrassment. They were still in Roderick's office, where they gave the illusion that he was a connoisseur to prospective clients. Henry discussed the matter with Celia: He could take them home, or put them up for auction at Parke-Bernet. She said, either one; just don't leave them for Roderick like a grand seigneur. That would have been his inclination, they both knew.

He went into Roderick's office on his last day. "The bronzes," he said. Roderick had not mentioned packing them for him... Had he thought he would simply leave them on loan, so to speak?

Roderick said, "Oh yes. I was going to ask you if I could buy them from you. Say five hundred dollars each?" Henry's eyes rolled up to the ceiling, but Roderick did not notice. He was already writing the check.

He had discussed with his bank increasing his monthly stipend. Ruth had hers increased concomitantly. Even without his salary, they could manage well. Henry went back to his scholarly reading. Ruth continued her writing, but he noticed that she was drinking more, and was dismayed that one evening after several martinis, her slender ankles bent under her, and in falling, she hurt her head on a kitchen counter, and had to wear a plaster for a week. He thought perhaps she was drinking more because she could not have a baby. Perhaps she felt it more keenly now than before. He could not discuss it with her; there was not a day that he did not grieve.

Henry and Celia had lunch together two or three times in the year that followed. Then Celia called one day, "I'm leaving this place, finally. I've been asked to join a partnership, and it's a perfect situation for me now, because if I need to, I can set my own hours."

"Need to?"

"I'm going to have a baby. No one's been able to tell, of course, but it will show soon. I'll be able to work at home if I have to, and there are three other partners. I think it will be all right. And now, I have a marvelous little story to tell you. Do you remember that fellow Roderick wanted me to give my office- to?"

Henry did.

"He just left the agency and took with him the accounts on which he was account exec. They were accounts I brought in, and Roderick simply handed them to him. Serves Roderick right. He and Julius want to sue him."

"I am taking to my new agency an account I worked on evenings, you know, too small for the agency. And I have another in the offing, a small conglomerate. The other partners have a few accounts, and we're beginning on the street floor of an eastside brownstone that one of the partners lives in. Very cozy and we pay rent only when we can afford it."

The news about the baby was what interested Henry. Celia, a quintessential career woman, he had thought...

"Did you intend to have the baby?"

"Oh, yes. I went for an annual physical, and had a lady doctor this time. 'How old are you?' she asked me critically. I told her and she was very indignant. 'What are you waiting for?' Well, she was right, of course. I love children."

Henry scheduled a lunch for a few weeks thence; he had a morbid, he thought, interest, in seeing Celia in a maternity dress. She was, as he expected, filled out but still neat in a two piece, conservative, dark green and black cotton print. "How are you feeling?" he asked, really wanting details about how she was feeling.

"It's been easy. No morning sickness, no fainting spells, no nothing. The only thing is I feel as if I have a fever,- for the first time in my life my hands and feet are warm, so warm I'm afraid to touch people. I wonder if that will last after the baby is born." She touched his hand, and indeed hers was much warmer than his.

The announcement came, finally. A boy, eight pounds. A big child for small, thin Celia. Henry went to James Robinson on fifty-seventh street and ordered sterling flatware engraved with the baby's initials, DRB, Daniel Robert Baron. He wanted to deliver the gift, and did a few weeks later, dropping by with a half-bottle of Veuve Cliquot to celebrate. He was a beautiful child, big and strong, holding his head up when he was on his belly on the floor. Celia worked part-time at home, she said, having outfitted part of the foyer as an office. For the rest, she had a pleasant woman taking care of Daniel and the apartment, and they were looking for new quarters.

An idea entered his head. He pushed it aside. It kept returning. He kept pushing it aside. Summer came and he and Ruth took a large, comfortable room in Provincetown at the Provincetown Inn, the only really posh place in raffish P'town. They were having a splendid time, breakfasting at the inn, spending the mornings prowling the streets and talking to the local tradesmen, lunching wherever they found themselves, spending the afternoon swimming at the town beach, and dining where the locals suggested. They got about in matching bell-bottomed trousers and striped French sailor jerseys and sneakers. On cool days they wore blazers. They lunched on lobster sandwiches in little snack shops, enjoying whatever conversation they came upon.

It was little Daniel's first summer, and Celia had taken a cottage on a lake near Forestdale, about sixty miles away. Henry called the cottage. "Why don't you come to Provincetown and dine with us at this marvelous Portuguese place where the food is very inexpensive and delicious. You could have linguica stew."

They did indeed, and little Daniel, as good natured as could be imagined, and larger than last time, slept in his carbed on a chair at the side of the table.

The idea returned. He did not share it with Ruth; she might not understand.

In the fall, he thought about it again. He called Celia for lunch, and made reservations in the very expensive and luxurious dining room of his favorite hotel, the Barclay. They knew him; he and Ruth stayed there when their apartment was being painted. He dressed with special care, regretting that he was no longer svelte and that his new barber did not cut his hair as well as the old one. He knew Celia was puzzled about lunch at the Barclay. They usually ate in dark little bars – whatever the proprietor cooked. But she arrived on time, as always, smiling and warm.

"How is it going?" he asked.

"Oh, the agency has its ups and downs, but it's nice being an owner, and not having to apologize for my existence. And Daniel is wonderful. He had been walking for months, holding on to fingers, but he's walking by himself now... I dote on him."

He was trying to rehearse, had been trying to rehearse, what he wanted to say. "This is going to seem very strange to you, I think. You know Ruth had a miscarriage years ago, and the doctor told her her pelvis was too narrow to carry a baby..."

"I remember," she said. "You told me once. It was very hard on you."

"It was. I've been thinking lately. Of all the women I know, it seems to me I admire you the most. You're so bright, and really decent. A very good person. Very kind. You're exemplary in so many ways. You're very pretty..."

"Henry! You never said that before..."

"Oh, well. That's not really it. What I mean is, I respect you greatly... and this is very embarrassing, but I mean it more than I've ever meant anything. I would be very grateful, and more than prepared to show my gratitude if you'd be so kind as to have a baby with me."

"Oh, Henry." She was clearly deeply embarrassed, herself. "I can't do that. I don't know what to say. I love and respect you, you know that, but I can't have your baby. I want you to know, though, how flattered I am that you asked me, especially since the time someone told me you called me 'the little Phoenician...' "

He flushed. "Don't. Don't. I did not know anyone like you then... I had never had any conversation..."

"It's not about that Henry; you know how fond I am of you... I would want to raise my own children... with Lawrence... what would he think? And all the other stuff: by orthodox Jewish standards, your child would be Jewish..."

He had not dared get that far, or anywhere past the point of having a descendant, his own child. Everything else could be managed, he thought. He changed the subject. She was, as usual, very nice, very tactful and did not bring it up again.

A year later, the first symptoms showed up: a progressive weakness and cramping of his legs and arms. He visited his Manhattan doctor, who did many tests of his reflexes and asked him many questions. He said, "Your nervous system is turning to - ah - ordinary protein - ah. It is starting in your feet, and may work to your hands. You will not have any problem of incontinence, probably, and you will retain your intelligence, vision... all that. It could take many years to incapacitate you, but you can adapt..."

Henry was cheerful. If he could read and think, he could put up with almost anything. And Ruth was, as always, her dear, devoted self. But his legs began to weaken and she insisted on his going to the Mayo. They flew to Minneapolis, and from there drove to Rochester. His brother-in-law was directly and amply concerned during the week he and Ruth spent there. It was no use, but served to rule out other possibilities. He heard them say, "Lou Gehrig's..." and knew then how bad it might be.

Two years later, he was confined to the bed he and Ruth still shared, and she had hired a nurse's aid to help during the day, bathing him, changing the bed, helping with feeding him. He had come back to the slim figure he remembered from his youth. He remarked how slim he had become, how slender his legs, how clear the bony structure of face, now that he was no longer pudgy. He looked very distinguished sitting up in his paisley silk dressing gown.

"Ruth, Celia and Lawrence and little Daniel are coming to visit Saturday afternoon. It will be so nice to see them. They are going to eat at Serendipity afterward, she said, so we'll only have drinks together. Celia said little Daniel is planning to have a foot-long hotdog there, and a frozen hot chocolate, and has heard about their nickelodeon. Did we ever eat there? Did you know they have a nickelodeon?"

Ruth did not think so; she did not know Serendipity and was not quite sure what a nickelodeon was. An early movie box, he explained, that had a succession of pictures on flipping cards, and when they flipped fast enough, and you watched through the eyepiece, you had the illusion of watching a movie. They were always short, comic or melo-dramatic, and great fun. She nodded. Yes, she had seen one in Minneapolis as a child.

Well, the intercom rang and they were announced from below. He was still in bed, but had laboriously donned his dressing gown. Lawrence asked if he might pick him up to carry him to the living room. Well, he was so thin now, it would not be hard. Lawrence carefully slid his arms under Henry's torso, and carried him into the living room, where he lowered him gently to the fauteuil.

Celia looked well; the same. Lawrence did not really interest him. But Daniel, now four years old. He inter-ested him greatly: a sturdy child, still platinum-haired and blue-eyed, to Celia's vocal astonishment. "When he was a few months old, I asked the pediatrician, will he really have blue eyes? And the pediatrician looked closely and said yes. Imagine. We both have brown eyes. Two recessive genes must have got together."

They had brought picture books for Daniel and a couple of small toys for quiet play. He looked contented on the floor, answered questions, looked at the fine things around him without touching. "Did you warn him?" Henry asked.

"Oh, no. He's been visiting the old lady across the hall since he was a year and a half old, and she has all those porcelain cups and saucers, and breakables on low tables and shelves everywhere... And she says, 'he's a wonderful little fellow, understands without being told what he can touch, and what he should not...' "

Henry began to tire after an hour or two. He was not as strong as he used to be. There was no reason to complain. He was very well cared for. Ruth was devoted beyond any expectation...

"We're going now," Celia said. "We've enjoyed the visit very much; I'm so glad to have seen you. It's always wonderful to chat; we have so much to talk about..."

Ah. Weaker and weaker. Now all that were left were his head and eyes. He thought about Osiris, the Egyptian god, the god of the tuat, death and resurrection; the god who had been killed by his jealous brother, Set, chopped into fourteen pieces for his wife/sister Isis to find and reassemble. The god who was always represented wrapped in the linen windings of a mummy, with his bulbous crown on his head. This god, represented everywhere in Egyptian hieroglyphics and wall paintings, had come momentarily to life, dead penis included, and coupled with Isis, who then produced the god Horus. Could he? A dead penis come momentarily to life with a fertile female body astride his, could he now, like Osiris, father new life?

But how ironic to be a Fellow in Perpetuity of the Metropolitan Museum of Art, when perpetuity ended with him. He sighed, again; breathed out his *ka*.

End

# NOT LEAST AMONG
# THEM

Victor Petersen applied for a job as secretary-typist with my small public relations firm in the late '70s. I had advertised in The New York Times, and hired him because he was an extraordinarily speedy typist (in this period before widespread computerized word processing), had decent references, and was more than willing to learn. He was in his early twenties, had graduated from high school in the town in the Hudson Valley in which he grew up (Cornwall, near West Point), and in which some of his family still lived.

There was no question that he was gay: he was a pudgy, simpering, overtly effeminate man. But I had no reason to feel negative about that: My firm, established in 1959, had employed homosexuals before, and I had found most of them fine people and very good workers. As I usually did, I asked his predecessor to stay on for a week to train him.

Victor turned out to be an exceptionally valuable employee. Not smart – no, in many respects he was, bluntly, stupid. But, good-natured, willing, very quick to learn what he had to learn, and a person who put every minute in the office to good use, volunteering to clean up lists, to transpose my personal and business phone directories to Rolodex files, to do more work than anyone in that job did before or after.

He was not perfect. With his fingers flying over the Selectric keys, his mind would sometimes wander, and he would type homonyms for the words in our original copy, creating sometimes hilarious errors. He would also, occasionally identifying too closely with me, speak as waspishly as I might have to suppliers who had failed us. They were less willing to accept such talk from him.

But work in my office was not all there was for him. He was an avid fan of soap operas, and contributed regularly to soap opera magazines, writing fan pieces about his favorite actors and shows. He knew I'd be interested in his success with free lance work, and I was. My office was then in my large apartment (designated semi-professional), and we worked there for another year or so till we moved into an office building a block away. Part of the fun, for him, of working with me was the fact that several tv soap opera people live in my building, one of them an actress who lives next door. Of course, he seized upon the opportunity to introduce himself to her for an interview.

Victor worked for me for three or four years, although after about two years, he started warning me that he was likely to move on. He had learned a great deal from me, he said, but his career needed new learning and new opportunities. I did not want him to go, I told him often. I was paying him well enough so that he could move out of a shared apartment into his own place only a block away from the office. He sometimes had a roommate, but these arrangements did not last, and when he had the opportunity to terminate them (with friends, acquaintances, lovers?) he did. Most often he lived alone.

During that period, too, he was able to afford to buy contact lenses to substitute for the thick eyeglasses his myopia needed; he bought better clothes, though his taste was not GQ-inspired. And he confided a few things about his family: his mother had diabetes, and was far from well; his family wanted nothing to do with him when it became apparent that he was gay.

He had no longterm lover: he was not pretty, he was not fun, he was not bright. The best he could do was an occasional short-term relationship. At worst, I gathered, he was available for one-night stands.

As I gradually realized this, feeling for him and with him in his loneliness, I also noticed that he suffered from gastro-intestinal disturbances every few weeks, usually after a weekend. With a degree in foods and nutrition, and plenty of consultative experience in food handling, I thought I could help. So, I'd ask if he made sure to refrigerate his food promptly, to wash his hands before preparing his meals, to be sure the restaurants he ate in were clean and not to return to those whose food he had eaten before becoming ill. I must have gone over this elementary stuff for two or more years before it dawned on me that the microbes introduced into his gastro-intestinal tract might have had their origins in his sexual practices. (Middle-aged, straight women are often dense). I debated with myself for days, not knowing if I could say anything, or how to say it, but feeling that I had to, that I would be irresponsible if I did not, even if the result was to make him angry. Then, I called him into my office. "Victor, forgive me. I have no business getting into your private life, but in the interest of keeping you healthy, I'm going to say something awful. Please, before you put it in your mouth – I know it's not very romantic – give it a good scrub with soap and water. And after, get up quickly and use a strong mouthwash." I apologized again for my bluntness and intrusiveness. Victor giggled and simpered to reassure me, "Oh, no, Ros, you're like my mother." (This was, of course, years before anyone ever heard of AIDS, and my understanding of microbiology was that the large intestine harbored many bacteria, and a few more introduced that way would hardly matter.) Victor's round face topped a body that was probably forty pounds overweight, and obviously had not participated in any kind of athletic activity, ever. A year or two after he came to work for me, he said he had to go to the hospital to have a hernia operation. I was worried that it would be botched because he was too good-natured to be critical about medical services. "Where is this operation to take place?" I inquired. He named the hospital widely considered, then, the best in New York. It has since lost that cachet with the unexpected deaths of several well-known patients. But, I was reassured. "And the doctor?" Apparently, he had credentials, too. The operation was a failure, and after a few weeks, Victor returned to work. "What was the matter?" I asked.

"They said I did not have enough muscle to sew up, and they want to try again in a few months."

Ever ready with correctives (I say this ironically), I recommended a bunch of exercises to build up his belly muscles. He listened politely. And went to the hospital after a while for another operation, which again was a failure. He said that his doctor had said the only way they could repair his hernia was to put in some kind of knit plastic tissue to affix the repair to. "What will you do?" I asked.

"Just live with it. It doesn't bother me that much." And that's what he did.

He announced apologetically in 1981 or 1982 that he was leaving; he had stayed with me longer than he had expected to, had learned a great deal, loved working for me, but it was time to move on. He had a series of jobs after that with a television association, with an animal care organization, and at Roosevelt and Mt. Sinai hospitals. When I met him on the street, he was still overweight, but increasingly natty, wearing three-piece suits, and having developed a large mustache with upturned ends. Always very cheerful.

As soon as the first news about AIDS began to appear in the public prints, I clipped or xeroxed the articles and sent copies to him. I invited him to our office parties, and he came when he could; I sent him my annual Christmas letter and in return received Christmas cards from him, and phone calls that told me where he was working and how well he was doing. I asked him once what he was doing to protect himself against AIDS, again apologizing for doing so.

"It's all right, Ros," he reassured me. "I'm celibate, now." But he was still in his twenties.

In the late '80s, the young woman who was his predecessor, now an art historian living in London, came to New York to do research for a book, and stayed with me. I thought it would be fun to have Victor and another man who worked for me during the same period come for a Chinese dinner, ordered in, so that the four of us would have a jolly reunion. He called me the day before to say he could not come, after all. His mother had just died and he was going upstate for the funeral. I told him we'd miss him, and we did, and how sorry I was about his mother's death. He said it was all right; she had been ailing for a long time. I believe that was the last time anyone in his family saw him. My vague impression was that he had two brothers and a sister, all of whom shut him out of their lives because he was gay.

In October of 1991, after I had retired, but was still living in the same apartment, my doorbell rang. It was Victor, whom I had not seen in perhaps five years. He looked different, a little older, now had a beard and a less flamboyant mustache, and was wearing sneakers, sweatpants and a jacket. Still overweight and with a flabby middle, but not as heavy as before. He hugged me, chatted briefly in his apologetic, lightweight voice, then asked if he could borrow a little money.

"What is it?" I asked. "Aren't you working?"

"Oh, yes. I'm in the hematology department at Mt. Sinai, but I'm on leave. I have some kind of liver infection, and my doctor says I can go back to work on November 1, but I'm on disability now, and I can't manage on what they send me. As soon as I get back to work, I'll repay you." He had used up his savings, he said.

I knew that the state's disability insurance was far from munificent, and sympathized. "How much do you need?" I asked.

"Is thirty-five dollars too much?"

"No, of course not." I had expected him to ask for a few hundred. I gave it to him. We chatted a while longer and then I said I had things to do... and he left.

Two or three days later, the doorbell rang again; he was back. He had run out of money, and needed... never more than thirty-five dollars, except when he had lost his contact lenses and had to have them replaced. But he was back at least three times a week. The doorbell rang, and there he was. He never phoned in advance, arriving during the day, during the evening, whenever he wished, interrupting what I was doing (I was writing a book), working on tax matters, getting ready to go out. I gave him money three or four times a week till the autumn of 1992 except for two weeks when I was away.

When the doorbell rang, I knew who it was; I was tempted sometimes not to respond. But I always did; he had no one else, he said, and he was so grateful. He could not go back to work in November. The doctor said December, then January, then February. He went to the hospital for treatment once or twice during these months. Early in this time, during one brief conversation, I asked, "Have you been tested for AIDS lately?" The answer was yes; he'd had two tests since AIDS became epidemic, one recently, and they were negative. His liver infection was cytomegalovirus. I looked it up in the Merck Manual. It was usually not of great consequence, but with AIDS patients...

After one of his hospitalizations, he reported that his doctor had said, "Your liver is like shit." He laughed as he told me. I asked him to make a daily record of what he ate. I thought if he were better nourished, got plenty of vitamins and minerals, his immune system would respond better. I went over his diet and marked up a vitamin catalog for him. I even suggested exercise, because research showed it enhanced immune function even for AIDS patients.

His boss at Mt. Sinai said that if he did not return to work by a certain date, he'd be fired. He could not, and was. Then he told me a new AIDS test had come up positive. He said he did not want to think about it; it was too depressing. I begged him to avail himself of the services of Gay Men's Health Crisis, which provided counseling, lunch, sometimes financial assistance. It took months to get him there – he did not want to be depressed by their other clients. Social service agencies kept promising him assistance and money, but their paperwork was constantly going wrong, and he was good-natured about that, too. (By this tine, we were into four figures of debt. And, on the few occasions when I was not home, he was borrowing money from another former employee who lived nearby.)

In the spring, he was back in the hospital, with a liver crisis and jaundice. By this time, he was on AZT and other medication. He was expecting a refund from the previous year's withholding to pay his rent, but he used it for other bills. His landlord changed the lock on his apartment and kept all his things, including he said regretfully, my various Christmas presents. He was perceptibly thinner by this time, but with what looked like a big fleshy tire around his middle. "It's my liver; it's enlarged," he said. "The doctor said it is trying to escape from my body." He did not resent his doctor's levity.

"Where are you living now?" I asked several times.

"In the men's shelter next to the Lutheran Church on Broadway. It's not very nice," he grimaced. I asked again, but he never gave me an address. When I walked up that way, I looked at the church, up the side street, across the street. I could see nothing that looked like a shelter. I looked every time I passed, but it did not seem urgent because he visited so often.

At the end of July, I went to Europe for two weeks. When I returned, I was met with indignation by the actress next door. While I was away, Victor had hit her for money and also the family of another actress and tv producer on a lower floor. I apologized, and said they could have refused. My feeling was that it was a matter of survival for him. I told him to keep coming to me, but please not to my neighbors. He knew how I felt, and hugged me for being like a mother on almost every visit. (Perhaps I should interpolate here that I have a son a couple of years younger than Victor, now a lawyer, who lives in a Western state.)

Then, without warning, his visits stopped and I did not know where to get in touch with him. He had expected to get Social Security funds for months, and I assumed they had finally started coming. One day, he left an envelope for me with the elevator man: it contained forty dollars in cash. I did not see him again.

I kept looking for the shelter, and trying to think how I could get in touch with him and find out how he was doing. Months later, it occurred to me that it might be the tall building like an ordinary apartment house next to the church on Broadway. I walked into the tiny lobby. Two men sat behind a makeshift desk. "Does Victor Petersen live here?" I asked. They looked at me blankly. "Is this a men's shelter, for men with AIDS?" I asked desperately. "I'm looking for Victor Petersen." "Who are you?" I explained that he used to work for me. One of them mustered a list. "He's not here." "Well, where is he?" They did not know him, never heard of him. One of them finally called the manager. "Oh, yes," he said, emerging from an office. "He died a few months ago." That would have made it early in 1993. "One of his brothers came from Queens to claim the body." I was devastated. I had hoped that like many victims of AIDS he'd live a few years after diagnosis, even long enough for some of the molecular biologists from NIH and elsewhere whose talks on their research I hear at the Academy of Sciences and Bard College to have developed a cure. But no. There was nothing special about him: he was an ordinary, decent, shallow man, who died alone, friendless, family-less. I had not found him in time to continue being his friend even if he no longer needed money from me. He was so alone that he did not think anyone might care. I do not know where he is buried. For me, this is his memorial, possibly the only one.

End

# CLOCKS AND BONDS

We do not become real friends or exchange confidences. We have learned over the years that it is risky to have a corporate colleague know too much about you. It tempers his objectivity, gives him a wedge into your weakness, ultimately makes working together harder. I've seen it happen: you get too close to someone, and you have to recommend a transfer or elimination of his job in a restructuring. You agonize over an ordinary decision. Or, conversely, a man gets to know more than he should, perhaps about his boss, and uses that knowledge to undermine and replace him. We work in a competitive world and we have to earn each other's respect every day.

Ervin Muller is my company's chairman and president. That makes him responsible for running a healthy, profitable organization whose results give pleasure to stockholders and analysts, with products that stay ahead of the pack, and whose people understand and work their markets. Management gurus like Drucker say the chief executive is the leader, articulating and orchestrating the corporate mission, and making sure the whole team hears the music and is motivated to play its best. So — no male bonding here, no buddies. That's only for anthropologists and the movies. Instead, we simulate friendship in talk about sports and scores.

weather and the stock market, sitcoms and other TV trivia, kids' accomplishments, blah blah. We all know it is blah, blah. An executive's life is lonely and wary.

There is bonding elsewhere in the company, but even that is time-bound. There is an up-down bond with mentors that frays when mentor and mentee near equality; there's a close bond, sexual or almost, between executives and secretaries. Long-term bonds develop between the upwardly mobile and the loyal second who rides his wake. But even the loyal second, in a change of life-pattern, sometimes takes off. Thus, any executive knows that cordial distance from co-workers is a key to his power. It was not so long ago that I tested that distance, and then by accident.

We were having lunch, a business lunch, to go over the marketing budget for the following year. That's what you do in September, fit the departmental budgets together with the overall business plan and goals you've hammered out earlier. Muller had meetings in September with all the vice-presidents. I've been vice-president, marketing and sales, for a couple of years, and been with the company for ten years, first as advertising manager, later marketing manager. Up the ladder with careful strategy development and cautious but smart execution.

We'd had the obligatory single drink to warm us up a bit, he consuming some plain grilled fish and vegetables to stay in shape, I thought, for board meetings. No man of fifty who faces a board wants the handicap of looking out of control. I'm ten years younger, but I have never had a weight problem. I eat breakfast, I eat meat and potatoes. Even dessert. We'd come to the end of our discussion about budget and expansion into Latin America, and we were waiting silently for the check. I left the next line up to him. The higher-level executive moves the agenda.

"Where did you go on vacation, Gerald?" he asked. Innocuous enough, usually.

"Club Med," I answered, wishing I had a fast lie waiting, but I never do. This was going to be hard.

"Alone? With your family to one of the family resorts?"

"No. With my wife to one of the singles places. We've been going for the past few years. I love them, the sports, the people, the attitudes and environment. There's nothing fancy about them, but you have the charm of a different mentality," I rose to the risk, "and the laid-back sexiness." I was talking too much.

He recognized a rare opening and nodded. "I've never been to one..."

It was an invitation to me to tell him more, but I reminded myself to keep it cool. "They're fun. I've been to half a dozen, learned to sail a boat, water ski, parasail, do other things I've never had time for. There's no embarrassment because you're with young people who make jokes, wear funny outfits and don't take themselves too seriously. And in the evening, there's homemade entertainment: songs and parodies, and everyone who wants to can get up and participate. Nobody cares who you are. The g.o.'s are foreign, young, adventurous and underpaid, and, whether male or female, a pleasure to look at. And the other guests: They're on the prowl for each other, and you can watch and imagine whatever you want. Sometimes, they even have the staff guys do a Chippendale's for the ladies, or the girls for the men."

Muller said, "It sounds like fun. What about your wife? Does she like it, too?"

"I think so. Or maybe," I reflected honestly, "she just wants to be nice. I think it puts her in the right mood, you know, all these youngsters flirting and making out. She loves talking French with the staff, and we both love the food, buffets for all meals — you sit wherever you please — and drinks, you buy them with beads. No cash."

"I'm beginning to feel I'd like it, too," he smiled. "What

do you do with your kids?"

"I wish we had some," I said, maybe more wistfully than I intended. "We've been trying for years, but nothing happens and time is running out."

He recognized the pain. Back to the vacation exchange. "We rented a house for the summer in Saugatuck — a Victorian mansion with plenty of room for us, the kids, a nanny, and a cook. Stained glass windows, a great view, but very damp. We finally bought a dehumidifier and had to carry it home!"

"Have you been to Saugatuck? It's an exceptionally nice town on the lake, with flowers everywhere and decent swimming unless the water is churned up by a storm. Then you get big waves like the Atlantic, and even strong swimmers get hung up on the ropes. It's actually dangerous, but I like the challenge. I go in and try to surf." I stared. I've been on the lake in a storm. What did he have to prove?

Here was the check. He whipped out the corporate Amex card, and signed and we could go. No harm done, after all.

Later in September, Muller and I made a trip to Chicago for a convention and meeting with our distributors. We were scheduled for speeches at industry meetings, entertaining at hospitality suites, and private meetings with our district managers. But, as usual after a couple of days of speeches and gladhanding, I sneaked away for a couple of hours to the Art Institute. I was rounding a corner in the Oriental section, not far from the great seated Kwan Yin, when I bumped into Muller. He looked shocked to see me, but pleased, too. "We're winding up tonight, anyway, aren't we? Might as well have dinner together. I always make a ritual when I come here of eating in a Chinese restaurant on Michigan. Is that ok with you?" I shrugged. I'd find something on the menu I liked. "They still serve shark's fin soup," he added.

Muller had ordered and was spooning up a huge, steaming bowl to the grinning approval of the waiter. "I can tell them from now till doomsday that I love the flavor. They grin anyway."

"Why?" I asked, not being too swift about Chinese cooking. I was eating chicken.

"They think it's an aphrodisiac. I thought you knew."

I laughed. "Put some in that side dish for me. I want to see if I like the flavor."

I had heard from his secretary months earlier that Muller dropped little poems on her desk once in a while — a token of gratitude for her hard work, patience and overtime. I do not think she thought it was a breach of etiquette to tell me, just a reflection of her admiration for his quality as a human being, and I liked hearing about it.

"Jeannette tells me you write poetry. Do you keep copies?" I asked. "I hope you don't mind my knowing. I used to teach 19th century English literature at Lehigh, and ..." I trailed off. Where did I get the notion this was an ok subject?

"I've been writing poetry all my life, even published some chapbooks," he acknowledged, "under the name Eugene Maske. It's no way to make a living, but it's nice to give form to a feeling. It's almost as good as a successful new product!"

I knew I liked him.

"I've been thinking about you and your wife, how great it is that you can go together to Club Med, and enjoy it. We don't all have good first marriages."

After the Business Week profile, I knew he'd been married early, divorced a few years ago and remarried to a younger woman. Well, almost fifty percent of American marriages end in divorce, and it was so common in corporations that nobody paid much attention. I even remember one CEO who embarrassed me after an introduction to his current wife, a very young thing who wandered off quickly, "I guess you think I have a new wife every time you see me." I didn't know what to say, and said nothing.

Muller looked disquieted. This was clearly something he

thought about a lot. "What I mean is that you're lucky to be in a good first marriage. I love my wife, but there's a generation between us, and moments when the time difference strains the bond. It's comfortable to stay together, as you have, changing and growing together, real contemporaries."

I was surprised. "You're a romantic."

"Why do you say that?"

"The romantics were my business before I went into trade." It amused me to put it that way. "Teaching is not much of a way to make a living either, and besides, the prospect of staying in school for the rest of my life made me feel as if I'd been 'left back'. Maybe the real reason was that I had to get away from where I was. Too close to a dying father. And that automatically made me next, another clock ticking... But, yes, you sound like a nineteenth century poet."

"Which one?" he asked.

"Hardy, Browning... I do want to read your poetry, if you'll permit it. But Michelle and I are not as comfortable together as you want to believe."

He looked puzzled. He had lost that thread for a moment. But, he recovered quickly.

"There are problems in every marriage, even the good ones. You find some way to deal with them." He was trying to turn me off.

Too bad. I was relaxed enough by the Tsingtao to barrel ahead. "We've been married a long time, eighteen years. I admire and respect her. She's smart and practical, and good-natured. But besides the fact that a marriage without children has an agonizing void at its center — you want a bond to the next generation — there's this reluctance to do it. Just to do it. I sometimes think the only way to get her into bed is to get her looped on wine beforehand." I shook my head. "No, sometimes you just want someone with an appetite for it. Not romantic. A sexy lady who knows what it's about."

He guessed, "You've found one."

"Maybe. But I don't want to talk about it."

We talked about art and about the impulses to get away that had led us both to the Art Institute. "I normally don't have time for art, but I remember loving it when I was in college," he confessed. "I want to paint when I retire. I like the freedom of gesture and the 'here now' feeling of the brush. Everyone has to have a role model, and mine lately is Winston Churchill who wrote novels and history, ran a country at war, and when it was all over, started painting. He was good at everything, even marriage."

I thought about Churchill. He had his failures, plenty of them. He had been turned out of office before he was ready to go, and all his life he had hit the bottle pretty hard. But, yes an accomplished man. I did not want to talk about him. I asked, "Do you have a way of seeing that means something to you, that connects you to feeling or another way of life?" I am always interested in creativity, in how people express their spiritual yearning to be part of something bigger. Like the march of generations. We all need to feel part of the universe, and to not have our part end with us. We want to leave something behind.

We were having lunch again two months later, to amplify the plan for Latin America. We were starting in Mexico, where we have an assembly plant but no real distribution of product, setting-up up two distributors, one for northern Mexico and another for the central part of the country. The advertising program was set to go. Our marketing people had analyzed Chile, Argentina and Brazil, and they looked good. We did not think the other countries' economies were ready for us. If we set up subsidiaries in Argentina and Brazil in partnerships with local companies, the subs' managers would find a way to penetrate the smaller Latin American countries on their own. It was my idea to proceed cautiously this way, but the partnership structure's costs might make us less competitive.

"Could we frame the distribution contracts to buy out the subsidiaries later?" Muller asked.

I had other things on my mind. It was hard to focus.

"Are you all right?" Muller asked, clearly embarrassed, but wanting to clear the air.

"Sorry. My mind was wandering," I apologized. "I hate to say this. There's no one in my family... and my friends are all her friends... this doesn't belong here at all."

"What?"

"You remember you guessed that I had a girlfriend ...."

He nodded, "I guessed because I knew how it was. All the joy goes out of life when you can't feel romantic with the woman you've vowed to stay with for life."

"They make jokes about middle-aged men, but we all feel time closing in on us, and when it seems too early ..." He was telling me the story. I listened, guessing at his motive. He had encountered this gentle girl on another restless excursion to an art museum — this one in Kansas City, the Nelson-Atkins. "I think by then I had realized that I wanted to paint those timeless Chinese ink and watercolor landscapes that are almost empty but put you in touch with another reality. Chinese painters copy traditional work all their lives. They don't have the same attitude to originality that we have." He looked embarrassed. "It has something to do with Buddhism. There was a girl copying such a painting in a corner on a pad, an artless girl, easy to address. I asked where was she studying, how long, did she come from Kansas or Missouri — you know. She had that mysterious quality... and classically, one thing led to another. I divorced my wife, giving her as much as I could, and married the gentle girl who was immersed in the timeless world. Meantime, as naturally and sweetly as she painted, she produced two new babies to add to my already grown-up family. That was it. I had done the wrong thing, thinking my happiness was at stake, and it meant the rest of my life, so it was justified. My older kids didn't see it that way. Young people think their parents' lives are over when they reach forty-five. I hurt them, I hurt their mother and it was too late. My new lady still has the bloom of youth, but my bloom is on the wane, and hers no longer matters very much. I am a wiser man than I was, and I have a deep sense of sin..."

It was not what I wanted to hear. He was trying to tell me not to use him as a role model. "But we're different. There are no kids; Michelle works. And this woman I'm seeing is very nice, attractive, smart..." I paused, "...sexy."

He nodded.

"She's pushing me to get a divorce. She's in her thirties, wants to have children, loves me, all that. I think we'd be happy together. Michelle and I have been together for eighteen years... Probably married too young. I was in graduate school, and she was so cute and eager... But I want children, a bunch of them, and time is running out... We'll probably never have any. What is life about anyway? Even Bertrand Russell said that the most satisfying thing in his life was his children."

"You can adopt," he said. "There are lots of great kids all over the world waiting to be raised by loving parents. You don't have to break up a going thing, do all that damage, throw away the good experience of eighteen years..."

"Don't misunderstand me, I'm richer in some ways than I was. I love both my wives, I love all my children, but my first wife did nothing to deserve what happened to her. And the older kids..." he shook his head, "they're in college or graduate school. I can pay the bills, but I can no longer say anything they will listen to. For them, I have turned into an uncontrolled old goat. That's not an argument against your doing it, but unless you really can't get along, stay with what you've got. You can get whatever else by adopting, by discreet... Ah, the hell with it. Let's get back to the distributor contracts."

"Okay. I'll talk to our general counsel and see if he can draft a buyout clause, maybe a progressive one."

We did get the kind of buyout clause we needed. In fact, at a seminar on Latin-American relations, the Commerce Department cited it as the way to go. It did the job, and I was still Gerald Haney, effective marketing vice-president, spending a lot of time on airplane flights, coordinating our advertising and literature in several countries, keeping tabs on the numbers, working out the pricing in many currencies. And arranging bulk deals in the home market in a way no one had thought of before. A good man for the company...

But that "deep sense of sin" line had really gotten to me. Muller cannot turn back the clock. I could see him at home, doting on his new babies, admiring them, being charmed by them as a mature man. Not irritated as he might have been by the first set, by the cries, diapers, tantrums. They are his. I wanted mine. I wanted to love them and teach them, grow with them as much as I could. "Deep sense of sin."

"Lunch?" It was months later on a Friday morning, and I had to talk to him.

"Not today?" He put it as a question, not a statement. "I was planning to go home and read the galleys on my new book of poetry."

"Please."

"O.K. We'll eat in Belleville, on my way home. Is The Pie Place all right? Catfish and hush puppies and cole slaw? I haven't been there in a while, and the courtyard is just right for today. I've put in so many evenings and weekends the past month, I deserve an afternoon...".

"I'm dumping on you, I guess," I said. "I need an older man's advice." We had driven separately to Belleville.

"Yes, you are. And I've given it already. Is this the same thing?"

"It's that carefully concealed intuitive side. The side that writes poetry," I said wryly. "I need it. I have a sad, long-winded story to tell you. If you can't stand it, just get up and go."

His face mirrored his distress. "Cordial distance, I've been told. I have a lot of respect for you, and I won't walk out, but I don't want this to go on."

"I hear you." I grimaced. "You remember where we last left this story... I told the lady that we were going to have to stop seeing each other. There was no way that we could fulfill her dream of getting married and having children, if it meant my divorcing Michelle, who in many ways, is my best friend. She was still young enough to find another man, and sexy, attractive, smart — she could make it. Women are having children well into their forties now, the clock has been turned back by technology. I said all that."

"Pretty reasonable. What did she say?"

"She wept that I love her, she loves me, why all these old-fashioned scruples about breaking up a marriage that was falling apart, that has no children to worry about... Life should be about self-fulfillment... What she said was not wrong but I had already talked to Michelle again about the possibility of adopting. I'd brought it up for years, and she did not want to, did not want to — it would not be the same. Who knew what hereditary disorders a strange kid would be carrying; how could you love a foreign kid, and there are no more American kids to adopt. Chinese, Romanian, Honduran... She hated the idea..."

"Back to the other lady," he said.

"Well it was a big, desperate scene, my responsibility, and I just had to stay with it, reassure her that it was not rejection, that in some ways I'm an old-fashioned guy who wants to be an honorable man."

"Was that why you taught nineteenth century literature?" he inquired. "Or did *I* force it?"

"Maybe. It doesn't matter. I did it, and I think it was

the right thing to do. She finally accepted that it was the end, or seemed to, but she was badly shaken and said she was going away for a week just to weep where no one would notice."

A week hardly does it if she was really mourning. I know.

"I did not hear from her again till Monday."

"This week?"

"A long, horrible story, I told you. She's pregnant, she says."

"Well, she consoled herself pretty quickly," he said. "Good for her."

I shook my head. "It's not like that. She says she was falling apart, collapsing, in her week away so distressed she could not think straight. A couple of days after she got to this hotel in Bermuda, it happened. Some guy came along in the dining room and asked if she'd have an after-dinner drink with him, maybe at a nearby hotel that had some music. A divorced man, affiliated with an insurance company or something..."

"Spare me," he said.

"They went to this rum and music place and listened for the rest of the evening, drinking those rum and fruit juice things that get you stupefied."

"That's what she said." He was skeptical.

"He took her back to the hotel, and she was drunk and a little crazy, and he seemed nice enough so..."

"And so, apparently by accident, he has no condoms, she has no diaphragm, neither of them has ever heard of safe sex... But as soon as she knows she is pregnant, it's you, so desperate for a baby of your own, to whom she proves she is fertile. What happened to him?"

"She never saw him again. It was just an accident. She only had his first name, he hers."

"What does she want?"

"She needs help. I'm the one she turned to." I felt a perverse pride.

"With what?"

"An abortion. She can't keep the child. She's a working woman. I told her I'd help her, but this opens up the whole thing again. Michelle can't have a baby, but ..."

"This other woman can, and she can prove it. Did it ever occur to you that this is a last-ditch effort to make you rethink the good-bye? Why is she involving you in her abortion? Is she asking you to pay for it? She's asking you to go with her as if you were the father. You say she's smart. Doesn't it seem to you to be awfully manipulative in a stand-up-for-herself, thirty-some-years old career woman?"

I was taken aback. "Okay. I'm sorry I told you. It won't be hard to find a legal clinic somewhere; it's less than three months. But you may be right." Was he? "It's a rotten job, helping her to get rid of a baby that's not mine, but could have been. If it had been..."

"I hate being the local cynic," he said. "We won't refer to any of this again. Strictly business from now on."

We would not be close again. He for his reasons, I for mine. You have to break some bonds to keep others. And every bond has its time, its clock. Ask the naturalist whose unnatural babies were the hatching ducks bonded to him because he was the first thing they saw after their eggs cracked. But they were hard-wired to bond, and it should have been mama duck they saw.

I did what I said I would. I knew I would even before talking to Muller. I reserved a date at an abortion clinic in Milwaukee, far enough away, and paid the fee in advance. I wondered as I was doing it. It was Anita's mistake, not mine, even if I was, in some way, responsible. A woman in her thirties should have a few hundred dollars in the bank. But I did not ask. It was the price of guilt. I understood her need to have me go with her, an old friend-lover, to give her comfort, to take care of logistics. But why did she not offer to pay for it? Was she working my pain to her own advantage? I did not ask.

We made solicitous small talk on the long drive to Milwaukee. "Are you all right?" I asked, wondering if her shivers were fear or chill. "I wish it were not raining. It makes this even more a funeral than it is," and instantly regretted it. "Let me know when you get hungry. We'll stop for sandwiches and hot tea."

Her solicitous small talk went like this, "Are you getting tired, driving so long in the rain?" and "I know how busy you are, and that I'm taking you away from your work for three days. I want you to know how much I appreciate what you're doing."

I had picked her up in late morning, and we got to Milwaukee just before dinner. The hotel rooms were reserved, too, guaranteed for a two-night stay with cash. I did not want any traces of this excursion on my credit-card bills. Michelle often paid them. Anita fortified herself with two drinks before dinner and a brandy after, and I had a few, too. What we wanted was speedy oblivion to this awful day and to be still a little blotto on the way to an early-morning surgical appointment. My room was across the hall, no connection.

"Stay a while?" she asked, when we got off the elevator. "Stay till I'm in bed?" This was worse than I imagined it could be. I sat in the chair facing the window, back to her.

"You can look," she said, painfully. "It doesn't show yet."

"I don't want to," I said angrily. I knew what she wanted, and it would only make things more complicated. I faced the window.

She smiled wistfully when she waved goodnight from bed. I shut the door firmly and went into my room, determined to do this right.

The clinic was genteel. Anita stared around her, was

careful to identify me as a "friend", not the father, as if anyone cared. She was out in a couple of hours, staggering slightly, but all right, and we had instructions to stay nearby, overnight, to be sure there was no untoward bleeding. Back we went to the hotel, and there in the room to which she was now confined for the day, the real agony erupted.

"I'll never see you again after tomorrow," her nose red, the tears streaming, she cried. "You used me, this baby-to-be used me; I'm alone, getting old, going nowhere, with nothing but pain, and a used-up womb." Not screaming. Just bitter.

There was nothing for me to say. I did not want to touch her, and it might not even be safe, but as usual when I see an attractive woman weeping, I had that stupid, automatic response.

We watched television, had lunch, Anita checked for bleeding. Then we watched television, had dinner, drank a lot, and Anita checked for bleeding again. Then we watched television, and finally I said, "Good night," relieved that nothing worse had happened, and that there was only one more day to go through. The next day, again, as if I deserved the punishment, I listened patiently to her weeping and to her saying it could have been mine, and to the pity of it, and that her having yielded to this importunate stranger was partly my fault, and wanting to weep myself, but that would have made me more vulnerable. It was a long ride to St. Louis.

Muller had been rough. He had seen me exposed to manipulation. Was he right? I did not want to know. If Anita could or would do something just to make herself irresistible after a kiss-off, that was conclusive. It was what I needed to stay with Michelle, "changing and growing." I would have, not too soon, to find another job, far away, perhaps in another industry.

Anita was history. Head-hunters are a fact of life, and I agreed to a meeting with the next one who called. More money. Another river town, Cincinnati, with a nice museum and a flourishing arts scene. And another industrial equipment manufacturer getting ready for expansion – a factory in Ireland and lots of exhausting trips, this time with jet lag because of the time differences — while I sorted myself out, not staying anywhere that I could open up again. In fact, with all the conviviality and toasts that came with the signing of agreements... with all the ordinary business dinners with bottles of wine and ceremonial port after dinner... and just being alone and foreign, it became de rigueur to keep a bottle in my room or rental car, and to have one even on an early flight. No one noticed. I handled it well.

Except for one thing. I thought it was my discouragement about not having children that was making my efforts at sex less frequent and less rewarding. Michelle did not mind. She'd never found it particularly fun. She just knew it meant a lot to me and tried to please. It happened with increasing frequency. I'd get home from a long flight, Dublin to New York, sit around the airport waiting for the connecting flight to Cincinnati, relaxed in the business flyers' lounge, sipping my new love, Irish whiskey, enjoying the sexy fantasies that come with the end of a hard trip. Michelle would meet me at the airport for an easy ride home, exchanging the news and gossip, and flirting a bit. "You've eaten, haven't you, on the plane? We can go to bed early!"

I'd nod. I'd been looking forward to this all day. And then... Nothing. Limp as a cooked noodle. Michelle would do something she'd never had to do, kissing, hugging, stroking, getting on top, using her hands... Useless. It didn't happen all the time. Just often enough. And I'd mutter, "Isn't this the worst thing?"

After a while, she'd give up, patting me on the shoulder comfortingly and kissing me goodnight. "It's all right. You're just tired."

Ervin Miller was history, too. Neither of us was a networker, a stay-in-touch kind of guy. We'd exchanged a couple of tentacles of sympathy, but could go no further. And even that, controverting business protocol, meant I had to leave when he judged Anita and her motives, sight unseen, so harshly — and maybe rightly, essentially conveying he thought I was a fool. I wondered then, "Does he want to protect me from a schemer? Is that it?" That made an affectional bond different from before. But perhaps he was just a careful man, a cynical man. A man who wanted no disruption in his marketing department. There was nothing more between us then or later. When I had to tell him I'd had a very good offer, we sat quietly in his office for a moment. He nodded. No counter offer. It was time for me to go, for him, too. A natural parting.

The boozing got worse, and I had to admit finally, that like my father, I had a weakness. The weakness was what made me impotent, not uncommon, I read. What precipitated it was a surprising scene in Cincinnati. A new neighbor there, a woman in the expensive development we had bought into, hit on Michelle: "You two are very attractive. Do you think you and your husband would like to join a few of us at a little party for a weekend? It's in the home of a couple we know, and we're all healthy and into having fun." Michelle got the drift. Swingers. Guilt, maybe, for my declining interest, an unstated wish to be there if I was going to indulge myself elsewhere, I don't know what it was. But she was willing, just as she was to go to Club Med.

Great, I thought, at the first one, looking around at the disrobed bodies, the women all pretty attractive, the men variable as men are. Michelle whispered in my ear about a couple of them, "Too hairy" and "overweight," as if to tell me I looked better to her. I liked that. I liked it even better when our hostess demonstrated with loud sucking sounds from her vagina, that simply by exercising her muscles, "Look, Ma, no hands" she was sexy enough to produce an orgasm for herself.

Everyone by that time was warmed up with several drinks and flaunting physicality but me. If it was the alcohol, a cure could not wait. I was not feeling well, I said, "I must have picked up a bug."

After that, it was, what the hell, medical leave in Minneapolis, where the drying-out came with psychotherapy and a lifelong commitment to drink tea and carbonated water. Psychotherapy: your mother, your father, your siblings, your circumstances growing up, your body image, your religion, all the things that made you to be put behind you. From here, you accept the things you can't change, enjoy each new day, recognize your success, your good marriage and loving wife. You work at balancing stress with a well-lived life. You develop a meaningful philosophy.

I was away for six weeks. Our European affiliates understood — mal de foie. Michelle understood, too. She quit her job and came with me on a number of the trips, planned museum visits and sightseeing for the little time off I had, looked spiffy so the Europeans were impressed, cute, smart, fluent French, what a lucky guy I was; "changing and learning," my best friend, a strong marital bond. I was lucky. I could even get it up again, but not with the neighbors.

Still, there was no baby in the picture. It would end with me, end with Michelle. Where was the renewal that a bond to a next generation created? I could go back to teaching... I was tempted. I had so much to offer tv-infected kids. I wanted to give them an antidote to passive watching — one that would last the rest of their lives, and be a real connection to the future. I thought, as I sometimes did, of Ervin Muller. He had it all: published poetry, two families, five kids ... A lucky man.

The body takes its revenge ingeniously. If you cannot drown your sorrows in ethyl alcohol, it says, punning, "Back." To what? It is not literal. I am in constant pain. I travel with Tylenol. I have no bonds to the future, no child, time is passing, what is it passing for? I am doing brilliantly, with raises, stock options, a reputation, money, a lovely wife. "Back."

Another medical leave, big surgery. Fused vertebrae, a corset for a while, physical therapy. A lovely, solicitous wife. "Back." Where? Or perhaps when? To the time of still-open possibilities.

Now, there is a buyout. My firm buying his. Analysis, negotiating, investment bankers, lawyers, the works. What kind of fit are we together? Who would know better than I?

I fly to St. Louis and take a limo to the old plant. They know I am coming. Ervin introduces me to my successor, a woman, tall, youngish, good-looking. I am lucky she does not work for me, and will probably leave as soon as the buyout is completed – with a healthy package, of course.

"Come to my office after your meeting here," he says and leaves. She has changed my office. Leather furniture, a designer desk without drawers, a computer behind her to swivel to, and portable phones. Completely "with it." I scrutinize the numbers and contracts extra carefully, just to be sure being with it does not work against them. But that is my usual caution. There is a team of consultants and lawyers working in other offices, examining the past, projecting the future.

But Muller. I am back in his office. He is full gray now, tubbing a bit in the middle, but a handsome man with an air of integrity and authority, a man to like and respect. We exchange conversation about how well we look, about our families, and finally about the economy and the new wave of mergers.

"You've fought this thing so hard," I say. "Ads in the Journal, hiring defensive lawyers and public relations people... "

"I wanted us to remain independent. We have a good, growing company, we're making plenty of money, we run clean plants and treat our people well. You know what a merger is: big downsizing, dislocation for people and their families and the towns whose plants are redundant. We didn't want any of that. We take our obligations seriously."

"I know," I say. "This company is a real prize. You are, too, and you'll be vice-chairman when it's over with gilt-edged stock options and a shot at running the bigger company."

"Not likely," his face is serious. "I fought too hard. There has to be some bitterness and that does not make for a collegial bond."

"Well, however it ends, I want to tell you something. Our huge firm of buyout lawyers thinks you're the finest executive they've ever met. They've had nothing but admiration for you from the beginning. We've bought other firms. I've never heard that from them before."

"In the end, nothing I did made any difference. The funds, the institutional holders, they could see a quick premium over the current price of the stock. Why wait? It's in their nature to take the money and run."

Maybe he is not altogether lucky. Is he bitter? Angry? "I want you to know I had nothing to do with this. It came from our investment bankers, not me. You know that, don't you? I told them you would fight a hostile offer."

"It's the time. Bigger is better, and the rush is encouraged by the profitable prodding of financial organizations. Maybe I just belong to another era." He smiles. "A romantic?"

Now, in defeat and disappointment he is making a bid for a bond. In our separate ways, we have been wounded by life. I feel for him, with him. Churchill, too, was out of power before he expected to be. "What will you do?"

"I have been ready, without knowing it. Now it's time. Time for art history and watercolors, time with the kids... even the older ones, if I work at it... and more travel. Maybe to the misty mountains of China, even if they are building a dam. I want to see where the poet-painters brought their arts together. My wife will love it, too. What's the the matter with a Buddhist passion to unite time and space, and leave the clocks and Confucian duty behind?"

"Only," I wonder, "is any man after years of action and power able to live out his life as a scholar-painter-poet?"

He smiles, pleased to know I've been doing some reading in his favorite time and space. My six-week drying-out in the Minneapolis clinic had pushed finding a "workable philosophy." I have been looking. Unlike Western philosophies, so preoccupied with words, the East, in all its variety, is concerned with living life. And I, a word person from the beginning, know where words have little left to say.

"Some Chinese mandarins," he responds, "left power when dynastic change forced them out. Retreated into poetry and painting. Often as political acts, but they did beautiful work. Not a bad analogy. Why not?"

"I'll stay in touch this time," I say.

End

# OUTSIDE/IN

I do not marvel, at all, that cooks have become chefs, and that chefs have become celebrities. Why should I?

It is like American cuisine, full of reversals of the ordinary. Ichabod Crane in The Legend of Sleepy Hollow talked about every roasting pig running about with a pudding in its belly and an apple in his mouth. Poultry and veal shoulders were formerly and routinely stuffed with bready fillings in America. The point was to "extend" the meat, to effect an extension of meat flavor to non-meat and cheaper ingredients. Now? A turnabout — inside-out — we "wrap" meat with delicate puff pastry or phyllo or whatever it is that new food wrap chains have discovered, making the already expensive ingredient even more so by clothing it in extra time and skill.

It is all style — really all fad — here in America, and I am a presiding genius of the frivolous in modern American cuisine. We "fuse" regional flavors, make gourmet items of earthy vegetables like turnips and beets, turn forgotten farmhouse staples into the "latest." But are we different from the happy cook who first stumbled on that institutional favorite: pineapple upside-down cake? Where the top is cooked on the bottom in a shallow skillet heated in an oven, not on top of the stove? Upside-down, inside-out food. Food.

It would not have been my choice, of course. But when you're drafted at nineteen into the army of an Eastern European country that fought on the wrong side in World War II, choices are not what you have. There is no real place for unfledged scions of rich, scholarly families. No place for exercising your *gymnasium*-honed fencing skills in a modern army. And if you're a smart boy, you give plenty of thought to what keeps you out of the kill-or-be-killed set.

I have read that as we age, an accurate sense of smell differentiates the potentially senile from those who remain alert. Has anyone tested the young? A good sense of smell is what differentiates the good cook from the not. I had it, I have it, I exploited it then for a job in the kitchen. I exploit it now for all the prestige, influence, riches and scholarly trappings anyone could wish. In my family, it is traditional that when a society rewards you, it is your obligation to give back. I do, with pleasure. I teach, I train, I do scholarly work. Not without controversy.

Today, I am keynote speaker at the first ever Chef-Laureate event at the Library of Congress. I am, of course, Chef Laureate, despite the never-lost Eastern European accent that leads me to say of my critics, *sotto voce*, of course, "Fock them. I laugh all the way to the bank." Food — like poetry, like art, like music — now has its critics. They write scholarly, angry tomes on the bad taste of bad taste.

Back to the smart boy with the good nose in the old-fashioned army kitchen, presided over by a hotel chef, now a cook/sergeant who dealt with his recruits the way noncommissioned officers do. Brutally, but you learn. In five years, I knew what he knew, and he had been a chef in the capital of our country where cosmopolitan visitors mingled with ex-nobility, where noodles were made by hand every day, where paprikas were a religion and veal was its sacrifice, and palascintas symbolized the resurrection.

I talk too much. My wife is a patient woman. From a

place in the world where female patience has not yet worn thin. I am grateful for that. She is grateful to be with me. I am her vocation. She was an antiques dealer when I met her, and although I do not yet qualify for sale, she appreciates fine things and the unique.

The war ended. The victors treated most of the vanquished with exemplary courtesy. No one in my country was a war criminal, except our dictator and he died, quite conveniently. I could not, after all, attend university. Like the rest of Eastern Europe, we were swallowed in the maw of the Great Bear, regurgitated after a while in unrecognizable flatness, our mountains of privilege and pleasure leveled by the sweep of his hairy paws into a dismal gray, universal poverty of spirit and flesh. The new regime made us all socialists or social workers wearing the expressionless mask of fear. Discretion and a few well-placed antiques found me a refugee camp in another country. Was it Orwell who said corruption is the last symptom of humanism in a totalitarian society?

No matter. Waiting on a dilatory bureaucracy to process our applications for elsewhere — in my case, the *nekulturny* United States — became a vocation. It had its casualties. People died waiting. But its successes. In four years, I made friends in the camp: Ukrainian lawyers and teachers willing to work at cleaning the floors in U.S. hospitals, at learning how to sell industrial starches to adhesive manufacturers, or to take courses in hematology and become blood technicians. Whatever the new country wanted, we would supply.

I, at thirty-one, with a useless gymnasium education in the literature of my benighted country, science that was already becoming obsolete, music (the art we all most loved); mathematics, with a vocabulary that I could not translate, a lean, shaved-head, bony-faced fencer with an unfashionable martial mustache. What use was I? More than most. I could cook. My sponsoring town found me a job in a diner in

Connecticut. A jolly job from 4 am to 9 pm, making toasts, scrambling eggs, grilling cheese, mixing meat loaves and pancakes. Not together, of course. All new and foreign. I was used to cooking for hundreds. The Army did not cater to individual orders. I was now cooking for one or two at a time, "short orders" all day, except when there were none. Then I mixed for the next spate of customers. I wore rented pants, a rented shirt and a rented apron, which I turned inside-out (or outside-in) when the first side became unsightly, but was not yet considered eligible for laundry.

Four years of valuable lessons in sharing an apartment over a garage, minimizing laundry costs, mixing messes now for later and storing them in America's huge refrigerators, putting a sprig of parsley on every plate, despite the fact that it was the one thing that was never eaten. And, because I was the "short order man", cooking behind a service counter and watching my food consumed a foot or two away by the fascinating truck drivers, retail salespeople, kids and factory-workers who ate at the counter. Some of them were lonely enough to talk to me. They had to be very lonely at first; English did not come easy. But I tried, and smiled (very undignified where I come from) to make up for my linguistic deficiencies, absorbed the vernacular, and pursued a liberal education in, as one of the critics says, "How America eats," while speedily breaking eggs with one hand, flipping them in a little pan so they'd be "over easy," pressing hamburgers flat on a grill to hasten cooking as I was taught, and watching their good juices drain away into the greasy trough I emptied at the end of my shift. I only worked five days a week there. I found a part-time job in a hotel kitchen for weekends when other cooks wanted "off" to be with their families.

We are in the anteroom of the auditorium where my speech is to be televised, recorded for the ages, and where I will speak to cooks and critics, cookbook collectors and perverse recipe pornographers. I am up for the occasion.

"Ladies and gentlemen," says the Librarian of Congress, "I give you our honoree, our poet of food and life, literature and the physical, art and eating, the earthy and the sublime, the newly-invested Chef Laureate of the United States, Serge Szenty." I am on the dais, a dusty platform in the Library auditorium frequented alike by lecturers, chamber music groups and laureates, but not by the maintenance staff of the library which "does" assigned areas, but forgets staircases and platforms. A restaurant kitchen floor so furry with dust bunnies would attract the notice of the health department.

I smile, wiggling my eyebrows and mustache in an actorish display of communal feeling with the audience that we have all heard something quite excessive. I nod, and begin. "Laurel leaves are intoxicants. The priestesses at Delphi, those hapless girls, ate or inhaled them to induce the visions and hermetic utterances that were called prophecies by the priests whose interest was, of course, collecting treasure from the gullible. I am here crowned with laurel, but do not plan to ingest it, since food is my business and I know better."

What was there to say? I could rattle along on a history of cooking from Europe, Asia, Africa, the related arts of pot-making and uses of shaped fireplaces and cooking tools in Neolithic times when raw meat, virtually on the hoof, was no longer couth; the shaping of cookery by society and vice-versa, the first cookbook by Apicius and a little digression into a recent annual dinner at the Archeological Society for which some of his recipes were ineptly reconstructed... I did. To be chef laureate in a library, you must be literate.

And while I talked and watched the historians, scholars, food writers and less vaunted chefs who were my audience for nods, smiles, frowns and faraway looks, the parallel track in my head that speeds along beside the overt track backtracked.

*1949. Honor and humility. The Jesuits in this temporary country took refugees in. The notorious libertine and fighting man who had founded them in a change of heart had formulated a fierce, not passive, ethos. They knew me instantly and made me their cook. My first stop after refugee camp, but still awaiting a visa. Fencing with one of them, a countryman whose family had migrated during an earlier dictatorship and who had left disputatious law for a Catholic bow to authority, availed me of lessons in French and foil, and kept me there two years exploring dualisms: fellowship and loneliness, exercise and indulgence, action and meditation, hot and cold, crisp and soft. The Jesuits are worldly, educators, scientists, writers and diplomats. I, too, became worldly, but not, after all, a member of the Society. I was still a cook, proud myself, menial to the world. Pride and humility. Not even an artisan; a servant.*

There is a reception afterward. I am being honored for contributions to American cuisine. Two of my enemies approach, a cranky aging journalist and his wife. They are interested only in the past. "Chef Szenty," he says. Is he telling me I am still, after all, only a cook? She, his wife, studied in a French school. "You have won. We congratulate you. The American cuisine described by Pegge two hundred years ago in which Europeans complained about how odoriferous American fruit was has come half circle: upside-down. Nothing has a taste any more, except what is applied to it." He is leaning on a cane; some nutritional or hereditary disorder has unhinged his joints. Does nothing have a taste because his taste buds no longer blossom, but have withered into senility, and his bile spills into his copy?

I fence with him, too. "You think original flavor is all it *would* be in a new land. I agree with Curnonsky: food should taste of what it is. But if it now tastes of other things, it is like writing or other art. A jaded palate requires the titillation of the unfamiliar. It is why cookery is a performance art, as evanescent as dance." I think he was once a theater critic. He does not acknowledge my riposte; waves his cane as if to say words are futile. His wrinkled wife steadies his elbow, staring the while at my healthy mustache and blooming cheeks. (I puzzle sometimes about how we Europeans do not develop the doughy complexions of natives, but keep our fresh color. Has anyone researched the question?) A horde of ladies, as aggressive as the Hun, overruns our conversation, breathing hard, sweating and demanding autographs. They are cookbook writers and editors, cookbook collectors. I autograph their copies of my latest book, *Good Taste*. Also my business.

*It was in the diner "dinner in the diner, nothing could be finer," that I aspired to leave the front for the back. My first taste of outside/in. I would be dinner cook for slow nights, Sunday to Thursday. Slow nights, sped by experiment. Beef, lamb, pork and chicken could be frozen if they were cared for and packaged securely, cooked not long after. But the hard work could be done ahead, speeding the cooking, speeding the table turnover and requiring fewer refills of the bread basket while people waited. Chinese cooks do such slicing, cutting, chopping early but they do it daily. I had seen Chinese cooks, but I wanted to do this for European cuisine.*

*One of my customers was the president of an electronics company. "We are expanding. Our employees have an in-plant cafeteria, like a big school lunch room. I want to create a private dining room for me, the board, the executives, and our guests. You will be our cook."*

*It was a promotion. I had been the off-night cook. Now, I was a corporate functionary, with a budget, a say about equipment, a staff and a responsibility for everyday gourmet lunch as well as on call for emergencies, meetings, cocktail parties and other events. A private life at last. I began to collect cookbooks, cooking utensils, and etchings, engravings, woodcuts, lithographs, an art and book collection centered on sustenance. Why? In my country and in all of Europe, princely families had their Kabinetts; my family, haute*

*bourgeoisie, intellectuals too, collected. Sarit learned to save*
*priceless ancient cookbooks and prints for me. I found her*
*selling incunabula and made her my expert and my love.*

I am finally back in my chilly midwestern city, where
hog butchers once reigned but now beef is king. My restaurant is in an old mansion; beautiful rooms, high ceilings,
exquisite paneling. A sketchy kitchen, but big enough, and
a varianced freezer in the back yard. Unlike other restaurants here, My Place has reasonable prices. I want people to
enjoy their food without fretting. The waitresses are good-
natured black girls whom I have trained to be impeccable
servers. I am the savior of their neighborhood. I take them
from poverty into possibility, teaching them, with my Thai
wife, the Tao of service. She presides over their accumulation
of grace. I teach their kitchen counterparts, men who do not
find it emasculating, the essence of cookery: combining and
timing. We take reservations, dinner only, six weeks ahead.
Because it is a mansion, My Place is a private club. There
is an application and membership fee even for a visitor. The
ingenuity that enabled me to barter antiques for freedom has
served me with the bureaucrats of this corrupt city. But I
do not escape my past.

The phone rings. Sarit answers, but I have inadvertently
picked up as well. "Sarit, it's Bode. You remember me; it
was not so long ago, Bode."

How could she or I forget? The nay-saying nemesis of my
foray into all-American catering. "I'm in a new company —
my own — I consult on food service..."

"You?" she asks. A loyal wife; she knows I am listening. The unasked question, "What do you know about food
service?"

"It is time for me to be an entrepreneur, and my first
client is on his way. I have been Serge's mentor. You two
owe me. I want a reservation for us tonight at My Place —
your place."

Sarit laughs. "We are booked two months from now. You are not a member of the club." She is good-natured, has a girlish way, a hard-to-define accent that shows up in mangled consonants. "You must join. I will send an application, and perhaps another time..."

"Today!" He insists.

I know she is shaking her head to go with her giggle. "We cannot. You go to Morton's. Very good steak."

Bode is used to getting his way. He is a very tall man. In this country, size counts. Bode is six feet-three; everyone else in the catering division of the bus company we worked for was well over six feet. Except me. Bode, foiled, whines. "I need a table for two at eight tonight. I need it."

Sarit is firm. "It is impossible. Ten-twenty, if you wish, but the kitchen closes at eleven."

"We'll be bombed by then." He gives up.

*In the dining room, very private, with its beautiful twenty-foot long, five feet wide Duncan Phyfe mahogany table and Regency armchairs, the guests are enjoying the cheese and fruit course of what has been a rare evening meal. They are investment bankers, underwriters for the electronics firm. One of them has an interest in a transportation company, he says, and wants to see the kitchen. I am presiding in spotless whites with a high toque. One helper. Two servers.*

*"It's tiny," he exclaims. "My kitchen at home is bigger. Show me how you manage it. We need a new way."*

*I think he is talking about airplanes. But no. Busses. Diversification. Catering. Bus stops. Restaurants. Microwaves. A new era. I think I do not "get it." But, finally, I do. A lot of money, "corporate research chef", a new title, a move to Detroit, and how soon can they have me "on board?"*

*We are happy here; we read in the libraries, take evening courses at the university. Sarit and I go to dances where we have learned the tango, a perfect dance for a fencer and a long-waisted Thai beauty. Sarit is the daughter of a Thai general, sent to Wellesley to learn art history, who found it easier to stay than to return home. Like me, she is a preserver of tradition.*

*It is a wonder that we have found each other, two people from opposite ends of the earth, both outsiders here, who share a love of learning, loyalty and art; who want to contribute seriously to our new culture, but who, like all outsiders, must study it to find where we fit in. Our life together is a shared closeness of affection, work and trust. We travel when we can, marvel at what we see, and enjoy what we do.*

*Detroit? Slums, automobiles, a chain of hamburger drive-ins called Big Boys, and the mediocre Detroit Symphony. But it is the American way. We move, taking with us antiques, forty cartons of cookbooks, and the good wishes of my former employer because I have trained my successor, another refugee, with great care.*

I do not hear again from Bode. It is all right; I am busy inventing new food fads. And publicizing them. I invite the press for a tasting on Tuesday morning two weeks after New Year's when they have nothing to write about. (Home sections are Wednesday and Thursday; restaurant sections are Friday for the weekend — everybody's interest is catered to.)

It is eleven in the morning. "We are sampling today, early, a new model for saucery. The coulis for the modern cuisine."

We have six in attendance. Just right around my chef's table. Two ladies with idiosyncratic eyeglass frames and heavy hips, a young food writer for an entertainment magazine, very slim and stylish, a hearty gentleman who barbecues for Esquire, an effete fellow whose interest is more in how I maintain my figure than in the platters at hand, and a food writer for an alternative weekly, a very snide man who will turn into a cranky journalist as he ages. Or perhaps into an Internet power.

I address the press, "I am a chef laureate who cannot rest on his laurels: I demand creativity of myself, a new 'style' in food like Dior or Saint Laurent in clothes." The ladies in idiosyncratic eyeglass frames nod. "Arthur Koestler, one of my countrymen, said when two old things come together in a new way, there is an 'act of creation'." I pause. "So — you do not put the sauce on the food, you do not drown it, you surround it with an artistic swirl of sauce, a coulis. It is like painting a platter." I show them how it is done with several dishes, using color-coded basters for my coulis. "These sauces are very concentrated and refined. The food is displayed in maximal beauty, framed." A few slashes of my knife, and they can taste morsels, lightly dabbing them in the magical sauce. They have new things to write about; I am, as always now, their darling. I show them a revamped menu, tell them about enhanced flavor, lower calories, buying larger platters for dinner service to show off the coulis to maximal advantage, recipe development for desserts which they will be invited to in a month, again on oversize platters, with fruit coulis. We make food excitement.

But, some of the popularity of My Place depends, as it always has, on charm: Sarit's, the waitresses, society cooking lessons, and on the most personal: the well-groomed chef emerging from the kitchen, greeting his guests, all of them, by name, asking about their families, their lives, and how they are enjoying their meals. I can do that, without rushing back into the kitchen. Most of the food is already prepared; it needs only to be finished. My clientele understands that I care about them, and that is true. I attend to my employees the same way, the right way. I was the first chef in the United States to come "out" of the kitchen. Coming "out" brought me "in".

*Sarit and I discussed Detroit. "It is not the same as a university town, where people understand difference," she says. "It is another culture, Serge." She is a little timid, but I will protect her.*

*"We do not have to worry, dear, dear Sarit. We are, yes, outsiders, but like most immigrants we know how to study the new place. We came with nothing, but we watched and listened..."*

*"But, sometimes we misunderstand," she said, worried. "Like Ahmed, who thought sex here so free... that it was all right to sniff his new girlfriend's armpit at a party, to show how much he enjoyed the new society..."*

*I laughed. Sarit and I, we are together, a cultural compound of two, homeostatic, self-correcting. Ultimately, that is what we know and trust for any strange place.*

*We moved to Detroit. The bus company had been overtaken by automobiles, by airplanes. "Our future is in diversification, we are bidding for contracts for rest stops on the highway, for operation of airline kitchens. And we will install our systems in our own bus stops. They provide us with a laboratory for system analysis. I want to introduce to you our research chef: Serge Szenty." It was the first time I was called "chef."*

*I bowed. One of the tall men in the front row laughed. I was comical, a cook, a servant. The others joined him.*

*"I've heard the Department of Agriculture has a new research project in school lunch," said a second very tall man. A deep voice, Research Director, my immediate superior. "They have funded a study of garbage, leftovers, to research what children do not eat. Is our research chef..?"*

*"Knock it off, Alvin." It was the man who first laughed. His distinction lay in being contrarian. He looked up at me quizzically. "What kind of research do you do?"*

*I was nonplused. I am a cook, a chef, not a scientist. "I am assigned," I said slowly, "to develop a series of products that can be marketed across the United States in our own and others' menus to create the illusion of gourmet food. They will be frozen individually or in small packages for groups for easy processing by the unskilled."*

*"Listen to him speak," a third tall man boomed. "Where you from, Serge?"*

*I had begun to hate them all. I did not answer. They were like the horsemen of the Apocalypse to me, harbingers of death and destruction. "I think it is time to think about where we are going, not where we come from." The feeling was mutual. Bode was the contrarian, vice-president in charge of marketing. He had been in charge of finance. I did not understand the connection.*

*I had been hired on an impulse by a board member — the man in "transportation." He was on the board of the bus company, too; a "professional" board member, an outsider in his companies, a board member with a broader view. But he was not inside to defend me.*

*My research was to begin with what American cooks wanted to serve without cooking it; predictably they had no idea. What could Americans want to eat when they ate out that the restaurants in mythical Podunk could not provide? What was the most attractive "gourmet cuisine?" French, North Italian, Hungarian? A bit of each. My library of books and techniques, kept at home, provided answers.*

My clipping service sends me the results of my little press meeting. Three-column wide, full-color pictures of my main dishes, some of the oversize platters painted with swirls of two or three coulis of different colors and flavors, the latest sensation for the stylish eater or cook. And a recipe for one. The others "still secret." My mail has an invitation to be the "performing artist" at a west coast hotel and nearby famous museum. It is a flattering six months into the future. They know I am in demand. I agree. But only for a few days.

Bode calls again. Sarit answers the phone. "Where's Serge?" he asks.

"Doing research," she answers politely, knowing he will

be offended. I am consulting a book a few feet away. We smile at each other.

"I have a proposition for him."

"I will tell him," she promises. I am there. She does not have to tell me. We are easy liars, having learned in our changed cultures that telling the truth was a luxury only the safe could afford. My successor in the executive dining room is a wonderful liar. He has told of his musical career as a concertmaster in Eastern Europe; his "training" in the kitchen of a famous gourmet chef, where he learned against all odds to put steak tartare on a grill for a minute on each side, and to season it with curry powder! His being hounded through the sewers of Warsaw (I saw the same Polish movie); we know how to impress our American audiences.

*Research meeting. All the tall men, Alvin, Bode, Louis, an exceptionally crude tall man who is their touchstone, a guide to the tastes of the customers and otherwise director of operations and production for the bus company.*

*"You're on, Serge."*

*"We should start with boeuf bourgignonne. Everyone likes beef and red wine," I say. No one argues. "Then to chicken paprikash, chicken in a cream sauce flavored with a fine paprika. Everyone loves chicken. Lobster Kiev, crabmeat Newburg, beef stroganoff, shrimp in coconut milk. We need at least ten fine specialties to start so that the menu-maker does not repeat on the same day of each week his last week's 'special' — or if he does, it is by choice, and perhaps he does not like something..."*

*"Nobody told us what research you've been doing. What..." It is Bode. This ignorant man is questioning my methods.*

*"I have asked the restaurant association's program director; they do an annual poll of what is the most popular dish in table service restaurants," I begin with dignity. "We have had no budget for this research."*

*Bode laughs. "Why didn't you budget research along with*

*your other ..."*

*"I have resources," I respond, nonplused.*

*"What kind of an answer is that? Who the hell are you anyway?" This is the culmination of months of needling. I would challenge Bode to a duel, with sabers, if I could. I want a big, heavy weapon that will slice his head off.*

*"Serge Szenty, at your service." I bow again. If you want to kill someone, it is important to be polite. "I have done careful menu research with restaurant association information, with my books about national cuisine and I have, for years, studied the American restaurant customer."*

*"You're a cook!" he booms. "You work with your hands like a tailor or a carpenter or a bricklayer. Every housewife does it; that's what cooking is, putting slop together. In the Army, we called it the 'mess hall'. We want you to succeed; it is our future, too. But what do you know about research?" The tall men are happy he challenges me. Spryness and agility do not count for them; they are hunters with cannon; a loud bang — what rabbit or deer survives?*

*I cannot say that my gymnasium was better than their colleges; it is true but unacceptable. "I am superlatively qualified to do research. When you have a Doctorate, you are examined for your capacity to do original work; when you have a Master's degree, you write a thesis examining the work of others. I have both."*

*They are flummoxed. For the moment. I pass a list of what I have determined to be our beginning ten dishes; with what accessory foods they are to be packaged. I have invented a multi-compartment package so that the dish and its accompaniment are not to come into contact with each other until the climactic moment of service. That is art. It is otherwise just what Bode said, "Slop."*

*"When are we going to see these, taste them?" It is Alvin. "So far it is all talk." That is true, but it constitutes a "go ahead."*

Bode calls again. "This cannot wait. I have presented an idea to a large investment banking firm, a buyout firm."

"They are not necessarily the same thing," I interpose, taking on his negative, contrarian strategy. It is a way of throwing him off stride. I learned it from him.

"They know I'm a food service expert. They have asked me for investment ideas and for fast-growing locations. I want you to come in this with me, now that you're so famous. There are big fees and stock options in astronomical numbers. That is better than cooking..."

He does not know. I write cookbooks; I edit a prestigious series on regional cuisine; I appear on television on a cooking channel and I am seen in the U.S. and abroad. I own real estate; I have huge, safe investments. I write syndicated food columns for the cities in which I do not appear on television. Airlines whose customers dislike them use my name to beef up their cuisine in first class, and offer the recipes to tourist class to take home and try. (There is always something important omitted. I do not give away secrets unnecessarily.) I laugh when I see the latest: Penne with "favorite meat sauce." It has twenty-five ingredients including Worcestershire sauce and sugar and includes a can of prepared tomato sauce. If they were not paying me so well, I would sue them for libel.

*I truly want my first experiments to be superb, fool-proof. I work diligently with custom wines, thickeners of blended waxy starch and natural gums, seasonings that cannot change in storage, everything of a purity and quality that I can be proud of. I have written my specifications for precisely portion-controlled beef, chicken grown, fed and slaughtered to order, veal that is only somewhat milk-fed; too much milk and the meat is too pale, anemic and flabby. I use fresh garlic, fresh peppers, fresh onions, basmati rice, custom egg barley, exquisite sausages. I taste everything to be sure. Five of my ten recipes are perfected. The double pouch packages*

*have been made in pilot plant production after I showed the
packaging company what I wanted. My prototypes were made
by Sarit, by hand, of heavy-duty plastic film. She sealed them
with an iron, a steam iron, at home.*

*I present them to a board meeting, at which Alvin, Bode,
Louis and the rest are present, and my "sponsor" is, too. The
others have developed the marketing plans, the budgets, the
factory drawings, the production schedules. Now it is time
to taste.*

*The pouches are dropped into pots of water. Pouches for
groups are heated in a steam unit. It is a moment of painful
suspense. My assistant sets up a buffet on a long table. She
slits open the first package, the boeuf bourguignonne. Ah.
The aroma is mouth-filling. Then the second, the third. Eyes
are sparkling with anticipation. Rightly.*

*"Congratulations, Serge." It is Alvin. "You have created
masterpieces that we will be proud to bring to market."*

*Bode nods. He turns to operations, Louis. "How long to
get these into production so that we can ship trial orders?"*

*Louis says, "A year from now, at least, for us. We farm
them out in the meantime, get a custom-packager to do it till
we're rolling."*

*I am stunned. I will lose control. "Who?"*

*"That's my job, production," Louis says proudly. "You're
the research chef—you do your cooking, Serge!" He thinks it
is funny. "Give me the recipes and we'll get them done."*

I tell Bode that I do not want stock options. No paper.
Money in advance, as a consultant, plenty of it. My name
is the only one anyone knows, and it is on the line, as they
say. "Make the offer substantial, and I'll see if we can create
a concept."

Bode has to go back to his principals, he says. "This may
not be what they have in mind. They like to do things on
speculation. But without you, who is there?"

"Faculty at the Culinary?" I suggest. He makes a face.

"They do not have your nose." He has learned that from me. "Or your Master's and PhD. What did you get them in, again? Which university?"

Why does he bring that up now?

We meet with his principals a few weeks later, in New York, in the boardroom in their offices in one of the stylish new glass buildings on the East Side. These investment bankers/buyout specialists are familiar names, disciples of the junk bond genius of the west coast. The elder, a beautifully-groomed womanizer who, with the help and brotherly attention of the other, a kinder, gentler version of ruthlessness, betrayed his family's frozen foods business into a succession of unrelated, mismanaged enterprises, each milkable for the next. Their magic has made them billionaires, while each of their companies has suffered a miserable decline into bankruptcy or acquisition by even more vulgar "investors." Now they are back in the food service business, which is indeed growing, but not at the rate of high-tech, which none of us understands. High-hype, however, is very familiar to all of us.

I am here first class; staying at Trump International, at their expense. Sarit and I are looking forward to an Eastern European opera at the Met and a superb Jean-Georges supper later (if he is in his kitchen, which he is usually not). I do not want this meeting to last long.

"Bode, here, says you're a culinary genius," says the elder, Wilson Spitz. His lieutenant, Dieter Ray, nods. "We want a concept, a concept that we can project into a chain of thousands of shops all over the country. Not McDonald's, but just as popular, just as profitable. Least equipment, least skilled people, best food. We'll call you our chef and you will be a stockholder with terrific options, be on tv, be quoted everywhere, invited to the White House and to the best places in the Hamptons. You'll be very rich."

"I am rich now," I say. "I am rich in books, art, music,

and love. I have a measure of fame. I am not sure I need this to round out my autobiography."

*Alvin comes into my research kitchen. "Where are the recipes, Serge? We've been waiting for weeks. Louis is impatient. He says you keep putting him off."*

*They are ready; they have been sequestered in a locked box, but I must surrender them. I visit the custom manufacturer with Louis; this I insist on. I am introduced to their "prepared foods technologist." We have brought with us samples of my production.*

*"Very nice," he says. "Good concept. We will have to develop a method of filling and sealing these little packages. No one has done this before. We will substitute protein hydrolysate in some of your sauces; we will use Minor bases for some of the others. It may be a bit more salty, but we will not then have to reduce... We will use waxy starch only for the thickeners, the gums are so expensive. We will start with frozen lobster and crabmeat, because that will make a more reliable supply..." he goes on but he does not understand what he is doing to my recipes. Every substitution will be an offense, an offense against flavor, texture, my love for my accomplished work.*

*"No," I say. "You are performing the death of a thousand cuts on my food."*

*"That's food technology," he says, very satisfied with his understanding of his subject. Louis, whose bad complexion attests to his penchant for take-out pizza for lunch every day, booms happily. "You let us know where you can achieve production savings. We are hoping to make this a profitable line right from the start."*

*There are battles in Detroit, with a phalanx of tall men advancing, blunderbusses pointed at the fencer who must be alert and wily. I have only wit as my epee; I flourish my Master's and Doctorate. The tall men are ignorant; they know it. I have chosen to cook because cooking incorporates everything civilization has developed: art, science, love, good manners. It is more meaningful to the average person to be well-nourished than to have his psyche explored. They retreat. No previously frozen seafood; no Minor bases or protein hydrolysates. I offer a little compromise: the waxy starch without the gums.*

*Bode has to reprice our offerings for less profit. "Your university didn't shut down during the war?"*

*"Of course not. Did yours?"*

*"Didn't they have a draft in your country?"*

*I give him my superior, educated, raised eyebrow.*

*Louis has done a good job; even the technologist has. We are putting out an excellent product, and I am rewarded with a huge bonus and stock options in the bus company.*

*"Now," I say, "we must keep a close watch on sales, watch when they flag, introduce new products on a schedule, eliminate the less popular of the older products, we have an ongoing task..."*

*After a while, customers catch on. Boeuf bourguignonne in Alabama tastes just the same as boeuf bourguignonne in Sioux City. It is good, but boring. They open a menu in Trenton and it has the same "chefs specials" as a menu in Cleveland. They retreat to prime rib, medium rare, eschewing our "development" of sweet and pungent pork with an excess of sugar and pineapple. I am not surprised. I have saved my money and it is time for My Place.*

I am home among my awards and citations, "Chef of the Century" at the Culinary; an honorary doctorate from Johnson and Wales and another from the University of Chicago; a gold medal at the culinary Olympics and another from the American Academy of Arts and Sciences for lifetime achievement. I am thinking about a possible concept for the investors, knowing that it will translate ultimately into another offense against nature and tradition. But, in the meantime, it is time to invent a new concept for My Place, and I have.

"Our European philosophers, Schelling and Goethe, called architecture variously frozen music and music in space. We have here the architectural, the frozen music, in food. We build upwards, and structure these new dishes to astonish and to hold up even when assaulted by fork and knife, retaining their harmonies to the last bite." The press listens, hypnotized. They know I am a scholar and a creator. Both. Everyone has heard about the famous chef with a Master's in history and a PhD. in psychology who has chosen to cook as his great service to mankind. My structure of eggplant, puff pastry, and meat, supported by underdone vegetables rises five inches from the plate. The lofty meringue, frozen in its lacy structure, provides the foundation for an exquisite seafood mixture, atop which an even more tenuous filigree of whipped potato rides. These verticalities challenge common sense. But that is part of their charm. I know how to do them, and no one else does or will bother to learn.

I am wondering if I can continue to invent into the indefinite future, even while my latest success is splashed on the food pages of Gourmet, The New York Times Magazine, and Vanity Fair. A biographical sketch is scheduled for The New Yorker, and my interviewer, a lady philosopher who is expert in photography, theater, fiction and cinema as well as in leaving a symbolic forelock of white in her otherwise harshly-dyed black hair, has sent me a copy of her draft. I find no errors. My Master's and PhD., my motivations, my early history are all correct.

Bode is coming with his "principals." They are bringing with them a lawyer who has drafted an international as well as domestic agreement. I have not yet said what I will do or what I want, when we meet in my office on the third floor of My Place. Of course, they are impressed. I see Wilson Spitz surveying the scene under drooping eyelids; Dieter's nods and smiling grimace show that he approves, too.

"You're ready, aren't you?" Bode asks. Big but insecure.

"I am ready," I say. "I have made a decision just this morning. Otherwise, I would be guilty of having deceived you into making this trip. I do not want to participate in this development. Even if it starts out with a good spirit and good products, in the course of time, that will change. Its very size will make it change. I do not want later to dishonor my products, products whose name and face I provide, like Col. Sanders, who, dead these many years, is still the trademark for Kentucky Fried Chicken. He was known to say privately of his, his, fried chicken, 'It's nothing but a fried doughball wrapped around some chicken' with a gravy like 'wallpaper paste.' My honor is important to me."

"Your honor!" Bode sneers. "What are you, some judge? You're a liar from the word go. That's why we intended to rely on you." Wilson and Dieter, and the lawyer from a very good firm look puzzled

"I finally got an answer from that university you claim to have gone to, that prestigious university where you received a Master's degree and a PhD. I had to write to them a number of times, finally found someone to write it in the right language. Enclosed international reply coupons to be sure they would answer. You never even took a single course, not one. You have no degree. None. You no more have a Master's degree or a PhD. than my fourteen-year old. Wait till this gets out. Your honor. You make me laugh."

"Why are you fighting with him now? You said yourself we need him, that he's a genius!" Wilson interposes, his usually expressionless face contorted with the anguish of a deal going bad.

"On the contrary," I say. "You make me laugh. Do you think your spiteful, angry, frustrated allegations will go very far? Will reach the editors of my biography in Who's Who in America, will reach the American Academy, the President of the United States, the Librarian of Congress? I am an

American hero, the substance of myth. I am taller than
Paul Bunyan, I grow to the height and girth of a California
redwood. Top that if you can."

I am "in" so far, that I can no longer — like the cat or
garbage — be put "out."

End

# THE SYSTEM

The guy's secretary called early one December morning. "Mr. Hoberman on the line."

I answer my own calls. "Mr. Hoberman?"

"Herbert Hoberman," she affirmed.

"About what? Oh, never mind. Put him on." I am not fond of the games of oneupmanship.

"I've been asking around, and I'm told you're a very good political consultant. I am planning to run in the primary for the Democratic party designation for Congressman in the 21st Congressional District, and I need a consultant to manage my campaign, handle the media, prepare all the literature... you know."

"Ah. Yes, I do know and what you're asking for is more than any one person should do. It's a more than full-time commitment. I'm flattered. But I can't do it."

"Why not? I can pay you."

"It's not money. It's my life. I do not want to have you and only you on my mind for nine months. We can talk about campaign management, or campaign strategy or just about media — advertising, public relations, literature..."

"How would it be..."

I interrupted him. "Mr. Hoberman, why do you want to run?"

211

"I have a lot to offer the political system. I'm intelligent, honest, and I care about the direction of U.S. policy. I want to make a difference."

I frowned. I could smell a loser. "Who are you?" I asked, pretty bluntly for a person whose stock in trade is being politic.

"I'm an investment banker, and what with bonuses, warrants, options, and fees, I've become a multi-millionaire. I know how to make money, lots of it. It's not interesting any more." His earnestness was palpable. He had a pleasant voice, deep, a plus of sorts.

"Have you run before for anything, worked on community boards, been a member of a political club?"

"No," he said, proudly. "I'm a public-spirited citizen with no baggage."

"Not even in school?" I inquired. No.

"How about connections? You'll have to raise money."

"I have enough."

"But spending your own money exclusively raises credibility questions," I said. "You want to show that other people are supporting you – colleagues, former clients..."

"I'll think about that," he said.

We made an appointment for a meeting. The most important thing in an intimate relationship like consultant/client is chemistry.

*Consultation I.* He was a tallish, youngish man, clearly fit and in control of his body, with dark wavy hair cut well by a premium barber, wearing a smooth, gray pinstripe suit and heavy brown shoes. About what I had expected. Eyeglasses with metal frames; cleanshaven, a long-toothed smile. He'd photograph all right, look ok on tv, might work well with the press.

What did he see? A woman, wearing a decent Bergdorf suit and Italian shoes, businesslike, approaching middle age. Nice-looking, maybe, but not making a point of it.

I could see that he wanted to be friendly but his friendliness was forced, that of a man whose daylight time required quick first-name relationships. Such intimacy would last long enough to take a small company public, let him get his fees plus whatever else the bargain entailed, and run. Run even before the first buyers flip their IPOs. Get on to the next one's due diligence before the payment from the earlier one clears. Quick smile, warm handshake, good body language, the friendliness of a man with financial know-how and contacts, a man who is busy. It was a friendliness that did not have to like anyone; just use them well. But, I reflected, that was what we were both about, wasn't it?

I ushered him into the livingroom of my apartment, a 2-bedroom flat where I live alone, using the second bedroom as a home office from which I coordinate professional work done by other paladins-for-hire. "Tea?" I asked. "The first consultation, one hour only, is free. After that, time rates apply."

"Nice place." Right. It was designed as background, not foreground. Comfortable old furniture with wood frames, upholstered not too long ago in stripes and damasks. Convenient side tables, a big coffee table and plenty of lamps. Dark oil paintings, landscapes and portraits. No distinction.

He did not want tea; had come with all the nourishment he needed.

"You want to challenge Al Broadus in the primary? He's the incumbent, and there's no groundswell of opposition," I said. "Why'd you pick him?"

"I live in this district," he said, as if it were self-evident. He did not seem to know about two ambitious guys who had migrated not so long ago from Manhattan to Long Island to run for Congress. Both had made it. One even became a senator later. After the Civil War, they called it carpetbagging.

"Yes, but what are your policy differences?"

For the first time, he relaxed. Crossed his legs, swinging one foot, and got ready for the kind of policy statement he might have made to a fellow Harvard Business School alumnus. "I'm with him in human policy — for all the protections that make it possible for the U.S. to have a color-blind, sexual-preferences-neuter opportunity for everyone. I believe in civil liberties. Where I differ with Broadus is the amount of intervention, the size of government, the importance of the right kind of education..." He paused. "Foreign policy. These are major issues."

I agreed. They are. "But there are problems. It's hard to get public attention to them. We have short attention spans, busy lives. A cynical electorate." Did I want to discourage him? I was of two minds. "Well, you seem to have given some thought to this run..." I was flattering him. I had decided that a few "last hurrahs" would, if I managed them well, furnish me with a substantial addition to my money-purchase plan, and enough to put a down-payment on a nice old conch house in Key West, with its raffish, shabby ambience and great weather. Then I could write my memoirs and recommendations for improving the political system. Or just hang out in a bar and go to the pier to watch the sunset.

We'd used up half an hour. "Ok. Let's get down to business. You will need a lawyer to make sure your petitions are all correct. The law in this state favors incumbents. Then you will need a program person, who arranges all your calendar activities, electioneering at subway stops, visiting clubs... A media person. I'll coordinate that, along with strategy and polls. Issues research. We've got to find an idle space for a temporary headquarters in a good location. We need a volunteers coordinator... A paid volunteers coordinator." I looked at him. "Do you still want to get into this?"

"My mind is made up." He looked solemn. "I need the challenge. I want it. I will do whatever is necessary."

"Well," I said. "You are going to need a fundraiser. People do not like the idea of a candidate who can buy an election out of his own pocket. The Village Voice will be poisonous."

"Is that still read?"

"More than ever. It's free now. Do you have a friend with good connections who will put the bite on big donors? The neighborhood kaffee klatches are not going to raise more than a few hundred dollars at a time, but they do introduce you to prospective voters ..." I stopped. "I like to do something other people don't do: define my role in a campaign on paper. A proposal."

"When will I have it?"

"Early next week."

It's a fussy way to do business. I know it. But without it, controversy between client and consultant escalates. I have never been sued, and that's how I want to keep it. Contracts are worthless in this business. If a client has lost precious time, he can't get it back. And if he doesn't want to pay, there's no way to force him. If he or she accepts a proposal, that becomes a working document, and something to refer to when the going gets rough.

I wrote it, outlining my role, incorporating the usual explanations of the process, the system, and knowing how poorly people read, took it to Hoberman's downtown office for our next discussion. Don't laugh: I read my proposals to prospective clients, trusting that if they follow the text while I am reading, they will hear as well as see what's involved.

Hoberman's office was in the financial district; a modest-sized space sublet from a major partnership whose main office had moved to Park Avenue before their downtown lease expired. He had opened his own consultancy, he said, to be sure no interesting deals went by just because he was running for office. It also gave him a place to work, be interviewed, have a secretary, and to fall back on, if necessary. But he was pretty confident. He signed the proposal "Accepted," and the date.

I had a lot of things to think about and not say. You cannot tell a candidate running in a primary against an incumbent that he will probably lose. You cannot say, "The ordinary voter does not come out in a primary. The party organization won't help you." You can not say these things because there are other possibilities. There are always upsets, illnesses, lucky breaks, or at worst, developing useful recognition for a later run, or achieving enough notice for a prestigious appointment. Even using the experience in a different way.

I try to give good, honest advice no matter what I am paid. But I do not say, "Don't do this. You're wasting your time and money." I have to earn a living.

*The Get-Acquainted Meeting.* I went to his apartment for our next meeting, a handsome building on Riverside Drive, a standard seven, three bedrooms, three baths, living room, dining room, kitchen and library-den. But not in the part of the building that had the view. It faced east to the back of a West End Avenue building, an uninspiring set of bricks, window glass and air conditioners. A good address, but a frugal choice in co-ops. The decor? Comfortable and not flashy: Leather furniture, smallish carpets on polished floors, "decorator" art — a tall, standing, semi-antique, wooden Buddha from Burma, an Italian modernist painting or two from Wally Findlay, and lots of family photographs. The wife, I thought, was a little special: a tall, warm, slightly homely girl, mother of two, wearing a plaid skirt and turtleneck, and clearly apprehensive about this latest turn in their relationship. She would back him well with all the Wellesley-bred niceness he needed. The two kids, polite boys who attended Collegiate, sat cross-legged on the floor in their school blazers and ties.

Across the livingroom was his elections lawyer, a familiar jerk named Brennan who lived in Scarsdale and enjoyed speeding up and down the state's roads to Albany and beating, by fast talk and guile, the almost inevitable third ticket that would deprive him of his license. At least, until the earliest ticket expired and lessened his risk. I had often wondered what other kind of law he practiced between elections. But he would do.

Also there was a campaign chairman, an old friend from the financial world who could be expected to find some outside funding. An east side guy, who had invested small sums in startups and made himself a pile, then started a hedge fund. Gray-haired, affable, unmemorable. The inevitable yenta, a neighbor in the building, a tall, brassy blond who had volunteered to recruit volunteers. I shrugged. Good enough to start: he had taken me seriously and found whom he needed, and our little meeting got under way.

He introduced us as formally as if we were a board of directors, but it was clear he was planning to be the CEO. "Is it all right if I start?" I asked. He nodded.

"This is going to be some of the hardest work any of us has ever done. We are going to have to start by making the man recognizable to a population that..."

He interrupted. "I want a flyer first, with my picture on the cover..."

"Of course," I said. "We'll make it a self-mailer with a back panel that can be addressed without an envelope, a single sheet folded in three to fit in a 3" x 10" envelope, that will say who you are, why you're running and enunciate your basic positions. Not too oppositional to start."

"Right, just what I want. How soon can that be done?"

"We have to get photos taken first. Then, a day to write, a day to change or approve, a couple of days to get it printed on a glossy paper that will do the photos..."

"Then?"

"We have to hold a press conference to announce you're

running, as soon as the flyer is ready. We have to prepare a press kit with background, extra photos, tidbits and ideas for special stories, interview points for radio and local television... I'll get that stuff together. This is going to be a race to the market like a high-tech IPO."

Hoberman nodded. The older of the two boys sitting cross-legged on the floor stood up. "May we be excused?" Nice kids. Too nice. Their privileges showed and they'd annoy the envious.

The yenta wasn't such a yenta after all. "As soon as he's announced, I'll have a thing in my apartment to introduce him to volunteers, a cocktail party. Then we'll start spreading through the neighborhood..."

"It's not so simple any more. The neighborhood looks like Gerry's salamander, from the top of Manhattan deep into the village, and with a little Riverdale and Brooklyn thrown in. We'll need some ethnics, gays..." I stopped. I could talk to her later.

"Research." I said. "Who's doing that?"

Herb said he was. "Why do you think I'm running?" he asked, cuttingly. "I have files and files of stuff about Broadus and his positions and about my own. It's all done."

"I'll take a look," I said soothingly. "Meantime, I have to get a photographer in to take pictures of you and your family, you in the neighborhood, you working on 'real world' problems as a financial advisor — or do you have some of that?"

"Some. I don't want an expensive photographer. We've budgeted this for the long haul..."

The petitions lawyer yawned. "You don't need me for a couple of months... I'll be on my way."

I wanted to discuss strategy, positioning him as a liberal alternative who understood the differences between yesterday's ultraliberal point of view — "The government can do it all" — and today's shadings all the way to "I earned it; I want to keep it" — "We have to help them to help themselves" — the New Democrat mentality. That and foreign policy were his best bets for differentiating himself from Broadus, I guessed.

"Not now," he said. "We'll have a private strategy meeting later."

*Pictures for the Media.* The young woman whose work I had spotted in a show of new women photographers at the "Y" would come cheap. A hundred fifty for the day, prints included, and we keep the negatives. Hoberman was pleased. (Not the last of the big spenders.) I had asked her to take candid pictures of Hoberman for a day, including the family at breakfast, plus a formal family portrait, then follow him trekking fakely around the district, stopping in a school yard for a shot with kids, visiting a smiling bunch of oldsters briefly at a seniors' lunch center, dropping into the office of the West Side Chamber of Commerce... standard stuff. We picked about ten good ones for real prints and I had them made as 5" x 8" glossies from copy negs. We had what we needed; the photographer was thrilled with her first professional assignment; Hoberman was exhilarated, too, by all the flattering attention: "What is this about?" and "Who are you?" on the street and in the senior citizens' center, but responded modestly, shaking hands and grinning.

*Flyer I.* "I'll write a draft," I said, " to introduce you to the district. Nothing too controversial to start, a good guy, bright, who cares and gets his money's worth. I'll get an endorsement or two, to fit the theme. 'Herbert Hoberman, there for the voters of the 21st Congressional District.' "

"Responsive, responsible — from this district, for this district."' Unassailable positions for education, civil rights, cooperative programs between the public and private sectors, healthy families, small business development, mass transit. And here's Hoberman, a homegrown guy from a family brownstone on the West Side, NYU bachelor's degree in history, magazine space sales for McGraw-Hill, off to Harvard Business School and hired by an investment banker to develop fledgling businesses, and meantime, volunteering his expertise to a worldwide microcapital fund for women's enterprise. And who's endorsing? Easy. A neighbor, who had, in fact, founded the microcapital thing, endorsing his "Clear vision, responsibility, constructive programs." Another endorser, the yenta, who, as it turned out was on the community board, appointed by the borough president, and therefore was useful on local issues and personages. (I acknowledged to myself that the yenta designation was only partly merited, and was more a matter of style than substance. I was ashamed of myself for even thinking it.)

Nothing in the copy was too specific, but it was all engaging and statesmanlike. It was printed in a week, the heads in red, text dark blue on white. (A little subliminal patriotism doesn't hurt.) During that time, we prepared the press conference: place, a press release, photos, talking points, invitations to the media, and a lot of Q & A rehearsals. I tried hard for a few local "leaders" but they were cagey. Did not want to appear for him and get on the wrong side of Broadus.

*First Press Conference.* Of course, it was set for 10:30 am. That way you get the dailies before the guys have to get to their desks to write their stories; you serve coffee and bagels and fruit for a low-priced event. You get the tv crews for the 6 o'clock news, and they have time to get comment from "experts" about the candidate's chances... We were holding it in a nice room in one of the hotels near Lincoln Center, not far from the place on Amsterdam Avenue where we had set up campaign headquarters in a storefront that had formerly housed an Italian restaurant.

Campaign chairman: "My friend, Herbert Hoberman, the best candidate for the democratic nomination for Congress in this district. I love this guy. Reliable, decent, hard-working, responsible. He'll tell you..."

Herbert: "This district is poorly represented now. The man who represents us hasn't had a new idea in thirty years. He thinks the only way to deal with anything is to have the government take over, doing your thinking for you. He keeps pushing for big budgets for tasks that private ingenuity can accomplish. That's not the way it should be. We need fresh positions, community, new coalitions..."

Mrs. Herbert: "We welcome the prospect of working with the women in this neighborhood as an empowered constituency..."

The yenta: "Volunteers have been recruited from West Side business groups, the Urban League, Fordham University, Local 32 and some PTAs. We're going to make Herbert Hoberman the man whose record and positions everybody understands..."

The microcapital man: "Herbert Hoberman truly understands the economy of the 21st century. He's the man we need to represent us as the world transitions (sic) to new forms of organization..."

They all sounded great. I had had them put their little pieces on index cards so even if they were not unfailingly spontaneous, they had only to look down at their cue words. This was going swimmingly.

Who was there? Hardly anyone but us. A tv crew from New York 1, a third-ranked kid from *The New York Times*, interns from two of three weeklies, and the president of one of the local democratic clubs — as an observer. They picked up the press kit with the news announcement and the portrait photo and leaflet, wished Hoberman good luck, munched their bagels and ran.

We still had the room for half an hour. "Why weren't they interested?" Hoberman demanded.

"No message gets through the first time. It has to be repeated and amplified and varied and repeated... We score

it for solidity and a few good surprises, and by and by, the
name is familiar, the positions are accepted. You can't be
too flashy on the first go-round. You want to create trust
and an open ear for the next message."

He was angry. "I hate spending money and time fool-
ishly."

I could see he was hurt. He had not been taken seriously.
I wanted to try a little "heart to heart" to let him know I
understood, but his bristling made it hard for me to open
up.

Instead, I said, "It's not foolish. This campaign has a
long way to go and it has to be built organically. It's not
an Internet stock. We've made a decent start, and we'll look
at the tv news tonight and the papers tomorrow and on the
weekend to see what they've done with it."

"But nobody was here."

"We sent the press release and background to all the local
media. Even if they didn't show up, something will appear.
We even did a Web posting. We'll follow up to arrange
interviews."

He was mollified. There was a flash of his announcement
speech and a sentence or so on NY 1, a sentence and still shot
on the 6 o'clock news on another local channel, a paragraph
in the Times, and photos and captions in two of the freebie-
hungry local weeklies.

I understood what he wanted. We all want magic, a
fairy-tale transformation from ugly duckling to swan, the
frog transformed into a handsome prince with one kiss; the
winning lottery ticket. You can create a buzz about a public
figure, but there must be a figure first.

*Strategy I.* "Now we have to start running hard and fast.
First, where's your research?" He opened a file drawer in his
office. I frowned. It was just a pile of crap culled from years
of clippings. No order, no notes about changing positions,
only a few off-the-wall pronouncements. Al Broadus had

been appearing at every left-wing meeting around, shaking hands, nodding and smiling. He had been hosting community forums annually on subjects that had little to do with federal policy or powers. This comfortable sloppiness about which branch of government did what went down well with community activists, and gave Broadus a substantial crowd to greet. But where were the real issues, the real research? Not in Hoberman's annals.

So, I shared my highly political Congressional directory with him. Broadus was a congressional failure despite his longevity. He was on dumb committees, chair of only one subcommittee, had introduced no legislation of any consequence, had a mediocre attendance record and unimaginative voting record. C-Span did not broadcast his rare speeches; in fact some of what might have been speeches were inserted as remarks into the Congressional Record without having been uttered. It was clear that neither the press nor his peers had much respect. That was a start. Herbert loved the directory's careful disparagement, its sarcastic tone about Broadus' unpopularity.

"But we need more," I said. "I can hire a part-timer, a political science major, to go through your stuff and the *Times* index... It's a truism in politics that it is easier to get people to vote 'against' than 'for.' Easier to mobilize anger..."

"Never mind. We won't need that stuff. There are so many new, young people in this district that there's no way they're going to vote for an old horse like Al Broadus. Everything he says reflects his first election: the concerned citizen of thirty years ago taking over from a dead man. This is going to be easy."

I shook my head. "Nothing's easy. Has anyone checked the demographics? How many new people are there anyhow?"

Herbert smiled. "You can see in the street. Look at all

the new stores catering to children, look at all the nannies and baby-carriages... Look at the take-out shops."

"Not good enough. We'll have to get the data from Henn & Groen and have them do a survey... I have to have a meeting with your volunteers coordinator and with your calendar person. You've got to get busy at subway stops. The leaflets have to be put into buildings... Everyone has to know who you are and why you're running. We must focus on getting the vote out. The hardest thing in a primary is to get people to the polls who ordinarily don't vote. Their interest must be mobilized." I could see I was boring him.

*Meeting the pollsters.* He insisted on coming along. If he was going to pay, he was going to evaluate them. No argument. I did not much like these two guys in their office on Third Avenue, the main room filled with maps and pins and boiler room pollsters, their private office blinking with television sets and computers. But they were as good as any others and currently favored even by national and international candidates. Of course, like all pollsters, they had their biases, theirs being democratic. No far right organization would hire them.

We talked to Groen. I had a list of the questions I wanted asked. How long had the voter been at his/her current address? What changes in occupants of his/her dwelling had occurred? What did the voter(s) think about current Defense Department expenditures, and about what kinds of warfare the Defense Department should be planning for? (Big, guerrilla, ethnic, aerial, etc.) What our stance should be vis a vis the United Nations — budget, peacekeeping, human rights, women's issues. What position should we take to former enemies, now somewhat down on their luck? What to third world development? How much should the federal government do to establish domestic education standards? What about health care standards for the general population; for Medicaid and Medicare? A few questions about tax

reform, and about social security; questions about long term
health care; term limits; mandatory prison for drug possession. I had phrased the questions to create a "difference"
between Broadus and Hoberman that could be used, and to
offer a spectrum of responses.

Ah, but H & G wanted to *use us.* Groen wanted to
piggyback on our little "universe" of 500 demographically
typical respondents in this congressional district, a bunch of
questions whose answers I had no interest in. He had his list.
I had ours.

"What's the idea?" I asked indignantly. "We don't want
those questions asked. The answers are irrelevant to Hoberman's campaign." It was clear that this extraneous research
was being done for someone else, and I had no doubt Groen
would charge whoever was paying for it full value, a bit of
piggery all too common. "Those questions are just going to
annoy our respondents, take too much time, bore them..."

Groen was adamant. He even partly persuaded Hoberman that his questions had value for him. I argued and it
got ugly. What the hell. It wasn't my money, and I smiled
gently at Groen, knowing I'd bad-mouth him at every future
opportunity. We'd get the answers to most of my questions
more promptly if I gave in.

*The Yenta at Work.* "We're introducing Herbert at a series of kaffee klatches to which neighbors are invited. Starting here, but fanning out through the district." At my sug-
gestion, she had prepared a "how to run a kaffee klatch"
information sheet, available on our Web site and at headquarters, with instructions to call the coordinator for dates
that were open.

Hosting a kaffee klatch was a one-time opportunity for
everyone who hoped to run for office in the future or solicit a
job or just "get involved." Another mutual use program. We
had coordinators on the upper west side, lower west side and
Brooklyn and way north, Washington Heights and Riverdale

and the north Bronx. Four kks per evening, with Hoberman being carted from one to another by a volunteer with a vehicle, who inevitably sacrificed her next day's "alternate side" parking space.

The instruction sheet: put a notice in the lobby "Come meet the candidate. Beverages and desserts." Twenty to fifty people per apartment, Hoberman's standard speech and handshakes all around, a pitch for funds as soon as he left by the "disinterested" host. A kaffee klatch was fun for everyone, even Hoberman. He got to meet people who were interesting, and even better, they got to meet each other.

Along with the checks, each kk got us more volunteers, leafletters and bell ringers, some of them high school kids, stuffing things under doors, piling them in vestibules, doing a better job of blanketing the neighborhood than take-out deliverymen with restaurant menus. A month or so after they started, we began a campaign newsletter with material from black and Hispanic neighborhoods, shopkeepers and the little committees we set up for special interests. We had posters in the barber shops, delicatessen windows, and fruit and vegetable markets. Now when Hoberman appeared at a subway stop in the morning or evening to hand out his leaflet and chat with passersby, he was "known." But a story appeared in the Daily News: Some unionized companies in the Midwest had downsized after a Hoberman-engineered merger. We put out a statement immediately that many more jobs had resulted from increasing the companies' competitiveness. We followed up with a Times op-ed piece about that.

*The Look.* I was getting complaints from a few activists. "He won't win with those button-down collars, repp ties, pinstripe suits and for God's sake, white shirts."

I made an appointment to meet him and the wife at home on a Saturday morning. I wanted an ally. "You're going to hate this, but it has to be done. You look too much like a financial type. Let's create a more universal image. What do you think, Patricia?"

She shook her head smiling. "You're not going to get me in on this."

I shrugged. "Okay. Let's loosen it up a bit. Colored shirts, occasional chinos and sports jackets. How about stripes? Brooks Brothers sells them."

"No," he said. "No way. I don't have colored or striped shirts or chinos or sports jackets and I'm not buying them."

"This is an electorate that wants to see in you 'their guy.' Don't you want to get the nomination?" I asked.

"Yes, but with my standards intact." My candidate had a really mulish streak.

"Keep your standards for the important things. Politics is a branch of show business. You have to look the part," I insisted. "You're going to be interviewed on tv twice next week; they recommend light shirts, blue or beige, not white."

He looked at his wife. "Herb," she said, "it's what *they* want. You can buy a couple of shirts and pants and a blazer. In fact, I think you'll look great in them."

He even consented to wear his new clothes at subway stops in the morning. And, they had a reciprocal effect on his campaigning. He loosened up a bit, tilted his head when he talked or listened. He was affable and sensitive on tv, and inspired some favorable comment. We were doing all right. People knew he was running, had a vague idea of his background and positions.

*First Attacks.* Broadus would not dignify Hoberman's campaign with an attack, himself. It was set up with the Village Voice first and then with the *New York Observer*'s, most lefty columnist. "Can Anyone Just Buy an Election?" asked the Village Voice. No, it answered. Look at Lehrman, Lauder, Forbes for starters. You, the electorate, are too smart. (Plenty of conjecture about Hoberman's real goals. He and his friends are rich. They want tax cuts, budget cuts, "waste" reduction and privatization to benefit themselves and their businesses.)

*The Observer.* "The Unrealistic Challenge — A Waste of Time and Money." A guy with no track record presumes to challenge a West Side representative with seniority in Congress. For what? So he can be a congressman-in-training on the house floor, take this up as a new hobby, exercise his ego, find a new source of power.

I suggested that Hoberman offer lunch and an exclusive interview to each of the writers. They would probably not accept. But if they did, he could point out that he was not obligated to anyone for funds, and ask who finances Broadus: municipal employees including teachers, the left-wing unions, socialists and social workers. They vote *their interests* in the system as much as anyone else. But, he had to focus on *his message*: there was serious opportunity for the whole society in new initiatives that did not need tax funding.

*Poll Results.* And now we had them. I brought the results with me in a visit to his office. I had a plan for clearly differentiating him from Broadus using them. There had not been as major a demographic shift as he had hoped. Only eight percent of the electorate in the district had moved during the past five years. But on the issues, the electorate showed a clear difference with Broadus. There were good percentages for charter schools and educational standards; for shared public/private initiatives in job-training and small business in depressed areas; for decriminalizing drug use, and offering substitutes and treatment; for rent-to-buy housing plans. And, a confused set of results on foreign policy: recognize Cuba, let business and international agencies work with Russia and eastern Europe; intervene minimally for major human rights goals, but yes intervene if necessary; professional negotiation of trade issues; participation in World Court and other international bodies but caution about ecosystems commitments, and a diplomatic formula for dealing with Taiwan and Tibet while preserving relations with China.

"You have a bunch of terrific points to make, Herbert. Broadus is out of touch on domestic issues, and even on some foreign policy. Now we can put out a press release about the results of the poll and how you differ with him so voters can see there is a choice. Plus, of course, we'll emphasize that you're as liberal as he is where it counts."

He shook his head. "I don't want the results of the poll made public. No press release, no interviews."

"What? After we spent all that time and money? These are legitimate differences that give the electorate a reason to vote for you! Or," a new thought occurred to me, "do you not want to be perceived as using a poll to direct your positions? We can use it without mentioning it."

"No."

"Then what? You have to stand for something — some serious differences — or no one other than party regulars will bother to vote." I was beginning to wish I had not agreed to take this nut as a client. "You have to compromise — politics is all about compromise. If you get to the House, you'll never find anything perfect there; it's all about finding a compromise that a majority can vote 'yes' to. There's no purity in human interactions. You give in on some issues in order to get something you care about on others."

"I'll think about it. What I want to emphasize in my campaign is character, not personality. I don't want to be marketed like snack foods. I want people to understand the meaning of integrity. Other candidates can do the polling and posturing. I think our electorate is smarter."

I was beginning to wonder if he was as simple and straight-forward as I had thought. And to dislike what I was doing with him and for him. He was paying my fees, and the expenses with his gentlemanly thirty-day holdback. He did not seem to think we had a quarrel about anything. In fact, he seemed pleased by our careful building of his recognition and momentum, the advice I gave, and the issues I suggested. But, I was deeply uncomfortable. He did not understand that he was working within a system that took its time with new people. It happens in every relationship. We suspend our differences to work together and they come back to haunt us.

*Petitions.* We had people going door to door with petition forms and expected to get at least twice the number we literally needed to survive challenges. There were tables set up in front of several Barnes and Noble book stores and in front of high traffic Zabar's. Not in front of Fairway or other fruit and vegetable markets. That would block the streets almost completely and infuriate prospective voters. The tables featured posters of the Third World women funded by microcapital; senior citizens smiling in a cafeteria line; kids in a school playground. Pretty and painless. We got our signatures; we'd survive challenges. Brennan did a capable job of examining the signatures for legitimacy, residence, all the rest, and by and by they were filed. Broadus' challenges were perfunctory.

He had other challenges, however: why were we featuring women's enterprise when everyone knew that women were already overloaded with home and work and what then for the family? Broadus concluded that some candidates are insensitive to the real world...

We countered with sound trucks but not the really irritating ones that yammer as they circle neighborhoods. No. Ours stopped at corners, opening with jazz or Mozart depending on the neighborhood, and our speakers, who'd been sitting on benches in the backs of the open pick-ups, stood up to address the crowds on the issues they thought were important, even attacking Broadus' record and failures.

*Endorsements.* It was time for endorsements. First, individuals. We called around, all of us, including the yenta. It was uphill work. No one was willing to alienate Broadus and his crowd, knowing how hard it was for any challenger to mount a credible challenge, much less to win. I tried an ex-mayor. Success:

"Herbert Hoberman is the kind of man we need in Congress in the next millennium: a man who can get things done — - and leave the wrong things undone. A man who thinks through the issues and finds solutions that can work." That was good.

A Hispanic councilman who had already staked out maverick positions on enterprise and housing and obligatory "equal opportunity" quotas: "Our people have so much capacity; they need a candidate who fosters enterprise not dependency. Herbert Hoberman understands the economy and what small business can accomplish."

Several real estate developers, thinking anyone was better than Broadus, especially a sophisticated financial type like Hoberman, tried to endorse. We could not accept their accolades; only their checks. We did, however, accept endorsements from many small shopkeepers, the West Side Chamber of Commerce, the head of the building workers union, a few clergymen and a gay business group.

The professional politicians, the district leaders, the council members, the state assembly people, the state senators were all ostentatiously neutral. We could not even get our phone calls returned. They knew that most primary challenges in our district are forgotten by the time the leaves fall. We did not have anyone with any influence among the tiny minority of registered voters who would turn out in a primary.

I met with Herbert. "We have to articulate our issues. This is a 'ho-hum' campaign. There's enough evidence in our poll that people are tired of the 'war against drugs'. If you come out, as some judges, the mayor of Baltimore, the Civil Liberties people, and some important doctors already have, with a strong statement saying the war on drugs is an expensive, crime-inducing failure; let's try offering prescription drugs at reasonable prices to people who want them as long as they participate at the same time in drug treatment programs. We can give drug users what they want and are already getting to the tune of crime and expensive disorder, and perhaps even cut back on the clogging of courts and prisons, while providing a future for now-dependent people. It would galvanize the electorate."

"I can't do that."

"Why?" I said, impatiently. "If you're going to lose anyway, you might as well show some courage and good sense."

"No," he said. "I'm hoping for an endorsement from the Harlem Congressman. Without the full-press war on drugs, he thinks his entire constituency is down the tubes."

"They know better," I argued. "They're the ones who are getting mandatory sentences for possession and being sent upstate to prison in droves. How about housing conversion with a rent-to-own plan; or a community health education program with neighborhood lessons in schools, churches, community centers on personal health care — diet, exercise, stress reduction, warning symptoms? A certificate would be worth a rebate on income tax or an earned income credit. Every three years a refresher with the latest... To reduce chronic and long-term costs, early death. You can offer really good ideas to a receptive community instead of doing nothing and losing. Why not give it a try?"

"Don't argue. You're my consultant; not my boss. There are plenty of women around who'd like to advise me." I had suddenly become "a woman," not a consultant.

I detected a little sub rosa lobbying by the yenta, and shut up about new programs for druggies, health care, and housing. I'd find a smart candidate who would understand these ideas, in the meantime, I knew the Harlem Congressman as a powerful, devious guy. He was never going to endorse Hoberman until and unless he won the nomination.

Then he might even campaign for him, but not much. His own constituents and future were a lot more important.

Back to endorsements. "Listen," I said. "What you really need is to address the clubs, all the clubs from downtown to Riverdale. They'll all be holding endorsement meetings and we want at least a third of them to go for you. We'll arrange meetings first with the leaders. You have lunch or dinner with them before the evening of your presentation and the vote. They will know you and feel comfortable then, and you have a possible favorable vote."

'How do other people get endorsements?" he asked.

"Well, one Congresswoman was notorious for her permanent floating 'packing' group. She'd send thirty or forty new people into a club a few weeks before an endorsement vote; they'd pay their dues; they'd be members of the club. Most clubs have maybe twenty-five active members. Comes the night of the endorsement meeting, the club is packed with new members who vote, outvoting the regulars. The new members are not seen again in that club — but yes, they manage to join every club in the district in turn, participating in the crucial debate, voting and disappearing. I think Lenin got the idea first."

He was horrified. "I can't allow that."

I nodded. "Then you have to visit with every club's leaders privately and discreetly, court them, pay attention to what they want, and assure them you will work with them."

We were sitting in his Amsterdam Avenue headquarters, he at the big rented desk in the back of the room, and I in the side chair adjacent. Around us, the phones ringing, the volunteers talking, piles of paper literature, posters, and note pads, lists of registered voters to be called, maps of the district, messes of Starbucks cups, plastic-packed food from Korean shops half eaten, and a campaign headquarters smell of nervousness, haste and eagerness.

To my surprise, he said, "Wait a minute. I've been speaking to Pete Headly."

It was a bombshell to me. Headly was a pontifical consultant who advised his clients to take the expensive media route to everything because he made his money on the commissions, not on fees. TV advertising, full pages in the *Times,* video news releases for the local stations and the same news releases sent to the clubs, along with rental equipment. Nothing paltry about his way. Did Hoberman understood what this guy's advice entailed? I could not ask. It would sound like professional jealousy. (Maybe it was.)

"He thinks it shows a lack of integrity, a failure of charisma to call on these guys. He's advising me to just sit tight. They'll have his videos and all that advertising and pressure from the members who will have seen ... Anyway, they know where I am. They'll come to me." He sat there smugly certain that they would. I did not think so.

"They'll never come. They do not need you. You need them. You must go to them."

"No."

Who else was talking to him? Of course, the yenta. She came into headquarters, tan (from where?), excessively blond, a little overweight, wearing high heels and a flowing dress.

"Herbert," she said, "I think the borough president will endorse you. She likes your message about women's enterprise, and about microcapitalism in poor neighborhoods, even about rent-to-own housing." (Ah, she had picked up an idea from me.) "She's ambitious, wants to be mayor. This will be a real breakthrough for you."

Was he listening? Did he believe this bullshit? I did not. How much of it had she been feeding him? Was she the Headly contact? I would not be a bit surprised. This was going bad. I hated the situation I was in, fees or no fees. I was reminded of another political yenta who, after putting on many neighborhood kaffee klatches for him, had become a WASP mayor's official yenta, his representative to women. Then, she had appeared at a Women's Bar Association meeting and taken the *negative* in a debate about whether women should be in politics. From there, it was an easy jump to running for office, herself.

"Herbert," I said. "We can't have so many conflicts about important matters. We will have to think about our next steps. Now, if you'll excuse me, I have to get back to my office."

It was all right, close to the end of August, the primary only a few weeks away. I had prepared a bunch of radio spots covering the music listeners' spectrum, with Hoberman's nice voice telling why he thought he should win the primary. They'd be placed, and do as much good as they could. We had agreed that television was wasted until late in the game if it was analyzed in terms of cost and spread and audience perception. But we had our tv material prepared and time bought for the last two weeks. What else could be done?

I stewed in my office waiting for the phone to ring. It did not. Hoberman had had no trouble substituting a volunteer yenta for what he perceived to be an interchangeable but paid yenta. And a full-of-it male consultant who had nothing to offer. It did not really matter. Ok, it did, a bit. I was upset and not upset. I am a professional: These things happen. I do not fall in love with clients, only with the work I can do for them. That's what I love: developing a strategy, thinking through the problems, creating solutions unique to each case. Clients come and go; they come back or go on.

Turnout for the primary was the usual twenty percent of registered voters. Hoberman conceded early and gracefully. He had won twenty-five percent of the votes. I was not surprised. If he'd been a mad success and done everything exactly right, it might have gone up to forty percent. That's how it is in New York. It's the way the system works.

I called Hoberman a few days later. "You've made a start. People know who you are. You have some contacts that will work for you in another election. Pick your spot carefully and you can win." I was saying this for closure, to tell him truthfully that it was salvageable, a downpayment on a successful future. But I did not think he would try again.

He confirmed my feeling. "No." I knew he was shaking his head. "I want to thank you for calling and for doing a very good job. But, it's not for me. I've been thinking it over and talking to my wife. I guess I just had to get it out of my system."

End

# OSCILLATIONS

Carey is getting old, he thinks. Who should know better than he what it means? But he is a young man, in his prime, a man who has risen quickly, coming from behind, to head the Department of Aging at the National Institutes of Health. He administers a huge and growing budget for research conducted inside as well as in grants to researchers everywhere. He is at the top of his heap, professionally and personally, knowing what it takes in showy brains, aggressive moves, occasional strategic retreats (*reculer pour mieux sauter*), and sheer focus on what he wants.

*     *     *     *     *

Carey has always known what he wants. At nineteen, he wants to be a dancer. He sees real men on the stage, beautiful, muscular and powerful; they leap, turn in the air, take more space than other men. He is in college then, near San Francisco, a good place to start. A lady-led troupe of modern dancers is so grateful for his strength they name him "the elevator" for his secure lifts. He acquires technique as he performs. The lady, Anna, sees to that. She supplements daily classes for the troupe with private lessons for him alone.

His *image* carries them as well: he uses a depilatory for his chest, exposing its beaming muscularity for dance fans, male and female. The audience swells with his pectorals. His father understands. Carey is in his body like few others. It is a sure way into his mind, and when the body's pleasures are fully explored, he has a fallback position. His father assures him there is enough money to give him time. He can finish college at twenty-nine instead of twenty-two, smart and healthy and with good habits. Dancing is beautiful and fulfilling, but Carey need not cling to it. He can take dance classes forever for sheer love of movement.

*     *     *     *     *

His next love is the elaboration of biochemistry, an elegance of long C-connected molecules, with shapely crowds of S- and N- , H- and O- groups affixed to make them work. In the course of finishing his coursework, he idles with a young woman, pretty, easy to take, not so easy to leave. Her parents have named her Muguet; he loves her name. She loves him, and makes a pitch.

"You are almost thirty, exposed all this time to women you wanted; women who wanted you, both. You will never love anyone as you love me. I am your woman for life, for marriage, for children, for now and forever. We can grow together, grow old together, play together. There is nothing to separate us. We have interests in books, science, skiing and nature. What else is there?" He is surprised that she is thinking so far into the future; she is a hydrologist, interested in ebb and flow.

Daunted, he can think of no reason to say "no," and to say "maybe" or "let's wait a while" feels indecisive, not strong. He agrees, "We do get along. It is better to have children when we are young. We will have a good life together." They are married at an expensive, formal wedding held at her father's friend's hotel in Palo Alto. Her parents are happy for her choice. They will have beautiful, smart children. The wedding is timed for a Christmas holiday trip to Rio and a week on the beach. From there, he sends a scrawled picture postcard to the leader of his former dance troupe: "Dear Anna: The spirit of dance moves here. As you know, Muguet and are finally wed. Will return in January for exams and more." Alarmed at the absence of the "I" in his coupling, Anna awaits developments.

*　　*　　*　　*　　*

The data are encouraging. He is grateful to the researchers at Harvard for the proofs that gene insertion in experimental mice creates more of the protein that enhances long-term learning and memory. This is expensive work, but it is important to know that aging does not necessarily result in intellectual deficits; that the learning channels can learn to stay open longer with the right stimulus. He calls the team leader at Harvard, "The results are unequivocal. Just what I needed. I'm getting a little flak here about budgets..."

The woman sounds alarmed. "It doesn't mean our funding for next year..."

"No. Don't worry," he soothes. "The budget is my responsibility."

End-of-the-fiscal-year data at Rockefeller University, too, are more than promising. Tomatoes and cucumbers, garlic and other vegetables have potent anti-aging properties, almost specific for some disorders. No gene modifications — just vegetables. Carey calls the technical advisor to the House Appropriations Committee. "Do you want to have lunch on Tuesday? We have some very promising results in from Harvard and Rockefeller University, besides our own clinical studies that are providing benchmarks for larger populations, especially minorities. That should be very popular... The labs are all counting on increased funding for next year and what we'd really like..."

"Don't tell me, please, " Dr. Hagerty says. "NIH, NASA, the Energy Department are all exploding with promising research, and as far as any of you is concerned, it's all too important to let slip. But I've been hearing rumors..."

"Absolutely not," Carey says firmly. "We are remaining within our budget. I just wanted to talk about the proposals for grants and where they're taking us... You're so good at this, your committee knows they can trust your judgment..." When did he start this blatant flattery?

\*        \*        \*        \*        \*

*Physiological chemistry.* The tall, slim Irish post-doc lady refers them to the latest edition of Hawks and Oser, which she herself does not need. She sprays her huge molecules on the chalkboard as gracefully as from a patterned vaporizer, but of course, they are from her head. Carey admires her greatly, wonders if he can visit her in her office, if her office has a sofa. He is interested in the piney scent of the young post-doc. In fact, Muguet who always wears muguet, a cloyingly sweet scent, as if she were duty-bound, is getting on his nerves.

"Darling," she opens, as soon as he comes in. ("Me?" he thinks.) "If you help me with the laundry, we can run up to bed earlier..." she smiles invitingly. They are living in a tiny married student duplex apartment in a eucalyptus grove. He is tired of the smell of eucalyptus, too.

"I can't. I have some oxidative pathways to explore before an exam tomorrow."

"You'll ace it," she says reassuringly. "Then we can go to Tahoe for the weekend..."

"I promised a long stint in the lab on Saturday. They're paying me to work up the results on the dog nutrition grant."

"All you do is work," she pouts. "We can get our work done and still enjoy life." He flinches. Was she always so boring? How had he not noticed?

Anna calls. "I thought I should give you a month to settle in after Rio. How's it going?"

"Pretty good," he says heartily. "We're into a new semester, and the work I'm doing is opening new pathways for me. It's not exactly the chemistry, I discover, it's the body. The body does the chemistry." He smiles to the phone, "Of course, the chemistry does the body, too." She always gets it.

"Carey, you have a passion for paradox. That's why you had that 'mystery' on stage. I wish you were still with us. Garcia is too small to catch a daring leap without staggering a bit. And I'm considering modifying my roles. I'm losing the elasticity in my calves and ankles."

That is interesting. Is she losing anything else? Muguet is listening; he cannot ask. Three months later he tells Muguet they cannot grow old together. He is leaving for Harvard, alone. Nevada is an easy trip for her during the summer, allowing her to explore the hydrology of the desert area during a six-week wait. In fact, she even publishes a paper on her observations, and her photos and drawings make a short piece for Natural History, signed with her maiden name.

*     *     *     *     *

Anna's troupe is performing in an auditorium in Cambridge, part of a series of avant-garde arts presentations to enrich academic life. They never came east when he was dancing — only up and down the coast to Portland and Seattle, to San Diego, and only as far inland, once, to Chicago. He is in the east now, and will stay. It has, as the French say, a different mentality.

Anna. She is only a few years older than he. He goes to the performance alone to lose no nuance. They are his old associates and he is moved to see them. Is he homesick, he wonders. No. His *old* associates. There are minute changes in their bodies, in the risks they take. The new choreography turns to story-telling. The dancers, from reveling in their power to do abstract work, now use their mature expressiveness to deepen audience encounters. And Anna. She says the ankles are the first to go. She saw it in Martha, she sees it in Merce. He does not see it, he tells her afterward in the dressing room, a hug allowed because it is a visit. Dancers sweat like horses; he likes the smell, fresh and pungent. "Let me take you out for pizza and ..." he says.

"You've forgotten," she says. "No pizza. We are never lean enough."

*     *     *     *     *

WHO's motherly specialist in aging is visiting from Rome. He knows she is not important. Only in a few countries do the aging have health clout. In others, it is assumed they will sicken and die, some later than others. But this pudgy old girl knows the demographics and is trying to alert the World Health Organization's powers to the next step – healthy old age. She wants his news. She wants him to lend his prestige to her quest for funds. Her work is at the beginning. The first task is to establish population benchmarks in many parts of the world. She has a few now. "There are amazing numbers all over the world," she says. "Life expectancy in India is ten years longer than it was thirty years ago. It is forty years longer than it was a hundred years ago." He is surprised. "In Mexico," she continues...

"Here, too," he agrees. He takes her to lunch at Jockey Club, intent on showing her she is important, to him. He values her respect, her need for him; he is pleased with his own power to do things for her.

He wants to help, has helped her in the past; but now he must be careful not to raise her expectations too high. "No one wants to spend money to build more labs, more experimental facilities. We thought the demographic argument would do it," he says. The lump crabmeat cocktail is delicious, as always. "Mayer was an expert lobbyist for new facilities, first a veterinary lab and then another for nutrition research at Tufts. He went directly to the congressmen with his elegant French accent... Everyone learned from him — Boston, Columbia, Northwestern, Catholic University, New Hampshire. But they hire lobbyists and get their appropriations — some of them ridiculous. Congress is flooded now with supportable research requests. They bypass us and our considered priorities. Whoever gets to them first — or last... We know so much more now about genes and metabolism, but I can't get a nickel for new facilities. They do not understand long-term research, and that some ideas come to dead ends..."

She nods sympathetically. "You've done so much for us."
She is Norwegian. Her face is unlined, but he knows she is
a grandmother. Good genes, he thinks. "Can I do anything
for you?"

"Maybe," he says. "Will you be here next week, Tuesday?
I will deliver my year-end report to the subcommittee and
you can echo what I say — that the U.S. is in the forefront
of such research and that its prestige and its products go out
worldwide, and wisdom and maturity ..."

She smiles. "I will do better. I have prepared a slide
presentation on productive aging in China and Japan. The
world has need of so much work, and even in Africa, a territory of the young, the aging are needed to help bring up the
children whose parents are dead or dying of AIDS..."

He nods. "We do not have a crisis to offer like the breast
or prostate cancer people or the AIDS researchers, but in the
long run, healthy, productive older people balance a good
society. We are beginning to have so much time between the
beginning of aging and its inevitable end. Can it be be put to
use in creativity, self-development, insights...? No one talks
about how society can leap forward if the aging feel good."

She grins, her blue eyes sparkling, pink cheeks round with
energy. "What a good idea! But we have some immediate
problems. We are being prodded from Glasgow — they want
you to update the recommended daily allowances, RDA..."

"That's not my role..."

"I know, but you must do it — for lifelong health. Those
old numbers were to prevent deficiency diseases." She speaks
English like Liv Ullmann, he thinks. "There is so much more
to being healthy. It is easy — more whole foods, fruits and
vegetables — and anyhow, more, much more vitamin C, vitamin E... They must go into the new recommendations."

"It's such a time-consuming, bureaucratic problem...
Those numbers are not in my budget. They are the National

Academy's..."

"We will tell them Tuesday," she says, confidently. He hasn't the heart to tell her those are the ghosts of Christmas past. He needs facilities for gene research, PCR, support for clinical work with the very old, muscle and brain research, coordination of mitochondrial DNA research in human beings... Can he pull it off? The labs are depending on him against a recurrent wave of anti-scientific lobbying by "greens", "goo-goos," and politicians who think of themselves as populists.

\*     \*     \*     \*     \*

It's medical school, after all. Harvard. He's a biochemistry whiz with a rare, intuitive sense of the body. He "gets" its intricacies, its connections of bone-muscles-hormones-neurons and systems and processes as easily as he gets a joke. He works joyfully.

There is a new girl, a cool girl, agreeable, but not fawning. He sees in her a calm competence, an acceptance of the world as it is. Jenny is a sculptor in residence at MIT. She teaches and works with her hands. They are companionable on walks and in bed. She shows him a new piece, kinetic, two hard plastic heads, cam-operated and timed to crash together at the forehead and then part. "What is it?" he asks.

"Us, eventually, but not soon."

"Never." He knows too much to let that happen. His power is dawning on him. She is a girl, accepting of life, nurturing, an artist. She will be a companion, a wife, a mother and do her work wherever he has to go.

He is offered residencies in Baltimore, New York, San Diego and St. Louis, all good hospitals, all with interesting aging communities nearby. He has made up his mind before he asks Jenny what she thinks about where to go; he thinks it is improbable her choice will be different from his. Yes, she agrees. The hospital is in New York, and they arrive to find that it is in Brooklyn in a neighborhood that is a mix of old Jewish and Italian populations, drab one- and two-family brick houses, poor transportation and wretched shopping.

"It's only a year or two," he says. "Not a problem, right?"

She nods. "I've looked in the papers. I can find a studio to share near the Bridge. Old industrial buildings are being recycled into artists' spaces."

He is not worried. His career is the main thing, they both know. She is sending resumes to art schools and universities, but is not even called for an interview or an examination of her portfolio. The only offer, finally, is from Pace College, a déclassé business school with a tiny, unknown art department. But she crows, "I'm right here in the center of the art world. I can see everything."

He has complaints, many, about his colleagues, the department, the hospital's aging facilities, his supervisor. He wants to be on his way. Jenny looks at work by Caro, Serra, Smith, Bourgeois. She gets a two-week summer internship in a barn in Dutchess County, working with artists from Canada and South Africa in big, gloomy spaces that smell of cut hay but do not even have fans against the summer swelter. She shows in a coop gallery on Atlantic Avenue, patiently serving her time there with a book on her lap.

*       *       *       *       *

There is nothing to smile at in the lean, tight face in the mirror. Carey has been hungry for a long time. Even now, there is always a little growl and gas to let him know how unnatural it is — thirty percent fewer calories — the magical horror story of geriatrics, of staying young. The first work was done on rats in the '30s, but research on monkeys, dogs and human beings confirmed it. Heavy exercise and a low-calorie, high-nutrition diet prolong youth and sexual activity, and may even increase mental acuity. He is his own best exemplar.

He tells his grim face, "I am not really hungry. It's just a periodic stomach contraction, as regular as a cuckoo clock." But since his move to Sarasota, there is a new pain in his gut. This emptiness will not be filled by food, and it is not only in his belly. It pervades his psyche. The mirror's aging man is suffering.

Sarasota is where the wealthy elderly buy property and stay to live, in the arts-and-culture enclave of the geriatric elite. He can swim in the Gulf, take classes in a local dance studio. He can run all year, with no possibility of ice or snow. He grimaces at the prospect of treating aging Rabbits, but it may be the best place in the country for him; he is needed and wanted.

Florida was an easy choice: Long ago, as a resident in Brooklyn, Carey shared meals and complaints with an incipient cardiologist. Medical meetings, a bicycle trip up the west coast, and occasional textbook consulting have kept them in touch. A single phone call to the cardiologist elicits an offer to join a lucrative group practice, a career move for the downhill slope to retirement. The group combines, as well, an oncologist, a neurologist, and an orthopedist. He is the generalist, a specialist in geriatrics, better late than sooner, a practicing doctor.

He is making all the right moves, as always. He has found a house, a mid-priced one with four bedrooms and an acutely empty, big-family kitchen. He eats his solitary meals in restaurants, following the rules: low fat, high fiber, plenty of fish and vegetables. But if there is anything he wants, it is to eat, even grossly, in the kitchen with Jenny and the kids joshing and horsing around at the roomy, round table. It will not happen any time soon. He is alone, trying not to imagine an empty future without family, without a career "next step", without love.

He is lying naked on the floor of a stage in a harsh over-head light, flattened by circumstance. He picks himself up, looking for cues from scenery, other dancers, music... there is nothing. It is up to him to improvise... to find new music... a costume... paint the backdrop... retrieve his company... go on...

Sarasota has a museum, an opera, a winter Philharmonic, a modest film festival, culture. They are his best talking points, he thinks. Schools? Jenny will ask. Florida's aging population does not support good private or, indeed, very good public schools. He must wait.

*     *     *     *     *

He and Jenny are ready to leave Brooklyn. She has packed their clothes and books, her new welded pieces and a few painted plaster figures of desolation that she cares about. "You're so good at that. I love watching your hands wrap-ping the bubble wrap, tying the ends up, insulating the pieces so that they will survive even a rutted road." He means it. Not everyone has good hands.

She smiles wanly, tired. She has found the boxes, bought the wrapping and the tape, labeled everything so there will be no searching. This is the second time. She has made the arrangements for another dinky apartment for the new job in Cincinnati.

"This one's for you," he says, knowing better. "It's the prettiest city in Ohio, on beautiful bluffs over a river, just across from Kentucky. You will love it."

"It's the middle west. I won't love it. No one will understand what I am doing. You are moving along..."

"It's just a couple of years again; then..."

"California, right. We'll be back where you started, where your old friends are, where you went to school, where you will find a hospital hospitable to your kind of research. I am happy for you."

"It's not like you to talk like that."

"No, it isn't. I'm feeling like a gypsy. My work is suffering." She waves at the packaged art all around them. "I'm doing kinetic sculpture captured by your medical work. It's interesting, and I'm beginning to think it may be a kind of multi-dimensional equivalent to Terry Winters' painting..."

He nods, sympathetically. "That's great. I love his work, all those beautiful life forms recreated. And I love yours, too. We'll settle in a few years, and you'll have been growing steadily in the meantime. I know you..." His arm is around her and she smiles, gratefully. He knows somewhere he is manipulative as hell, but he has to be.

They are going to take the risk, now, relying on his father to supplement the residents' pittance. He wants a family, and they have made a ceremonial occasion of his taking a week off before the timed moment to be sure he is well-rested, and she, too, at optimal readiness. Of course, it works. He rules chance and diet; there is no wine, little fat, plenty of veggies and fiber, calcium tablets and vitamins. Jenny is the picture of health, until her hormones misunderstand where this pregnancy stands, and she is in premature labor, delivering a two-pound baby in the emergency section of the unfavorably viewed local black neighborhood hospital. The baby and Jenny are transferred to a hospital with better facilities for preemies, and then there is the grueling two-month wait while the baby is tested and tested again, patched with sensors, fit with extra light, weighed and measured, cuddled and gazed at anxiously. She finally reaches five pounds, and they deem her ready to go home to a hovering, anxious Jenny, who cannot work for worry. He sees her looking at him quietly, not blaming him, but yes, betrayed by her body, betrayed by his sureness, betrayed into pain and fear. He knows it will take a while.

He is busy on muscle research on older people, has been working on a grant. The hospital has recruited elderly men who need the money to allow snippets to be taken from then-working thigh muscles. It is the most minor surgery, healed in a week or two, after neat stitching. He is co-author of the paper, telling the world that old muscle does rebuild, that the slow contracting muscle fibers grow with exercise. The problem is that fast-contracting fibers do not rebuild, just keep disappearing as the body ages. Is this why older people are unsteady on their feet? This, rather than the proprioceptor system? Follow-on research will tell, or begin to tell. The paper is heavily cited in others' research. He is called to speak at a Cleveland medical school.

"Anna. I just had to call you about this. We don't know when it starts — we have to do some longitudinal research — but we have these old guys pedaling bikes in the exercise lab and I'm delivering a paper about how aging muscles rebuild but only with slow-contracting fibers..."

"Carey. You're a valuable man." Her voice is warm, as always. "How are things with Jenny and Jody? Are you still taking classes?"

"Yes, with a slim, aging, black lady, named Diane. I love her work. Full of dance-stories and feeling, and with jazz music. We work in a community center, and once in a while, if she needs me, I do a little." He means performance, and wants to be modest.

Anna doesn't ask again about Jenny and Jody. "You'll

send me a copy of your paper? We need this kind of information."

While they are in Cincinnati, they take day trips in the little Ford they can afford to Indian mounds, to Mammoth Cave, to the first fortified town of early settlers in Ohio. There is more than either of them had thought, and true to form, Jenny's sculpture picks up the look of the cave lit by torches, the feel of an underground cavern carved by eons of water, sculpted mineral deposits. It is very strong stuff and she knows it. The Whitney invites her to enter a piece in the biennial.

\*       \*       \*       \*       \*

He was worried about being bored by an ordinary geriatric practice, dealing with people of failing senses, muscles, minds, putting them through the routine tests, checking out their bone density and colons, looking at sagging, lumpy flesh. But no. The population in Sarasota is surprisingly salty and smart; even, he discovers, cute. They fool with their computers, enjoy vivid sexual encounters, swim, bike, hike, run off to Elderhostels and group trips to Africa or Turkmenistan that they are pleased to discover are not as groupy and dull as they were afraid they might be. And most of them are extremely well, visiting only once or twice a year for routine maintenance on almost the same schedule as their cars are taken in for service. He would love to tell Jenny... But Jenny is not listening, will not listen.

He plots his next visit to Washington, actually to northern Virginia, with the care that he once gave to testimony before a Congressional appropriations committee. He will wear comfortable chinos and a tweed jacket from Burberry, a cashmere crewneck over the pinpoint oxford shirt that is designed to be left unbuttoned, and rubbersoled moccasins that will squeak slightly on the waxed floors of the old house. He will invite Jenny and the three kids to Williamsburg for the day and they will eat dinner by candlelight... He will talk about finding rare shells on the beaches of Sanibel; and the Frank Lloyd Wright architecture of a local college. There is a lot to learn and know in Florida.

*     *     *     *     *

It is moving time again. They are heading, as he anticipated, to California where he has a grant to study movement again. There is a new theory to play with, that aging is a failure of maintenance; when it goes too far, it results in "disease." That where the problems arise is not so much in the nuclear DNA but in the mitochondrial DNA that has less "junk" for unscheduled breakdown and is damaged more readily. That maybe "inflammation" as a process is causing everything from Alzheimer's and Parkinson's to losses of structure and function at the neuromuscular junction.

Of course California is wine country and what the growers want is research to prove red wine's benefits in reducing chromosomal damage. He does not want to be labeled an academic whore like Frederick Stare whose results were always what the guys who were paying wanted. There is a real problem in designing the study and authoring the results. But it's California, hundreds of miles, not thousands, from home! He has an appointment in San Diego where the Navy's healthy, handsome retirees are more than willing to participate in longitudinal studies.

Another baby, this time a boy, full-term, eight and a half

pounds, big from the start, unlike Jody who is still a peanut at three. This one was easy and Jenny's response to Alex is relaxed and doting. She is still thin and pliant, a figure he admires. And now her work is shifting again; embarking, in a way as his is, to dynamic studies of movement; he with the aging, and she in encounters between the young and the very young. She is working in clay, the quickest medium for evanescent attitudes, doing studies of her own unself-conscious children, preparing ultimately for bronze "encounters," and considering acrylic alternatives. The Los Angeles museum buys an acrylic piece, two kids caught between familiarity and the mystery of the other's being.

His research is important, important to him. His lab cohort marvels at his discipline as he reduces his calorie intake to the level of discomfort. He suggests it to Jenny, too, but she says, "Not now. I need all my energy for the kids and my work. You can do as you please, but I have other things to think about." His choices for dinner are respected, and he has no complaints.

Exercise. He runs early in the morning, even participates in a marathon or two taking the unnatural punishment on knees and ankles as a way of assessing for himself the damage on joints of a lifetime of overuse. But really, he has to visit Anna. Word about arthritic hips in early modem dance pioneers suggests new research. Jane Dudley has had two hip surgeries; Sophie Maslow walks with a cane. Does anyone escape? Anna will know. It is a weekend trip to San Francisco, and a dinner out on Fisherman's Wharf. They order, she Pacific salmon, and he vegetable soup, crayfish, rice, salad. She says, "Let's get a bottle of chardonnay to celebrate this reunion."

"No way. It's too much wine. Too many calories, too much alcohol," he says. "We can have a glass each."

She makes a face, and he sees it is becoming habitual. The fine lines near her mouth and eyes are trained to go that way. "I like wine with dinner. It's good for you," she is being defensive. "Anyway, I'll pay half the bill, so don't worry about the expense..."

He frowns. "One glass each. That's all." She does not argue, not wanting to spoil their visit. Susanne Farrell has had a hip replacement, too, she tells him. But not Maya Plisetskaya, who can still perform daringly. So it's not ballet vs. modem dance. It's not female vs. male. Is it in the training? Is there less damage with Cecchetti than with other ballet training? It was clear a long time ago that strength in the hips and thighs was greater for ballet dancers than for football players. They talk bodies and dance, endlessly interesting. Anna says, "After next year, I will stop performing, stick to choreography. I don't want to be remembered as a heroic old mess." He laughs; that will never happen.

Anna does not talk about her husband, the investment banker, who has made it possible for her troupe to tour, to train, to achieve longevity in the dance world. Carey does not talk about Jenny or Jody or little Alex. He is more interested in weight training and longevity and in increasing flexibility and yoga. She confirms that dancers are doing yoga and even incorporating yoga positions into choreography.

He kisses Anna goodnight. She still looks beautiful to him, but he sees no sign that she will collaborate in bonding their long friendship and affection with a night in a hotel. She knows what he is thinking. "We'll be better friends for not."

*       *       *       *       *

Before Carey leaves San Diego he publishes more results:

about the correlation of memory with motor deficits, and about the possibility that lots of vitamin E, strawberries, spinach and blueberries can even reverse or retard development of Parkinson's and Alzheimer's; that exercise, aerobic exercise, increases brain fitness. He is appointed head of geriatrics at Michael Reese in Chicago. Jenny is troubled, "I know it's a plum. But the climate is so terrible — I hate cold and wind."

"Just a few years. We'll find a beautiful house in Glencoe. The schools there are about the best in the country. For Jody and Alex... and we'll find a great nursery school for Nora. And you can work full-time; Chicago loves sculpture. Look at the Dubuffet and Picasso in the public areas. Look at their support of wonderful architecture. There are very good galleries, the really big annual art fair. It's your place." He is not lying, but he is, he knows, presenting great reasons for doing what he wants.

Jenny says, "Not till summer. The kids will finish their school year here."

He's won. He can be generous about timing,

\*     \*     \*     \*     \*

The kids are glad to see him. Jenny has kept him alive for them with photos, clippings, little stories. He is grateful for that consideration. It has been a couple of months since his last visit, and this time he has proposed a ride to the Catoctin Mountains, and a hike through the woods with a healthy gourmet picnic lunch he has packed himself. He is wooing them with everything he can think of, wooing the kids with interest and love, wooing Jenny with respect, consideration and even more love. He kisses her "hello", kisses and hugs her as often as he dares, knowing somewhere that one misstep will condemn him for life.

Jenny asks, "How is your practice coming?"

He smiles. "I love it. I love the one-on-one dealing with individuals. I'm making as much money as before — but you know that, don't you? — and I do not report to anyone but the IRS. I have time for dance classes again, twice a week, a terrific ballet bar and a modem floor work and exercise class, really the best. Keeps your mind at work, and it is the best body conditioning with a good teacher..."

"And if not?" she asks.

He nods. "Then you hurt yourself. But there is always that potential — either in the body you came with, a moment of inattention, or an inadequate warmup. You can do big damage. But it's so good for you, new neurons, new muscle fibers, better balance, you have to take a few risks. We all do while we live."

She nods. "Taking risks. Yes. Doing what we think is right."

He knows what she means, and changes the subject. "How is your work coming?" It's been a long time since he asked.

"You know some of the federal building contracts allocate a portion of the money to art. I'm getting some commissions — sculpture in front of court houses, federal office buildings. Big projects. I love big projects."

"What are you working in?"

"Stone. It's the hardest. You make a mistake and ..."

"It takes courage. You have it." She hears the conciliatory, respectful note, and acknowledges it with a smile. He is getting somewhere.

*     *     *     *     *

In Chicago, they experience a terrible winter and spring: snow, subzero cold blowing in from the Arctic, a chill that brings freezing temperatures into the end of May. Carey insists that the thermostat in Glencoe remain at 60 degrees even when they are home. "It is healthier to be chilly. Your body adjusts and you get fewer colds, fewer cases of flu." Jenny wears thermal underwear everywhere, even in bed. The kids wear thermals to their well-heated schools and are told they stink of sweat by their classmates. They come home to complain. Jenny takes their part and there are some terrific fights, ending with Carey's imposition of his will on them all, "I'm the doctor. Everything I do is for your health, your immune systems, your longevity: careful eating, plenty of exercise, hard work. You'll see that it will pay off in a long productive life."

Alex screams, "You're a tyrant!"

Carey says equably. "That's true. But it's my house and I pay the bills." Nobody argues about that.

$$* \quad * \quad * \quad * \quad *$$

He is summoned to a meeting with the Secretary of the Department of Health and Human Services and the Director of NIH, and assumes it is a budget meeting for the next fiscal year. A budget that will wrap up body-mind research for the aging. He is even including some work on biofeedback for blood pressure research at the Bird S. Coler Hospital in New York and experiments with controversial drugs like MDMA for depression in the aging. He thinks they will show how much using your mind prevents losing your health and that consciousness is the new frontier.

The Secretary is a woman, not much respected, but a

good politician; she came from the presidency of a multi-culti university. The director is himself a researcher and former president of the National Academy of Sciences, a good man. "Carey, we have something important to talk about." It's the Secretary.

"You've been doing an amazing job, opening one frontier after another in the years you've directed the Institute on Aging. We've looked over your new budget, and again, you're going beyond the ordinary. There is no question about it. WHO gives you high marks for cooperation and for advancing an important agenda world-wide."

"But," it is his boss, the director, "we've been making up out of contingency funds the really gross excesses in your spending. You've been way over budget year after year, and we've warned you over and over. You just do as you please. Well that ends now. We are asking you to resign, effective immediately."

He is motionless, unprepared. "You just said... groundbreaking, new paths, important..."

"Your deputy will recalculate the budget; we'll exclude... you know. We've spoken to him and until we have a new appointment, he'll be acting director. The press release will say, 'resignation for personal reasons'..."

"No! That's as good as saying I was fired!" He has finally found his voice, and is raging.

"Well then what?" The Secretary wants no public sign of internal dissent.

"Say I'm resigning because the Congress and the Department do not understand the importance of real research into aging, that we live half our lives now after middle age and that we want them to be good lives, and that our research points the way..."

"You're a little crazy," his boss says mildly. "There are more urgent problems..."

"No, there aren't."

"Carey, we'll put out what we want to put out about your resignation. Right now, we want you to empty your desk, leave your files here and leave them alone, and exit. We're notifying Security that you're out."

He is out two hours later, with Security to help him pack and his face a cold mask until he is alone in his station wagon. He is on the road before he begins to weep and scream. But, it is an hour's drive across the Potomac into Virginia and by the time he arrives home at four o'clock, he is composed.

He is at the kitchen table, drinking a cup of green tea and eating a small portion of frozen yogurt when Jenny arrives with Jody, now in high school, and Alex and Nora both in grade school.

"You're home early." She is not asking a question.

"I've resigned. It's time for me to set up a practice in Florida, and I've called Steve in Sarasota. He's in a small group of practicing gerontologists, specialists each in their own fields, and they need me. We'll be moving in a few weeks, as soon as I find an apartment or a house and we can arrange to have this one sold."

"No."

"What do you mean 'no?'"

"What I said. We are not moving. You can go wherever you like. We are staying here. This house is not for sale."

"You're my family, you have to come with me. I can't stay here."

He is staring at her as if he has not looked at her lately. Indeed, he has not. Her face is not angry, not contorted with rage or violence, the same face, with a few ordinary lines around the mouth and nose, the faint lines that pull the brows together and crease the forehead. She is still slim, still wearing her suburban jeans and Lands' End turtleneck, sturdy hiking boots to protect her feet when she goes into the studio... What is she thinking? He has not ever asked, comfortable with her calm assumption of responsibility, tidy housekeeping and childraising, choices of schools, furniture, guests...

"This is the moment, Carey. Remember the two crashing heads?... 'Us, but not soon.' Us, now."

"How will you live? Why are you doing this?" His anguish is only now being felt, only now coming to him. He is amazed at the pain. He wants to walk away before it shows, but cannot while he can possibly change what seems to be a sudden, lunatic response to what should be a settled circumstance. "We have to move. I can't stay here." He is repeating himself.

"We don't have to move. It's early in the school year. Nora and Alex and Jody are happy in school. It's too hard for them to transfer. I love this house and my studio; I have a gallery in Washington that sells my work, and I'm negotiating for representation by a good gallery in Seattle. There's a dealer in Soho who is interested in putting on a one-woman show and I have a lot of work to do during the next few months. No. We are not moving. We are getting on with our lives, and you can get on with yours – wherever it is."

"Well, you can stay till the end of the school year, and by that time I'll have a comfortable house for us, and" — inspiration strikes — "we can get a vacation place on Sanibel or share with Steve and his family... and we'll have much more time together. We can take family vacations... to Alaska and Banff, to Europe. Wouldn't you like to go to Italy? I'll have more time, working in a private practice, my own boss..."

"You have always been your own boss..." she does not say "and our boss, too." But he hears it.

"No. We are separating, Carey." The kids look surprised. This has been very sudden. "Dad and I have a lot to talk about now, and I wonder if you three would mind getting on with your homework. You can take your snacks upstairs if you want to." They hear her and because she is always reasonable, even he admits, do as she asks. Jenny puts a container of milk on a tray and a box of cookies, and they thump up the stairs.

"Did you know this was happening?" he asks incredulously.

"How could I? No. It is just that I knew the next time we had to move, I would not. I have done my best. I can't do any more."

"Is this permanent? Do you really want to end the marriage? I love you and the kids. I need you to be with me. It is too hard to go to a new place, start over without you..."

"You did not ask me about resigning. It is not my problem. You will keep up the payments for the house, for the schools, for us to live. We are not poor and I do not want our separation to create poverty..."

"It's only a civil service job; not a high flying private practice..."

"No doctor is starving. We have money stashed here and there; you have money in bonds and mutual funds. And you'll make enough. I am not worried. And I make some."

"I don't want this to happen to us. What am I going to do?"

"Whatever you think is right," she says firmly. "I trust you to do that."

He has not told her the unbearable truth. Perhaps if he had, this second unbearable thing would not have happened. He cannot, yet. If he told her now it would be a bid for family solidarity motivated by pity. No. He cannot.

\*　　\*　　\*　　\*　　\*

His father is not surprised. "Carey, you've always done

what you wanted to do. You've been so lucky in Jenny. In the long run, if you work at it, I think it will be all right. But you must work at it. It'll be hard. But, if you need..."

He shakes his head. "I don't really need money, Dad. I..." He is weeping again, and his father says, "It's all right. Go ahead."

\*       \*       \*       \*       \*

"Anna, what are you working on? I'm here for a week's holiday before starting a new practice in Sarasota. I've left the Washington job and..."

"Carey," he can hear the delight in her voice. "I was looking forward to seeing you when we toured to the East Coast in a couple of months. I even set up a night in Columbia and another in Richmond so we'd be sure... Why don't you come for the rehearsal today, and then we can have dinner in the studio together. I'll order in some Chinese..."

Anna's new piece is jarring. It is about the death of responsibility, people who do not care, about work, family, obligations. A mosaic of theatrical, story-telling episodes, united only by the indifferent shrugs that mark their climaxes. He is shocked. "How are you going to end this? Will something happen to unify them in caring?"

"I haven't decided yet," she admits. "I think I want the dancers to decide."

"You haven't usually left it to them... maybe a little individual movement, but not the real thing..." he is puzzled. "Why?"

"I think I want their collaboration. I'm not the boss; in a way, the leader is the follower."

He watches the dancing, and wishes he could join them,

but he is not part of it. He is not part of anything.

They're on the hot and sour soup, one of his favorites, when he says, "I was looking forward to seeing you. I'm having a bad time, weeping all the time. Do you think I'm going mad? It's a kind of emotional collapse. I guess I'm old enough for a mid-life crisis, but I never thought..." There is a pause.

"Carey. What happened?"

He tells her (a) and (b), two terrible events in one day.

"Well, of course you're weeping. We weep when we mourn. You have something awful to mourn."

"But why am I crying all the time, all the time...?"

"You're mourning the uncaring Carey, the self that was: The man of power who always won; whose every dance was a victory dance. You're mourning the man who controlled the action, at work and at home. He's gone. You will have to learn a new program, a new technique, new steps, a whole new repertory of roles." He squeezes her hand.

"Thank you."

"What are you going to do?"

"What I have to. I want them back. I will do what I must do: I will woo Jenny, woo the kids, make it their decision that we are happy together, and make sure they never regret it. I can do that."

* * * * *

It takes three years. Jody goes off to college to William and Mary. The others are happy in Sarasota. And Jenny: He is glad he is in a real practice when they need his colleague, the oncologist, for a frightening lump. During those weeks, the pendulum swings back — but only partway. He knows now that there will probably be a few more oscillations, each through a smaller arc, before it comes to a complete halt.

End

# TRUST

"I want you to go with me to Pittsburgh on the twenty-third. A guy there has a piece of equipment we may be interested in. If you think it's good, we'll buy it." The speaker was John Warden, president of the food equipment division of a company that also made machinery used in printing, sports, textiles, and autos in a bunch of low-tech factories it had accumulated in the past twenty years. He was way east in Rhode Island, and telling me he'd drive to New York, meet me at La Guardia and we'd take a plane from there. I marveled at his confidence. He was saying he'd make a major investment if I said to do it. But then, I thought, he trusts me because we have worked together for a long time and he knows I am knowledgeable, honest and discreet.

We were booked on a 9 am flight for an all-day visit to Pittsburgh, leaving there at five in the afternoon and returning to LaG at about seven. Some of these ambitious executives push themselves very hard. He might even have planned to drive back to Rhode Island that night.

John did not tell me more on the plane. He talked, instead, about the bakery section's new semi-continuous line for mixing bread doughs, panning them and pushing them through a slow ride in a proofer before baking. What did I

265

think, he asked.

"Sounds good to me," I said. "Continuous processing is always more efficient than batch. But sometimes you sacrifice quality. The mixing and temperature controls have to be very good or there'll be holes in the bread."

He nodded. "Thanks. I'll discuss that with the engineering group. Now, we need to extend the line of Moverators beyond school cafeterias and hospital meal-assembly lines. Any ideas?" He was paying for my time; he was certainly entitled to pick my brains. I suggested a transport system from central kitchens in factories and warehouses with simple recommendations for temperature- and contamination-control for foods as well as clean dishes and trays. Four months for a study and report, for a fee I knew would be acceptable.

"Any other ideas?"

"Sure." I made suggestions about other materials handling equipment that was well within their manufacturing capabilities, mostly careful old-fashioned metal-bending. It was a nice, businesslike discussion. Nothing about where we were going or why. That was all right. John Warden wanted to watch my face when we arrived. We taxied to a suburban area and walked into a small fried chicken place.

"This is it," he said deadpan.

A trim black man of medium height with a neat haircut and mustache was standing at the door in the functional whites of a counterman in a coffee shop. "Muriel Harris, this is Joseph Reynolds." I held out my hand. His was clean and dry, warm enough. Then he started talking and lost me pretty quickly. He had a southern mountain accent, not standard English, and talked so fast that while I was still puzzling over what he had said, he was several phrases ahead. And mixed with the speed and the unfamiliar accent was a memorized scientific jargon that I recognized but that I was sure had been acquired in bits and pieces for the snow jobs necessary to a black man working in a white world.

The place was pretty typical. A counter for sales fronted on a small waiting area - - a few straight-back chairs and a couple of small tables — for people picking up their boxes or buckets of fried chicken, fried potatoes and homemade cole slaw. There was a glass-front vending machine for sodas, and that was it. All white, neatly painted. Above the counter was the schedule of prices for various numbers of chicken pieces, all white meat or all dark meat or mixed pieces, buckets or boxes, and a few "sides" — potatoes, French fries, cole slaw, corn. Simplicity, itself.

But Mr. Reynolds was not much interested in his retail facility. He took us into a spacious back room, talking all the while in a jargon I was having a hard time following despite its familiarity. He waved at a big table, some frame-bound screens that seemed to be for sifting, then to some other oddly homemade-looking devices whose use I could not easily determine, and then to what I guessed was a deep-fat fryer, the likes of which I had never seen before: two deep vessels, piping, compressors... I heard "Pulse vacuum-pressure," "lower fat absorption," "health benefits," "food cell structure," "lower fatty acids," "no toxins"... What was this about?

Ah. We were going to have lunch, and eat his products. Great. I was starving. Our low-rent flight had not provided so much as a bag of pretzels. Like most women, I worry about calories, and fried chicken and French fries are not what I eat for lunch. He had set up a small dining room, with ironstone plates, stainless steel flatware, glassware, and place mats. Very thoughtful.

He excused himself for a few minutes and I looked at Warden. "What are we here for — the fryer?"

He nodded. "The guy has a different kind of equipment, invented by him and patented. He claims all sorts of benefits that could open the fried chicken and fried potato choice to people who are afraid of them. He claims fish can be fried in the same machine and the oil won't absorb any fishy odors, that he can do tempura vegetables, whole meats and fowl... I want to know what you think. Can we make the machine, and is there really an advantage to it?"

Mr. Reynolds was back with a steaming platter piled high with chicken and potatoes and a company-sized casserole of cole slaw. Everything smelled good. And he was saying, "I grew up in Kentucky in the mountains" (ah, I was beginning to get it) "and my family had a bunch of kids. Fifteen. I was the only one who got a stomach ache after every meal. All that grease made food indigestible to me... That's why I invented the PV cooker. I can eat everything it cooks. My enzymes simply float it away."

I smiled. This was not the time for asking — What was PV? What made it different? Was he engaging in inventor's hyperbole? Probably, but at this point I'd eat anything.

The meal was delicious. Nothing greasy, none of the heavy breading that falls off in large oil-soaked chunks. The cole slaw was freshly made, crisp and tart. Reynolds ate with us, as a previously invisible young man came and went to pour more water into our glasses, and, southern style, to re-fill our coffee cups during the meal. Mr. Reynolds continued with his incongruous discussion of free fatty acids, of mercury and other minerals in fish magically reduced, of PCBs, of lab reports that agreed his process eliminated heavy metals and pesticides from food cooked with it, and purged them from any possible contamination of the cooking oil. This all sounded like specious nonsense to me.

"When we've finished, could you show me the lab reports, Mr. Reynolds," I inquired.

Warden tried to help me. "Muriel is a world-class consultant. I brought her here to help us evaluate the PV machine. You can trust her."

Reynolds returned with a sheaf of papers in his hand. "There," he said proudly, "you can see right here how pesticides and heavy metals are eliminated, how the fatty acid content is reduced... ”

I was appalled. The lab reports were on the letterhead of a local testing laboratory. And they did have numbers, about tests of salmon, swordfish and tuna fish for mercury and bacteria. But some of the results showed more mercury after cooking than before (obviously the samples had shrunk), and the only conclusive data were that bacteria were reduced by cooking. But they always are.

I fumbled for words, embarrassed to be the bearer of harsh truth. "Mr. Reynolds, these are not good lab reports. A proper lab report tells you about the samples and their size, how the tests were done in detail, then the results, and offers a conclusion or suggests further testing. These little number lists don't do any of that. I can't really tell what was done, how or why, or what the numbers mean."

My distress must have shown in my face.

John Warden broke in. "Do you have other test results?"

Plenty. All terrible. Mr. Reynolds was being taken advantage of, paying for laboratory work that was unscientific and useless. I felt ashamed that I was part of a white society that would do this. Mr. Reynolds was still not sure what I was driving at.

"But you see," he said, "the lab tested earlier for chlorinated hydrocarbon chlorine and found that my process eliminated it."

"Chlorinated hydrocarbons — pesticides?" I asked. "Where is that?" He could not find the lab reports.

"I'm sorry, Mr. Reynolds. The food was very good. But you must find better labs that do an ethical job. These people are taking advantage of you."

"Could you give me your card, Ms. Harris. If Mr. Warden trusts you, so do I."

We spent the rest of the afternoon looking at the patents and ongoing applications for refinements to the fryer. I was delighted by Mr. Reynolds' clever breading equipment, and several other handling devices he had knocked together to make his shop efficient. They showed an inventive mind and were applicable to other facilities, I thought, and would be good things for Warden's company to manufacture and market.

"Besides," I said to Mr. Reynolds, "someone should commercialize your 'breading'," a thin wash of milk and egg with a dusting of seasoned flour. "It makes such a nice crisp shell that absorbs very little fat." He nodded gratefully.

I sent my report to Warden. "The pulsing of pressure is a very effective way of cooking. Blowing the fat out of the chamber before the food is removed prevents its soaking the food unnecessarily. But, the equipment now is cumbersome and needs reengineering. His systems thinking is admirable for materials handling and for automatic filtering of the fat after each cycle." I suggested ways of reengineering the fryer to make it more flexible. Then said, "I can't tell you if the fried product is better than that of any other equipment. It has to be compared side by side with other pressure fryers in a lab that specializes in frying, a lab that can do controlled tests, and do chemical and textural analysis. Send it to Rutgers and ask them to evaluate it against the competition. Regardless of whether the PV comes out on top or not, I think you should hire Mr. Reynolds, put him in a lab and tell him to develop all the food handling equipment he can think of. Pay him an annual salary and commercialize everything he comes up with. He will produce a lot of value for you." I wound up saying, "With a little help, perhaps he would not have to improvise so much 'science.'"

A few weeks later, Mr. Reynolds sent me a thank you letter with a new batch of lab reports from the U. of P.'s toxicology department. His letter implied that these new tests were favorable, but, again, he had not really examined them. Cooking their samples as much as three hours at the elevated temperature of a pressure fryer, the lab noted virtually no change in mercury levels in the fish samples, just as I had expected. The new reports were as lousy as the others. And anyway, who cooks 50 g. of anything three hours?

Months later, Mr. Reynolds phoned me. He was bitter. "Everybody takes advantage of a black man. Do you know what that big company did?"

I said, "No. I told them to send the fryer to Rutgers and have it tested against other pressure fryers by a competent lab. Then they'd know. I also told them to hire you, put you in a development lab and commercialize all your very good ideas."

"They sent my fryer to a machine shop and told them to copy it. They weren't going to pay for it, to recognize my patent. Just copy it, and figure I was a poor, dumb black man who could not do anything about it."

"Are you sure? Who told you?" I asked. "Mr. Warden is a very nice man..."

"Maybe to you. Not to me," he interrupted.

This was agonizing. I believed him. Warden never said a word to me about it after our visit. Nor in fact, could he. His division disappeared in one of those spasms of downsizing that conglomerates are known for and I never saw him again. I worried to myself: "Maybe he did that in a last desperate hope that with a ready-made 'winner,' his division would survive." Even so...

\*       \*       \*       \*       \*

"Ms. Harris," it was a year later, and the voice on the phone was familiar. "I'm coming to New York and I want to see you. Can you have lunch on Tuesday?" It was Joseph Reynolds, of course. He appeared at my little office on unfashionable Broadway at 11:30, dressed in a well-fitted navy blue suit, handsome polished shoes, a silk pocket square sticking out of his jacket, and gold cufflinks in his shirt cuffs. Downstairs at a meter was a Lincoln Continental. I could see it from my second-floor window. He must have rented it at the airport.

I thought he had gone to a lot of trouble to impress me. My office had nine people working in about a thousand square feet, with ordinary furniture, bookcases, equipment. Some of my employees complained from time to time that we looked too unpretentious for the quality of work we did. They wanted a prettier reception room and carpeting. It didn't matter. The only people who came to me already knew the quality of work we did and were glad we did not waste their money.

Mr. Reynolds looked around. "Very nice. You meet a payroll."

I nodded, introducing him to my mostly younger staff, wondering why he was visiting.

We were in the restaurant — a Thai place with a six-dollar chicken lunch special — when Mr. Reynolds began, "You're important to me. I want to keep you abreast of what we're doing. The State Department is sending me to Africa and the Near East to demonstrate my equipment. I've made a little unit that can be used in small places to sterilize food that is full of contaminates..."

He rattled on about the world food situation, that so much food in underdeveloped areas spoiled en route to markets... That starving people could be fed at modest cost if only his cooker were used, that he had packed fish and meat in pouches and sealed them after cooking and that they lasted without refrigeration for weeks... I listened, and as always found his ideas and words full of minor mistakes, the mistakes of a man who was trying hard without the educational background he needed. He said international aid organizations wanted him to go to people who looked like him and demonstrate his technology. I wondered whether those people had a source of electricity or gas to power even a small piece of his equipment. He could demonstrate the equipment in a city. How would it work in a rural area? An ordinary pressure cooker on a wood fire would sterilize food equally well, except at high altitudes. International aid organizations were always being attacked for funding impractical ideas: heavy industry before light industry, huge dams that displaced rural populations... But their experts did not understand local cultures and geography, and truth did not catch up in time to foil new schemes. I felt there was a kind of rough justice to Joseph Reynolds' benefiting from official naivete. Besides, the waste of resources was small.

I nodded, voicing none of my misgivings. "It will be an interesting trip, and I hope your technology does improve the food situation. Who's running your shop in the meantime?"

"My two oldest kids. They're home from college for the summer, and I've taught them..."

"Two oldest? How many are there?" This was none of my business, but it seemed safe.

"Five," he said proudly. "I'm divorced. All of them will go to college and to professional schools after if they want to. I'm a hard-working man." He paused. "What about you, do you have kids?"

I am wary of personal conversation with clients or business acquaintances. I had made a mistake. "One."

"Boy or girl?"

"Boy."

"What does he do?"

"He's in college." I looked at my watch. "I have to get a report finished this afternoon... If it's all right, we should go."

"You're a very attractive woman..."

"Thank you," I said briskly, turning to get my jacket off the back of the chair while Mr. Reynolds hastened around the table to help me shrug it on. I walked him to his car and wished him a safe journey.

Months later, there was another phone call. Mr. Reynolds again. "I have received a substantial loan from the SBA, and another loan is coming from the Office of Minority Business and I am putting together an organization... I want you to be a part of it. We will have enough money to pay you. Can you come to Pittsburgh again? The others want to meet you and we must make a plan."

The address was different. He had a new corporate name, and his facility was now called "Joe's". I did not remember the name above the door of the earlier one. The front was larger, with a few tables for diners: and in the back, a larger private dining room where I met three white men: a retired mechanical engineer, Mr. Hayes, portly and informal; a pleasant, slim patent attorney, Mr. Marsh, and a custom equipment manufacturer, Mr. Clay. Plus one black man, youngish, smartly outfitted, Benjamin Vincent, who had an MBA from Wharton, and was the comptroller of the new corporation.

"This is Muriel Harris, a world-class consultant," he said. "You remember that newsletter where she was quoted on new energy-saving technology for cooking." They nodded, as uniformly as the bobbing heads we used to see in the rear windows of cars.

I nodded, too. To say "hello." We had a huge lunch of fried fish, chicken, squash, potatoes, then a fruit cup, and as before, coffee with. They asked how was my flight, how was the weather in New York, did I travel a lot, which was my favorite city...

I was interested in the more compact design of the new fryer whose unitary housing concealed and remodeled its previous clumsiness. "Did you reengineer the PV, Mr. Hayes?" I asked.

"Yes. Do you like it?"

"Very nice." I turned to Mr. Clay. "How many can you build at a time?"

"About five. We batch the orders."

"They're selling?"

"We're selling them to fast food franchises behind the backs of their principals." It was Reynolds answering. "I have six 'Joe's' also."

"Pretty good. What else is going on?"

I realized after a while that Reynolds had sweet-talked Mr. Hayes and me, that Mr. Marsh was a volunteer and that Benjamin Vincent was being paid a small salary and a promise of stock when the company went public. Mr. Clay's arrangement was to schedule PV production for slow time in his plant. Reynolds was reimbursing his outlays for materials and labor. He, too, was promised stock before the company's IPO as compensation for overhead and profit, and for the risk of waiting.

Reynolds was trying to sell us all on the prospect of getting rich from early shares in the corporation before it went public. He thought Mr. Hayes and I could wait until we had our stock options. But, harsh experience of plausible promoters and dreamers had scarred me. I knew that lots of new companies tried to preserve their cash until they could see a profit. They did it by distributing warrants or other gifts of stock in anticipation of a public offering.

"Mr. Reynolds, I can't afford to work that way. I do not expect to get rich, ever. But I do need to be paid for work and reimbursed for out of pocket expenses." I did not say, "Yes, new companies sometimes get by on pie in the sky. But not with me. I am not a gambler, and I do not trust a future I cannot control."

Reynolds nodded. "That's all right. We can pay your

fees on a monthly basis." He wanted from me a full-scale
plan for everything: corporate development, venture capital placements, marketing, literature, public relations, and
finally a business plan and underwriter contacts for a public
offering. Benjamin Vincent would do the numbers for the
business plan. I would do the text.

I laughed. "One thing at a time, please. My office is very
busy."

"Can you give us an outline?"

I promised an outline, time line — PERT chart, essentially — and estimates for a year's work, in six weeks. Reynolds said he'd be in New York to go over it with me.

I was feeling a little sick about committing so much to
him. Why was I doing it? I had plenty of work for clients
who were established, who did not need everything. The
answer was always the same: It was the right thing to do;
somebody had to do it. I could see the same impulse in
the patent attorney, in the retired mechanical engineer, in
the manufacturer. Life was not fair to black people in the
U.S.; it was part of our sense of justice to repair a bit of the
damage.

Mr. Reynolds sent an autobiographical statement; and
a fat sheaf of official papers from various government agencies that "proved" his integrity in the face of litigation I had
not previously heard of. I read all this with mounting dis-
may. Banks, loan officers, the Pennsylvania department of
enterprise, the Treasury's International Development group,
the UN's economic development unit... had all discontin-
ued working with him amid claims, investigations, hearings,
clearings... Nothing solid. Just a record of many efforts
that had brought him grants and loans and then a tapering
of confidence and money that led to failure. These things
happened, but I did not want an association with a "con"
man.

All of Reynolds' new associates, and probably the earlier

ones, too, wanted to believe in him. We needed to do the right thing. Was it possible that if it was hard for a black man to succeed, it was not so hard for him to "game" people into working with him? Of course, the idea occurred to me, and probably to the others, too. But, we would have betrayed ourselves if we acted on it without proof. I went on trusting him, giving him the benefit of the doubt.

There are always problems of this sort. One of my colleagues had taken up with an inventor of amorphous semiconductors whose company always had losses, who spun off other companies that also got lots of press and funding and also experienced nothing but losses, whose technology was touted endlessly in its variations, and optioned by many major companies, and still had nothing to show for years in the public eye. It was a white man's company. The white man claimed a new technology, a new insight into the structure of materials... and no one knew for sure if it was bullshit or truth. President Reagan had been seduced similarly into throwing billions of taxpayer dollars at Star Wars, when engineers who understood the technology knew it was not workable. Poetically named "brilliant pebbles" were no more than elegant fancies.

I had to behave "as if," as if I believed. Give the man his chance. I prepared the complex proposal. A year's work for fees and expenses was going to run close to $100,000 and I knew that was impossible.

I called Mr. Reynolds. "I don't think you need to come. I'll mail the proposal and then if you want to discuss it we can have a meeting or talk on the phone."

He was clearly disappointed. "I like visiting you, a good-looking woman."

I shook my head over the phone where he could not see it. "It's better this way. You can go over it at your leisure, talk it over with the others." I had done the right thing and made a substantive contribution to his enterprise in planning and know-how. Now, I wanted to be out of it — cut my losses.

*     *     *     *     *

A year later, another call. "We're ready to put the whole
thing together. I'm negotiating with a major appliance company for manufacture of a small unit; and I have a half million dollars in loans from an industrial group formed by Jesse
Jackson and..." He appeared the following week at my office,
beaming. "It's so nice to see you again, Ms. Harris. I've
missed that." I raised an eyebrow. He was wearing a new
soft-cut suit and Italian loafers. "I have other news: I'm
married again."

"Congratulations." I was quite sincere.

"I didn't want to do it till there were no more kids at
home. It would not be right for them." He told me about
a teacher, a kid in medical school, an accountant, and... He
believed in education. I was impressed. I had not realized
that he was raising his children. "But," he said with a smile,
"I am certainly still interested in you, you know..."

"Mr. Reynolds, you've just remarried..."

"She's a good woman... But she doesn't have a flat belly
like you," he said, wistfully. I laughed. What else was there
to do?

We did most of the coordinating for the PV public announcement by mail or phone. Mr. Reynolds was responsive
to deadlines, interested in how it all came together. Two
days before the press conference he and his team came to
New York for rehearsals of their talks, and for the q. and a.
that a curious and sometimes probing press would insist on.

"I am not very smooth, Ms. Harris," he said worriedly.

"That's all right," I replied. "People will see you're the

genuine thing and respect that."

We had a very successful press conference in a three-story tech center, where we could do it all. There was a huge press kit, a color brochure, a slide presentation, talks by Reynolds and Hayes and Marsh, even a lunch cooked with the new technology. The PV had been trucked to New York and installed in the kitchen where Reynolds' kids did the cooking. The tech center's theme helped to focus the attention of press, video, business and popular media.

There was a two-page story with photos in Business Week, excellent coverage in the tabloids, video news sequences, and even a half-hour on a food channel. We could hardly have been more successful.

To follow up, I found a manufacturers' rep for overseas sales, a really reputable man. I had leads to venture capital sources. I set up a regional rep organization for the United States, and planned for Reynolds to address a meeting with them at the National Restaurant Assn. annual convention in Chicago the following month.

Reynolds paid the fees for the first couple of months, and I was feeling confident that I had made the right choice. We kept to our program and for once, the fact that he was a black man played out in his favor. I marveled at our and his successes, and was ashamed of my earlier misgivings.

We were meeting monthly, mostly in New York, and mainly for media interviews that I had set up, when a sexual harassment complaint by a black woman in a famous broker-age house achieved front-page exposure. She was suing, and he asked me what I thought. "Things like that happen all the time. These guys let their minds wander and figure they may as well try."

"Does it happen to you?"

I smiled. "Of course. When I applied for membership in a consultants' society not long ago, the committee's chairman came to see me, and said, 'You'd better be nice to me or I

won't vote favorably on your application.' 'Forget it,' I said.'
He didn't make an issue of it. I was admitted anyway."

"But that girl isn't a sophisticated city woman like you,"
he protested. "She is a country girl from West Virginia..."

"I don't care where she is from. The men in West Virginia cannot be so different. If you make it clear you're not
interested, they stop. A suit is unnecessary, and gives you
a black eye for the rest of your working life. People have
to get out of the habit of feeling like victims..." I stopped,
embarrassed.

"I never thought of that," he said.

Not long after, I started worrying about the new corporation's lateness in paying its bills, especially for the out
of pocket expenses: design, printing, mailings, etc. I always
paid these directly because I did not want slow-paying clients
to poison relationships with purveyors I trusted. I started
writing stern arrears notes on the bottoms of statements.
Mr. Reynolds' firm was fifty-thousand dollars behind.

A few weeks later, I received the projections for a business
plan for venture capital placements from Benjamin Vincent.
I did not look for a while at the spreadsheets. It was my job
to prepare a narrative: the company, the executives, market
numbers, a marketing plan extending to five years out. I
started writing what I knew and had in my own files. Then
I opened Benjamin's sheets. My heart sank. All my doubts
about this enterprise resurfaced. There was no coherence
from one spreadsheet to the next, the numbers were way
off, the time periods were incommensurate, as if they'd been
improvised by a playful child.

I called Mr. Reynolds. "Benjamin Vincent's numbers
can't be used. I can't figure out where he gets them. I'll
have to redo them all. It will be weeks..."

"Do what you think best, Ms. Harris."

I went back to the current state of affairs: sales, manufacturing, staffing, and costs, hoping they were right. Then

I laboriously traced my way into a plausible six months from now. Then a year, two, five years out. It took weeks of thinking and planning.

"Where is the business plan, Ms. Harris? We need it desperately here. We have a possibility of investment by a major steel company to diversify..." Mr. Reynolds was pushing hard.

"It's almost done, Mr. Reynolds. I had to revamp all Mr. Vincent's numbers. They were crazy. Is he really a Wharton MBA? I will send you one copy only, and it will be clearly marked "copy". You will not be able to copy it and I will not send you an original for reproduction until you pay a substantial part of the arrears." There. I had expressed my mistrust of what was going on, flooding my head with all his past problems. They had to have meant something beyond prejudice. "I am sorry to do this, but I have to be paid." (I was suffering the pain and guilt of crippling his effort when he might have had a chance, but I knew perfectly well that for a few hundred dollars, he could have had the whole thing redone on a computer with spreadsheet and word processing programs and he'd have his own original. He never did that. I do not know why.)

Meantime, he said, "I understand, Ms. Harris." He sounded humble. I did not want that. "Just send what you can."

He did not pay any bill and I sent the copy and kept the original. He called a few weeks later to tell me he had fired Benjamin Vincent.

My firm stopped all work on his account. The organization I had put in place for reps nationally and internationally was functioning well, but his own followup was lacking and the enthusiasm we had engendered was dying. I worried endlessly about my role in this. I had become the villain, holding him up for money when the business plan was crucial to his future. He had not explained where the money went, and why he could not pay me. I clung to that. And he did not press me further.

*     *     *     *     *

Another year went by, and Mr. Reynolds called. "Ms. Harris, I have a big package coming to you by Federal Express.
I want you to read it and call me collect with what you
think." I did not want to think for, or about, him any more.
He still owed me close to sixty-thousand dollars. But he was
sensitive, too. "Call me collect."

It was a huge box, with a series of binders, detailing work
with a major fast food chain over a period of almost thirty
years. It would take weeks to digest what was in them, and
then only with copious notes and indexing. I did not want to
read them. I did not want to. I dreaded further involvement.
But Reynolds trusted me to do the right thing, and I had to.

The binders averred in a history section that Mr. Reynolds
had invented the PV cooker and filed a patent application
years before he went to work for the company. He had had
lab jobs, quality control jobs; it was hard to determine what
he'd been doing. Then he left and opened his own shop.
But he and a patent attorney, (not Mr. Marsh then), and
an assistant had had a series of meetings, all documented in
memoranda, with the top technical and administrative people at the fast food chain's headquarters to sell them the PV
concept.

There were agreements, there was testing, there were options on the equipment, there were pilot programs. The
chain was bought by a conglomerate and negotiations fell
apart for a while. Behaviors were ambiguous and mistrust
was clear. The company's people wanted fullest possible dis-
closure before paying for much. Mr. Reynolds wanted to

reserve his trade secrets for when he'd been fully paid or had a final, signed agreement. They jockeyed back and forth over years. Stopped. Started again, different players, same problems.

I read on and on. Sometimes it seemed that an agreement was imminent. "We like the equipment. We are in favor of it. We will license it to manufacture. Just..."

Then, "pending new tests" "comparing it with an in-house unit we've been developing independently..." The conglomerate sold the chain to another company that was amassing a chain of chains, even planning that they supplement each other for time of day sales, a donut and coffee chain to be housed with a hamburger or fried chicken facility for twenty-four hours of maximum business. Another halt in the negotiations while the headquarters executives were brought up to speed.

Each time, I realized, the chain reserved the right to keep its options open while foreclosing Mr. Reynolds' possibilities of selling the equipment elsewhere. They were paying him so little that, essentially they kept him on a string, while they worked around his patents on their own equipment. No wonder he was bitter. He had kept all this back.

I called him, "collect" as instructed. "I'm writing a letter so you'll have this in writing. I think those people have been diddling you in the hope that your patents will expire before the game is up. It is hard for me to take this all in, but it is what the file says."

"I thought you would say that, Ms. Harris. I know you. You do what you say you will do." My alarm signals went off again. What did he want?

"This is my last chance," he said. "I am suing them for negotiating fraudulently while avoiding a real agreement. I have a lawyer who is handling the matter and we are filing the case in a federal court. My lawyer thinks we have a good chance of winning."

"Yes?" I asked.

"I want to avoid court maneuvers. Their new owners have deep pockets and can go at it indefinitely. You carry so much weight; everyone knows who you are, if you write to their headquarters legal department and ask them for a fair settlement in light of what the file shows... When we get the settlement, we'll be able to pay you and everyone else..."

"You want me to negotiate for you?" I asked incredulously. "I'm not a good negotiator. I hate trading advantages, I yield too quickly, I dread conflict, and I do not have the patience... Anyway, if we get to that, how much do you want? How much do you need?"

"Just to pay off my debts, six million, Ms. Harris!"

"Six million to pay off debts? That's a lot, but considering the fast food company's balance sheet and the prospect of unfavorable publicity if it comes to a newspaper story... They would not want to seem to have been trying to cheat a poor black man when a large proportion of their sales are to minorities... "

"Yes," he said eagerly. "I wanted to tell you about that. You know the publisher of the Amsterdam News in New York; there's another paper in Brooklyn; do you know the editor of Black Enterprise?"

I interrupted. "I know his former girlfriend."

"Good enough. There's a black Coca Cola bottler in Philadelphia; I've been in touch with Andrew Young..."

I did not like this. It smelled of blackmail. "Wait," I said. "I'll write a letter. I'll explain that I've read the file, that a settlement is to everyone's advantage, a bit of biography so they'll know I'm respectable. I'll send the draft to you and to your lawyer so we'll all be on the same wave length."

I wrote the letter as his advocate. But with misgivings again. Had Reynolds failed at organizing and promoting his company to success, although other entrepreneurs had? And had he filed a suit charging discrimination as his last resort?

I had read his file, accumulated over years — but was there more to it? I did not like being a party to manipulation of a big company's sensitivities. I knew Reynolds was pushing two of my buttons: the need to be paid, and the feeling that there might be a good reason for the suit.

Reynolds made no changes in my letter. His lawyer proposed some idiotic additions that I refused to make. It was my letter, after all. I sent it as I had drafted it.

I did not have to make a follow-up call. Their legal department had taken me seriously. A quiet, gentlemanly voice phoned the following week.

"This is Pier Reston from the legal department. We know who you are and that you are a sincere, honest person. But practically all that Mr. Reynolds alleges took place when our company had no interest in the food service chain. We only bought it a year ago."

"I know, but the ongoing business is what you bought with its liabilities as well as its assets." I was pleased with myself for thinking of that.

"How much does he want?"

"Isn't that in the suit papers? I don't know what he is asking for."

"The real question is what will he settle for?" The man was direct and reasonable, I thought.

"I don't think I can speak for him."

"Ms. Harris. We want to end this. It's hard on us. We don't think his suit has any merit. We've hired one of the largest law firms in the country..."

"You have? You're not handling it in house?"

"No." He named a very famous, successful firm. "Mr. Reynolds hasn't a chance. What will he settle for?"

"I have to talk to him. Call me Wednesday next week."

I called Reynolds, collect again. "I want you to send me a schedule of what you must have... To give you a reasonable new start, to pay off your debts..."

He sent it. He wanted a million for himself; not so bad, but not really much for all the years and wasted opportunity, and I found myself in an alphabetical list with a lot of familiar names. I was still at the original sum, no interest, but there.

"Six million dollars," I told Mr. Reston the following week. "To pay off his debts and to give him a little bit to start again. It's been a long haul of frustration and bitterness for him. He's a good person and he's not young any more."

"Too bad," Mr. Reston said, unsympathetically. "Why didn't he go elsewhere with his invention?"

"Your guys kept taking options, tying him up..." I had become his advocate even if I was not sure I believed the whole story.

"What will it take to make him go away?"

"Go away?" I had never heard that expression.

"Just go away. We'll give him two million just to go away. We don't think he has a case."

Then I had a letter from Reynolds, asking me if I would reduce the amount he owed me. It was years later. I had added no interest to the original sum. I called him on my own dime. "Mr. Reynolds, why do you want me to reduce this sum? I have not been dunning you. What you owe me is one percent of what you owe altogether. If I wiped out the debt completely, you would still owe ninety-nine percent of what you owe. What are you thinking of?" Anyway, I recommended that he take the two million and run.

Reynolds refused. "No," he said. "You and the others trusted me, and I want to pay my debts." I never asked him what happened to all the loans and grants he had received. Did the money go to clothes, a house, a fine car? He liked those things and had them, clearly felt he needed them to get more loans and grants and business.

The suit had to proceed as it was. It shifted to a different court in a different state. Reynolds' lawyer was trying for a sympathetic judge; the opposition was trying for a different judge; Reynolds' lawyer thought he'd like a jury trial, where people would be sympathetic to a poor man taken advantage of... Discovery was endless...

Then, months, years later, it was over. The corporation's high-priced lawyers had prevailed. The suit had been shifted to still another court, and the judge there dismissed it with a summary judgment. The end. Reynolds called me. Nothing for him, nothing for anyone. "I'll be ok," he said. "I have my health and my family, and even a little business..."

I felt terrible. I had long since given up hope of repayment. I had to rethink my own behavior. Had I let myself be involved over and over when good judgment would have called a halt? Yes. Have I done this all my life? Yes. Why do I not learn? On an impulse, a few days later, still not able to drop it, I called Mr. Hayes, the retired engineer in Pittsburgh. Had he heard? Yes, most of it. Did he know about the suit? A little. What did he think?

"No matter what, we did the right thing. We had to trust him, and hope it would work out, Muriel. You and I — we glue the society together."

A little postscript. Another phone call years later - this time from a woman I did not know, a litigator who said Reynolds had sent her his files. He wanted to sue a sterilizer company for infringing his patents, she said.

"They've expired."

"He has new patents for refinements and improvements," she said.

"Did he tell you to call me?" I asked incredulously.

"No. I found your name in the files. What I want to know is would you advise me to take the case?"

"Not unless you want to be a volunteer. He won't pay you."

"He says they're using his pulse-vacuum process for ster-ilizing."

"Pulsing is not novel; his patents are for a fryer. If you want to help him and trust him, go ahead. Otherwise, if this is simply another case, and you need to earn a fee, forget it," I said. "I'm sorry." Yes, I am.

End

30643129R00186

Made in the USA
Middletown, DE
01 April 2016